Doll House Copyright © 2020 Ashley Lister

www.ashleylister.co.uk

Published by Chorkie Press September 2020

All rights reserved. This book or any portion thereof may not be reproduced or used in any manner whatsoever without the express written permission of the publisher except for the use of brief quotations in a book review. The unauthorized reproduction or distribution of this copyrighted work is illegal.

This book is a work of fiction and any resemblance to persons, living or dead, or places, events or locales, is purely coincidental. The characters are productions of the author's imagination and used fictitiously.

(A version of this story was previously published by Caffeine Nights.)

#1

The doll stared at Tina.

From the moment she awoke in the morning, until she finally managed to creep out of the bedroom and escape its insistent glare, the doll fixed Tina with its sightless open-eyed gaze.

The doll stared at her whenever she revisited the bedroom in the day, either to find a change of clothes for a dinner engagement, or simply to collect a thicker jumper to stave any early evening chill that gripped the cottage. The doll stared at her when she returned to the bedside cabinet to retrieve whichever book she'd fallen asleep reading the previous night. The doll stared at her as she drifted uneasily to sleep on the lumpy comfort of the sagging mattress.

One eye was a muddy brown. The other, the one that always drew her attention, was impossibly blue. On a human child it would have been described as the blue eye of a cherubic angel. Poets would have called it the blue of an unpolluted ocean or the blue of an idyllic summer sky. Tina had started to think of the eye as satanic-blue. She had started to think of it as satanic-*evil*-blue with a slight hint of psychotic malevolence. Compared to the acrylics she was currently using, Tina thought the closest colour on her palette was manganese-blue, although that seemed less disquieting than the shade she saw in the doll's eye. She would have agreed it was impossibly blue, but she would never have said it was a blue that could be associated with something pleasant like an ocean or a summer sky.

She awoke just after three in the morning to find the doll glaring at her. The satanic-blue eye was sharpened by a red glow. Tina told herself that the additional colour was nothing more than the reflection from the LED on her bedside clock. The doll's eyes were glassy and round and she figured the orbs were likely to collect and reflect any light in the room.

It was a conversation she had often had since moving into the cottage.

She told herself there was nothing creepy or supernatural about the way the doll glared at her. She told herself the doll wasn't really glaring. It was only a doll, and dolls didn't have the ability to glare. That was a humanising talent she had bestowed on the thing with her own hyperactive imagination. Her agent, John, had said as much when she told him about the way the doll glared.

"Are you doing too many pills?" he'd asked. "Or not enough?"

"It's creepy," Tina insisted. "It glares at me."

"It doesn't glare at you," John said. "It's a doll. It's inanimate. It can't glare."

But John had said those words in daylight. He had said those words downstairs at the kitchen table, away from the doll, where it was easy to believe such plausible truths. Now, it was the middle of the night and she was alone with the thing. The darkness in the bedroom was broken only by a sliver of errant moonlight and the red glow from the bedside clock with its figures showing 3:10AM. Despite everything John had said to her, Tina knew the doll was glaring.

"If it disturbs you so much, why don't you get rid of it?" John had asked.

"It was a gift. I can't get rid of a gift."

"My first secretary gave me the gift of herpes," John said. "I've been trying to get rid of that for the past sixteen years."

"It was a gift from Marion," Tina told him. "I couldn't get rid of a gift from her."

"I'm not suggesting you throw it in the bin," John back-pedalled. Hearing the defensive tone in his voice, she knew he would never have suggested such a radical response if he'd realised Marion Papusa was the giver of the gift. "But you could stuff it in a drawer or lock it in a wardrobe, couldn't you?"

"She'd know," Tina said glumly.

John had nodded in agreement. Marion would know.

Tina had considered various solutions but none of them seemed quite right. She had thought about 'displaying' the doll in one of the downstairs rooms but that would've meant having to suffer its glare throughout the day whilst she was painting. Worse, she could imagine on a night, rather than being woken by the glare of its sightless eyes staring at her slumbering form, she would instead be roused from sleep by the rumbling patter of the doll's little wooden shoes scurrying across the polished floorboards in the rooms below. Even worse than that idea, she might have heard the heavy tromp of the doll's shoes climbing the cottage's stairs as it made its way towards her bedroom.

The idea made goosebumps prickle down her spine.

"Put a cloth over it," John had suggested.

Tina had tried variations on that idea several times.

The doll seemed able to shrug the fabric away.

Coincidentally, on those evenings when Tina had 'accidentally' covered the doll with a discarded blouse, she had found it easy to fall into a comfortable sleep. She had found no difficulty in dropping off, and the first half of her night had been untroubled by any suggestion of nightmare or disturbance. But the second half of the evening, usually a little after three o'clock in the morning, she had woken to find the satanic-blue eye with the flecks of red glaring at her. Inevitably on those nights, she clawed her way back to sleep whilst cowering beneath her quilt. And yet, even then, her rest was made grim with diabolical dreams of disembowelment and stomach-churning notions of graphic and miserable suffering.

"Can you just put up with it?" John had asked.

Tina had shrugged and said that was what she was trying to do. But it wasn't a perfect solution. She constantly felt as though she was being watched. She constantly felt as though she was being judged. The presence of the doll meant she couldn't invite a lover to join her in the bedroom. It was like being the centre of attention for a sinister voyeur. In truth, the presence of the doll had put her off masturbating since she moved into the village of Sandalwood. Not that she was a habitual bean-flicker, but everyone needed some form of release. The doll made her feel as though she was being watched in her most intimate moments by a small and malevolent stranger. The idea of meeting that satanic-blue eye whilst she buzzed out a *happy* was enough to make Tina feel dirty and shameful.

Since moving into the cottage she didn't know whether it was safer to go to sleep drunk, so she could no longer focus on the glare of the doll, or if it would be better to stay sober so that her imagination didn't trick her into believing that anything unnatural could possibly occur. Some nights she worked as long as she could on her paintings in the conservatory. It didn't matter that all natural light had been bleached from the sky, or that she was exhausted and unable to focus properly on what she was doing. All that mattered on those nights was that she spent as long as possible downstairs in the cottage and away from the glaring eyes of the doll. She worked until she was falling asleep, sometimes she worked after she had fallen asleep. She remembered jolting awake one night and had almost completed a particularly difficult piece of shading on the partial study of a clown's face she was painting. She had been standing up, in the conservatory, facing her easel and completing a painting. Asleep. It had unsettled her to discover she could carry on painting when her consciousness had gone. The idea seemed an affront to the notion of being an artist. Surely she needed to be conscious to do something artistic?

Staring into the doll's eyes now, she wished she'd spent longer in the conservatory this evening working on her current painting. She wished she'd maybe had a drink. Or several. And she wished she'd fallen asleep whilst painting downstairs. It wouldn't have mattered if she was painting or simply curled up in one of the conservatory's armchairs. All that mattered was the idea of being away from the doll's mesmerising stare.

The eyes seemed larger than she remembered.

Were they larger or was the doll closer?

That idea made her bowels ripple as though they were filled with loose water. She sat up in bed and squinted into the shadows. She was suddenly sure that she knew what to do. She had to get rid of the doll. She could put it in a suitcase and then lock the suitcase shut. That would stop the damned thing from glaring at her and it would mean she was able to get a proper night's rest. She could maybe take it back to Marion and say, "It's very kind of you to give me this gift, but I'm not a dolly-person. Being honest, I'm a little bit scared of dollies."

As ideas went, she knew it was a brave notion. She suspected it would be one of those ideas she wouldn't dare to carry out in the light of day. The prospect of telling Marion Papusa that her doll wasn't wanted was frightening, because no one ever refused Marion Papusa.

But Tina told herself that was what had to be done. And before she did that, she needed to stop the doll from glaring at her whilst she tried to sleep.

Tina tossed back the quilt and threw on the bedside light. Climbing easily out of the bed, marching with an authoritative confidence she didn't feel, Tina stamped over to the chest of the drawers where the doll sat. She reached for one of the doll's bare arms and lifted it in the air.

"Mama?" cooed the doll.

Tina dropped the doll and shrieked. She stepped quickly back, conscious that her bare feet were exposed on the bedroom's cold floorboards.

"Mama?" the doll repeated.

"I'm not your Mama," Tina hissed.

She knew she was overreacting. It was just a voice-box in the doll. Lifting it up by its arm had activated those sensors that made it speak.

It was insane to think there was any other reason as to why it was talking. Angry that it had made her react in such an irrational way, she drew her foot back to kick the doll across the room.

"Don't kick me, Mama," the doll insisted. "Please don't kick me, Mama."

Tina screamed.

#2

High atop a hill in the centre of Sandalwood village, visible from every twist and turn that John's car took, there stood a decrepit, gothic building. With the fading twilight behind it, the house looked like something where the *Addams Family* would live, or the home of Norman Bates. It was tall, dark and so obviously spooky, Ben thought it could have been snatched from the opening credits of a *Scooby-Doo* cartoon. It was easy to imagine a flutter of black bats or a white-sheet ghost flapping from the high-arched doorway or one of the sinister upper windows. Ben didn't want to be intrigued but he couldn't help wonder about the building.

"Where are you taking me?"

"You sound like a fucking kidnap victim," John yawned.

"It worries me that you know what kidnap victims sound like. Where are you taking me?"

"I told you where I'm taking you," John spoke with weary resignation. "For the next three months I'll be giving you what every lazy writer needs. I'm putting you in my personal country cottage. You'll have the solitude and the isolation necessary to finish your latest novel. I'm taking you back to your writing career."

Ben stared out of the window. He scowled at the sign saying 'WELCOME TO SANDALWOOD.' They drove past a cemetery-fringed churchyard, a police station and a pub. He saw a library and a pair of shops that were closed at this late hour of a Sunday evening. The houses they passed, all yellow stone beneath slick slate roofs, were packed tight together and lurked behind prettily floral front gardens. As the darkness took hold, the streets were lit by the archaic yellow glow of mock-Victorian street lamps. Ben thought it was the sort of location that would likely have village fetes, a secret history of animal sacrifice and some sort of deserved reputation for bestiality or inbreeding. Or maybe both.

"I don't want solitude and isolation," Ben grumbled. "I want alcohol, caffeine, nicotine and maybe some class *B* drugs. Those are the things that help me write."

"Yeah," John agreed. "You've had those for the last year and we're still no closer to seeing the final book in your trilogy, are we?"

Ben continued to stare out of the window. Sandalwood looked like it was in the middle of nowhere. He could see none of the familiar signs he would have expected, telling him there was either a bank, a McDonalds, an ASDA or a Carphone Warehouse lurking on the high street. He was beginning to suspect that the two shops, as well as the library and the police station, might well have been all of Sandalwood's high street. It was, he thought, something akin to Third World deprivation. With his heart racing he peered more furiously out of the window and tried to see something that suggested they were still in the twenty-first century.

"Where is this place?"

"This is Sandalwood," John said. "You head up north for a couple of hours past Birmingham and then you turn left for a bit. What does it matter where it is?"

Ben shrugged. He stopped himself from saying that it mattered if he was going to try and escape. He was still staring out of the window but the light had faded so much now he was treated only to glimpses of his own unkempt reflection.

There was a week-old beard dirtying his jaw. His hair was an untidy tangle beneath the cowl of his oversized hoodie. His eyes were hidden in deep shadows borne from too many late nights and too much excess alcohol. With high cheekbones and an unlined brow, it had once been a handsome face but now it looked like the reflection of an ailing party animal.

An ailing party animal that needed a kindly vet to end its suffering.

He pushed that thought aside. Not only was it depressing but it was a cheesily extended metaphor that made no sense.

John pulled the car to a halt outside a pair of tall, imposing gates. He stepped out of the vehicle and stood illuminated in the headlights as he fumbled with a lock and chain. He was an angular man: tall and slender and unnatural in his gait. In his corduroy slacks, sports jacket and a Harris tweed flat cap, he looked like a man who knew how to dress for the countryside even if the environment seemed not quite right for him.

The Daimler's engine continued to purr softly.

The chill of the encroaching night crept into the vehicle and began to caress Ben's cheeks and hands. He hadn't realised how warm and comfortable the journey had been, the sinister chill of the evening was unnerving.

This is your last chance, Ben thought to himself. *If you want to get back to the city, and escape from this three-month exile to the middle-of-fucking-nowhere, this is your last opportunity to steal John's car and drive away from here.*

He didn't act on the idea.

He had nowhere to go and no reason to escape. If he didn't write the final book in the trilogy he knew he could give up on any hope of ever writing again for publication. If he stole his agent's car it would likely put an end to their working relationship and Ben knew, afterwards, he would be lucky to be left with the option to self-publish on Amazon.

John climbed back into the car, shivering a little as he settled himself into the driver's seat. "It's nippy out there," he grumbled. He slammed the door shut and then drove the car slowly up the driveway. "I'm hoping it will be warmer in the house."

Overhanging trees made the route a dark tunnel. Ben could hear the scratch of talon-like branches snatching at the paintwork of the car. The tyres crunched at loose gravel. Noisy shards of the road were ripped from the ground and spat up at the metalwork beneath his feet.

"You've got property with a driveway?" Ben muttered. "You must be loaded."

John laughed. "We're up north. You could buy this entire village for the same price as some garden flat in London with an attractive postcode. If this place was really valuable do you think I'd be using it as a dumping ground for fuck-up writers who can't honour a simple contract?"

"Don't bother sugar-coating those thoughts. Tell me how you really feel."

John parked outside the cottage. The building had only been visible in glimpses of headlamp beams as they approached, but he could now see it was a majestic brownstone structure, set in its own grounds, with lights on in a handful of the windows. At one of the upper windows he thought he saw the movement of a figure, although he wasn't sure if that was simply a trick of his imagination or a passing leaf shed in the early autumn fall.

As though reading the unease in his expression, John said, "The lights are on because Mrs Scum has been in there cleaning all day."

"Mrs Scum?"

John shrugged as he made his way to the rear of the vehicle and retrieved Ben's suitcase. "That's probably not her real name," he called. "She's the cleaner. I never bothered learning her real name. I figured 'Mrs Scum' worked as a suitable *nom de guerre.*"

"Classy," Ben muttered.

John made a sound of indifference as he hefted a suitcase and a rucksack from the boot of the car and dropped them by Ben's feet. "Grab those and follow me," he said, climbing the stairs that led up to the door. "Let's get you settled in."

Ben did as he was instructed and followed.

He watched John slip a key into the main door and then push it open. The scent of home-cooked food struck him as soon as he stepped inside. The fragrance was so strong and appetising he felt weak with hunger and angry at himself for being so easily won over by a mere aroma. He was salivating like a Pavlovian dog in a doorbell factory.

"Step inside," John encouraged. He seemed either oblivious to the smell or spectacularly unimpressed. "Step inside and make yourself comfortable. You're going to be here for a while."

Ben closed the door behind himself.

The opulence of the house was inarguable. The walls were a rich and bloody vermilion. The floors were original boards polished to a glossy lustre and occasionally covered by stylish rugs. A large grandfather clock, glistening as though it had only just been polished, ticked a sonorous welcome as they entered the building. The hall was lit by glittering chandeliers hanging miles overhead. In his tatty trainers, comfortable dark jeans and cuff-frayed black hoodie, Ben felt grubby and out of place.

"This is the hall," John explained. "The stairs lead up to your main bedroom, the spare bedroom and the bathroom. I think there's also a linen closet up there and maybe access to the loft. Down here you have a study to your right, a dining room to your left and a kitchen at the rear of the building. There's a conservatory leading off the kitchen and there's also a door that leads down to the cellar."

"Where's the toilet?"

"That would be in the bathroom I mentioned before," John said, pointing up the stairs. "Try to follow what I'm saying here. It's not exactly rocket science."

Ben left his case and rucksack at the base of the grandfather clock and climbed up the stairs. The stairs creaked beneath each step, but the sound didn't make him think of antiquity or disrepair. It simply sounded like part of the house's welcoming repertoire. As much as it galled him to admit the fact, Ben found he was looking forward to living in the house.

All the doors on the landing were open save for one. He saw a large, sumptuous four-poster bed in the first room. Knowing there would be time to explore the bedroom later, he walked on to the second open doorway. This one was all white tiles with black trim, a showerhead over the stand-alone bath, and a large and somewhat imposing lavatory.

He closed the door behind himself and peed.

The tiles sparkled as though they had recently been polished. The sink was laid out with a full bar of virginal, untouched soap and a highball tumbler holding a safety razor and a blue toothbrush. With scarlet flannels by the side of the sink, and a matching scarlet hand towel draped over the radiator, Ben thought that Mrs Scum was clearly being undervalued by John.

He was trying not to be impressed by the appearance of the house, but it was difficult. The place was stylish. He washed his hands on the bar of Imperial Leather soap and dried them on the scarlet towel from the radiator.

The bathroom window, over the lavatory, looked out towards the centre of the village. He could see the creepy old house he had noticed when they first entered Sandalwood. Against the backdrop of a velvet blue sky it was now a black silhouette. The shapes of its high roof and turreted chimneys were striking. It no longer looked as childish as he had thought on his first glance. Now it made him think of the homes that had housed real-life lunatics like Ed Gein or Jeffrey Dahmer. He suspected it might have a basement worthy of Josef Fritzl. There was a yellow light in one of the upper windows. It chilled him to think that someone was actually living in the old place.

"Have you fallen in?" John called.

"I'm on my way," Ben said, flushing the toilet and heading down the stairs.

"Mrs Scum's prepared a meal for us," John called from the kitchen.

Ben followed the sound of his agent's voice. His footsteps creaked on each step. The clock tocked every passing second. And the welcoming repertoire of noises continued to make him feel as though he was going to enjoy living in the cottage.

"I don't know why the crazy old bitch has prepared a meal," John complained. "The woman's employed to clean the shitter so why she'd think anyone would want to eat food that she's touched is a mystery to me. But there's a simmering beef joint sitting in the slow cooker if you want to experience the taste of dysentery for yourself."

Ben glanced around the kitchen.

Like the bathroom it was meticulous. The tiled walls shone beneath the muted glow of kitchen lights. The work surfaces had the sort of glossy lustre that he would have expected to see in designer catalogues and other expensive product brochures. The entire room looked clean, welcoming and wonderful. Coupled with the scent of the food, Ben didn't think he'd been anywhere that seemed more like a home in the past decade.

It was a strain not to show interest in the slow cooker. He'd had a roadside burger on the drive up and it had tasted processed and unpleasant. The fries that had come with the burger had been cold and brittle. The whole meal had felt less like food and more like punishment. It was a huge contrast to the splendour of the roast he could now smell.

John stood before the large double-doors of the fridge-freezer and talked Ben through the contents. The right-hand side was all frozen goods. The upper half of the left-hand side was given over to milk, eggs, vegetables and cold cuts of meat. Beneath the cold cuts were chilling bottles of beer.

John pulled out two bottles and passed one to Ben. "I should show you a couple of small details before I leave," he said as he opened his drink.

"You're not staying?"

"I'll be back at the weekend," John said. "I'll be back every fucking weekend until you've finished this book."

"For the next three months?"

"Unless you finish it early."

Ben closed his mouth tight. There was no point going through the argument again. He unscrewed the cap on his bottle of beer and took a slow swig. It tasted cool and satisfying and reminded him that he was hungry. He glanced towards the dull red glow of the slow cooker's light and wondered if he could find a way to mention his need for food.

John gestured with his bottle of beer and led the way through to the study.

Reluctantly, Ben followed.

The study was a magnificent room dominated by a large wooden desk. In the centre of the desk there sat a huge, bulky typewriter. The words '*SILVER REED*' were written in worn white on its black lacquered surface.

"What's that?"

"It's a typewriter. It's like a computer only with less internet porn."

"Are you kidding me?"

"You're here to write for three months. I don't want you getting waylaid by any distractions."

"Are you kidding me?"

"There's no PC in this house. You've got no TV. There's a small library of books there," he said, nodding at a meagre shelf on the study wall. "But most of the texts are references. The sum distractions here in Sandalwood are the village pub and whatever local trollops you can get to suck your dick."

"For fuck's sake, John. You can't seriously expect me to-"

"No," John broke in. He spoke with a forceful authority. "This book needs finishing. If this was your first title, if you'd simply let me down with your first book, I'd let it pass. If you had a reputation for being a diva or a tantrum-thrower, I'd strike up the missing book to your inexperience and we'd rake in publicity from you pretending you've got writer's block. But you're a solid writer, Ben. You're a solid writer and I'm not letting you fuck up your career by producing a trilogy of two books."

Ben silently glowered.

"Victor Hugo followed a similar regime when he wrote *Hunchback of Notre Dame*," John spoke in a coaxing tone of voice. "He managed without clothes, so he couldn't go out even if he wanted."

"Yes. But did Victor Hugo write *Hunchback of Notre Dame* without any internet access?"

John considered him in silence until Ben realised the question was pretty stupid. He chugged his beer sullenly.

"I bought you a mobile," John said, pointing to an unopened box atop a locked cabinet.

On top of the cabinet was an empty crystal decanter, half a dozen highball glasses and a series of stained rings that now looked to be polished into the woodwork. Ben guessed the locked doors of the cabinet housed John's stash of quality drinks. He made a mental note to find the key to the drinks cabinet as soon as his agent had left for the night. If he couldn't find the key he figured he could spend a happy evening picking the lock. He wasn't much of an expert when it came to picking locks but, with enough time and appropriate motivation, he figured he would be able to get a result.

"Focus," John said, snapping his fingers and pointing at the box on top of the cabinet. "This is your new mobile."

Ben scowled at the picture on the package. "It's pretty basic, isn't it?"

"It does phone calls and text messages. There might even be a camera on it, but it does no more than that. I didn't want you getting distracted by the internet, gaming apps, Faceook or anything else. Once it's charged and set up I want you to put my number in there as the number one speed dial."

"What happens if I just walk?" Ben asked. "What happens if later tonight I get pissed and decide I don't like being held prisoner in the middle of nowhere? What happens if I decide to walk out of this house and then catch a bus back to London and quit being a writer?"

"Ben," John said quietly.

He paused and, in that pause, Ben could hear the constant tick-tock of the grandfather clock. It was an impressive sound that added gravitas to the moment.

"I've kissed a lot of publisher arse to get you this reprieve," John explained. "You've got three months to finish the script and, if you manage that, you can breathe a huge sigh of relief and move on with your life. The publishers will allow you to keep the advance you took from them for a trilogy of books. The editors I work with on a regular basis will no longer think I deal with writers who are a bunch of fucktards. And we'll all live happily ever after."

"But," Ben insisted. "What happens if I walk?"

John studied him with an unflinching gaze. "If you walk, and it puts my reputation in jeopardy, I have friends who can cure you of that walking habit. Do you understand?"

Ben understood. He struggled not to shiver.

"Any more questions?" asked John.

Ben glanced at the study's main window. He could still make out the shape of the old house. Its upper window remained brightly lit, shining like gold against the darkness of the night. More than anything else, he wanted to ask John what he knew about that house. But he shook his head and told John he had no further questions.

#3

Half an hour later, John had taken Ben through the house giving him a cursory explanation of each room and outlining what would be expected of him whilst he was residing in the cottage. Now, sitting in the kitchen, Ben swigged thoughtfully at his beer whilst he helped himself to a generous portion of the slow-roasted beef. John declined the offer to share the food, scowling at the slices of meat Ben was placing on his plate at the kitchen table.

"Mrs Scum will be here in the morning," John said. "She'll be here every day to clean the house and do any shopping you need. She's also paid to sort out your laundry. Do me a favour and try not to fuck her."

Ben cut himself a small piece of the beef and savoured its rich, meaty taste. He had no idea how long it had been cooking but the piece was so tender it all but melted in his mouth.

"Don't fuck her?" he repeated. "Is she fuckable?"

John shrugged. "Not in my opinion but I'm not a writer. From my experience writers do two things: they wear black and they fuck anything with a pulse."

Ben glanced at his dark jeans and black hoodie. He suspected John might have a point. Frowning he asked, "Don't writers usually *write* as well?"

"If you wrote, I wouldn't be dumping you up here for three months isolation."

Ben winced. It had been a low blow but he should have expected it. After chewing another mouthful of meat he said, "You never answered my question. Is Mrs Scum fuckable?"

John shrugged. "I'm never going to fuck a northern cleaning woman. You're a writer and I know you writers will fuck anything. Just don't fuck Mrs Scum."

"Does she live here?"

Ben asked the question when he remembered the shadowy figure he'd seen in an upper window when they pulled up at the house. John hadn't mentioned anything when they'd been touring the property but Ben got the impression there were lots of things John wasn't mentioning. Was he expected to share a house with a stranger for the next three months? That was an idea that he didn't particularly care to entertain.

"No. Mrs Scum has a hobbit hole in the middle of the village. She'll be here early tomorrow morning so don't go trying to fuck her when she does get here and don't try and get her to deal weed."

Ben forced himself not to raise to the bait of John's taunting. He didn't think he was so dissolute he would really try and get the cleaner into bed. Nor did he believe he was so involved in substance misuse he would try and get the woman to deal weed.

"You're back here next weekend?" Ben asked the question around another mouthful of beef. The flavour was delicious. If Mrs Scum was responsible for this food, he knew he would have to say a proper thank you in the morning.

"I'll be here around Saturday lunchtime. I'd try and get here earlier but there's a ceremony on the Friday evening and one of my competent writers is expected to receive an award."

Ben tilted his half-drained bottle of beer in salute. He was impressed by John's casual use of the 'competent writer' remark. Given the way he had let his agent down by repeatedly missing deadlines on this latest title, Ben figured he was in no position to argue with John. He could be called many things but 'competent writer' was not an accolade he was ever likely to receive from John's agency.

"I'll see you on Saturday," Ben said softly.

John lingered in the doorway. His gaze flitted around the tiled walls and he frowned as he studied the counter that housed the kettle and the sink. His expression was so intense Ben wondered if John was remembering something important that he'd once seen there. He was about to ask if that was the case when John wiped a hand across his face and abruptly spoke.

"I'm expecting ten thousand words a week out of you, every week for the next three months. I know you can do it. I know you could manage way more than that if you try. This place is useful for the isolation and the solitude and I'd advise you to take advantage of that." His expression turned solemn as he added, "But there's three things you need to be wary of. Don't try and befriend the locals. Don't take an interest in the history and heritage around here. And, above all, don't get taken in by the superstitions around these parts."

He gave a final nod and then disappeared out of the kitchen.

A moment later Ben heard the front door slam closed and he figured he was alone in the house. From faraway he heard the sound of John's Daimler starting up and then growling down the driveway.

Brilliant, thought Ben. *He blurts out some clichéd horror story hook and then leaves me here to brood in my solitude.* Ben wondered if John expected such a plot development to occur in the novel he was supposed to write. Considering he was still bereft of ideas for how to finish the story, and not drowning in ideas for how to properly start the story, Ben figured he was in a position where he could steal any story-worthy crumbs that were thrown in his direction.

Lazily, he sipped a mouthful of the beer and then ate a little more beef. According to his wristwatch it was nearing nine-thirty pm. It was automatic to yawn when he saw the time, but he didn't feel tired. Slowly he ate as much of the beef as he could manage and then washed up his plate, knife and fork.

Alone, he was almost tempted to dwell on the fact that his life was of such little importance he could take three months away from his usual routine and no one was even going to notice that he was missing. He had no living parents. His only sibling lived half a world away and communicated on the necessity of birthdays and Christmas. His last two girlfriends had found out about each other and decided they wanted nothing to do with him.

The only other person he had ever cared about was dead.

His social circle had dwindled over the last few years to nothing more than a couple of local barmen and a pair of dependable dealers. Draining the remnants of his beer bottle he tried to think of anyone in his social circle from the past five years who wasn't a person he'd used for drugs, sex, alcohol or money.

The sound of footsteps drummed loudly in a room above his head.

He ignored the noise at first, sure that he was on the verge of some alcohol-induced revelation about his personality type. It was only when he remembered he was supposed to be alone in the house that Ben's stomach folded with quiet unease.

He slid himself slowly from his seat at the kitchen table and went to the cutlery drawer. Selecting a sturdy butcher's knife from the tray, constantly watching the ceiling in case it gave up a secret whilst under his scrutiny, Ben tested the weight of the weapon in his palm.

It had an aged wooden handle. The flat of the blade was dull from time and too many washes. But the edge looked keen. The word *'Sheffield'* was stamped onto the hilt in lettering that had turned black with ingrained dirt. It wasn't a perfect weapon, but it would work to help him deal with whatever unknown lurked in the room above.

"Hello?" he ventured warily.

"Hello… hello… hello…"

Echoing weakly from the kitchen walls, his voice sounded ridiculous to his own ears. Gingerly, he made his way out of the kitchen, into the hall and up the stairs. If it was a burglar, were they likely to shout 'hello' back to him? If it was someone who believed they had a right to be in the cottage, weren't they going to think he was a dick for shouting a greeting? He opened his mouth to call out again but this time he couldn't bring himself to shout 'hello'.

"Who's up there?"

Silence.

The only things he could hear were the sounds of his own accelerated heartbeat and the creaking of the stairs beneath his feet. Had he imagined the footsteps? Was he going to be walking around an empty cottage all evening, looking for the source of a noise that hadn't really happened?

At the top of the staircase he glanced along the landing.

The place was brightly lit from the chandelier above the hall, but that only made the shadows darker and deeper. The doors to the spare bedroom and the linen closet were both closed. Ben hadn't bothered glancing behind either door on the brief tour of the house and he thought he remembered his agent closing all the doors. But now he was no longer certain.

The door to the bathroom was ajar.

The door to the master bedroom was wide open.

"Is there anyone there?"

No answer.

He stepped into the master bedroom and glanced briefly around. His suitcase now sat at the bottom of the bed. His rucksack was in the chair beneath the window. He could see that the room looked exactly as it had when John showed it to him. There was a painting on one wall, a sinister looking thing that showed a clown's eye staring morosely into the room. The shelf opposite housed a collection of teddy bears and disturbingly lifelike dolls. Ben had decided he would need to make some cosmetic arrangements to the décor. There was no way he could sleep with those creepy eyes glaring at him throughout the night.

"Hello?"

The scuttering of heavy feet on wooden boards made him turn towards the doorway. He wasn't sure the sound had come from behind him but he knew the noise wasn't in the room with him. It could have been in the loft or on the landing. He twisted on his heels, expecting to find some lunatic bearing down on him wielding a weapon far more capable than his own kitchen-drawer knife.

His heartbeat quickened and he heard himself whimper with fear.

There was no one there.

He hurried out to the landing and saw that everything was the same as it had been before. The bathroom door was ajar. The other two doorways were both closed. He shut the master bedroom door firmly behind himself and glanced in the bathroom.

It remained a bastion of glossy tiles and polished surfaces. John had clearly used the bathroom before leaving and he had left the scarlet towel balled in the sink. Other than that, with its liquid black windows and daunting white porcelain, it was exactly the same as when Ben had last seen the room.

"Scruffy fucker," he muttered, unhappy with the untidiness of the towel. He folded it neatly, placed it over the rail, closed the bathroom door and studied the upper landing again.

"Hello?"

No response.

He tried the spare bedroom. It was empty. This was the room that John would be using when he returned the following Saturday. There was a large, functional double bed. The décor was more modern than anywhere else in the house. The painting in this room was another large oil on canvas similar to the glowering clown in the master bedroom. This one showed a shovel in a midnight forest. The silver-metal blade of the shovel glinted in the moonlight.

"Artwork from the Horror Channel," Ben grumbled.

He had expected his nervousness to dwindle a little as he searched one room and then another. But, instead of abating, his anticipation remained keen. His anxiety left an acidic flavour sitting tight at the back of his throat. He could feel the beef and beer shifting uneasily in his stomach as he opened the door to the linen closet.

His fingers fell on the door handle. He eased it slowly downward. With a sudden rush of energy, he pulled the door open.

A pair of bright yellow eyes glared at him.

Too shocked to move, Ben stared in horror as a cat, black as an oil slick, bolted out of the room and hurried past him, along the landing and down the stairs.

He only shrieked a little.

The sound was enough to make him feel unmanly when he replayed the moment in his mind later in the evening. Then he was trembling with relief and staggering down the stairs to see where the cat had disappeared to. His heart was beating fast enough to make him sober. His hands shook on the bannister as he tried to support himself down the stairs.

"A bloody cat?" he chuckled.

He couldn't see it in the hall or the study. It wasn't visible in the kitchen but, when he got himself a fresh beer, he poured a saucer of milk and placed that on the floor near the sink. If the cat was still lurking around the house, he figured it would find the drink.

Sure enough, a moment later, the creature came stealthily padding into the room. It glanced at Ben with suspicious yellow eyes and then warily stalked to the milk. Delicately, it lapped at the liquid.

"Cool," said Ben. "I'm a writer with a cat."

The thought was empowering. Etta had always wanted a cat. He knew that Hemmingway, Twain, Bukowski and Poe were all renowned cat lovers. He tried to tell himself that the presence of a cat would add literary gravitas to whatever shite he managed to spew out with the typewriter. He was now a writer with a cat and his work would get completed this time, he told himself, this development would help his writing receive the critical acclaim that he knew he deserved.

The cat farted.

Ben sipped at his beer and glanced at the cat-flap in the kitchen door. He didn't know if the creature belonged to the house but he could see there would be no advantage in putting it out for the evening, or whatever the hell cat-owners were supposed to do with cats. Resigning himself to the idea of sharing his accommodation with the creature, secretly pleased about this development, Ben found a second saucer and then pared off small pieces of the beef from the slow cooker. Placing the food beside the saucer of milk he stroked the creature lightly on the head. Etta had always said, if they ever did get a cat, she would name it after her favourite literary heroine of all time.

"Enjoy your supper, Anastasia," Ben told the cat.

The yellow eyes considered him coolly before the creature returned to its feast of milk. Deliberately, it ignored the beef.

He visited the study and played briefly with the typewriter. He was used to working only with a computer. The stiff weight of the typewriter keys was cumbersome and ungainly. He rolled a sheet of blank copier paper behind the platen and typed out a handful of words to make sure everything was working properly. After two minutes he decided the only things not working properly were his imagination and his fingers. Because of the few words he had typed, the muscles in his hands felt as though they had been subjected to an Olympian workout.

Anastasia slipped into the room to watch him whilst he typed. The cat jumped easily on the table and sat unperturbed as he slammed down one noisy key after another. Eventually, it lost interest in him and Ben noticed it was licking itself.

"I might not be able to write like Hemmingway," he grumbled. "But I can follow his other example and sit at a typewriter whilst watching a cat lick its arsehole."

He yawned, finished his beer, and decided he had endured enough excitement for one day. He'd abandoned London for the season. He'd committed to finishing the trilogy. He'd travelled to the back end of nowhere. And now, it seemed, he had adopted a cat. It made sense to go to bed, get some sleep, and make a proper start on the writing in the morning.

Anastasia joined him as he settled beneath an unfamiliar cover and rested his head on a too-soft pillow. The cat purred. He closed his eyes and stroked the creature as it walked within his reach. It was only as he began to drift off to sleep that it occurred to Ben that the cat was relatively stealthy, yet the thing that had alerted him to a presence in the house had been the stomping of heavy, hefty footfalls.

#4

"Eh bruv. You looking for anything?"

Tom glanced up and immediately knew he was being addressed by a dealer. The man was a scruffy-looking guy in a dirty grey hoodie. Tom conceded that there wasn't technically a uniform for dealers to wear, but this guy was sporting a pair of scuffed trainers, he was poured into a pair of skinny jeans, slung low at the crotch, and he wore a hoodie with a marijuana leaf on the back. With his unshaven jaw, and his bloodshot eyes peeping above the rims of John Lennon shades, he could not have looked more obviously like a dealer if he'd had the word *DEALER* tattooed on his forehead, or a badge on his breast saying - *YOUR LOCAL DEALER: always happy to supply*. Silently Tom prayed to gentle Jesus that the man would be compliant and not confrontational. If it could be avoided, Tom didn't want to hurt anyone. Tom never wanted to hurt anyone.

"Eh bruv," the dealer repeated. "I asked a question. You looking for anything?"

His speech was slightly slurred. Combined with the blank stare in his eyes and the light twitch of his jaw, Tom suspected the man was either drunk, seriously into a weed high, or cruising on amphetamines. Amphetamines seemed most likely from what he knew about current fads in local drug use. Tom had seen the symptoms before. Over the past few months he'd become an unwitting expert.

Tom considered the dealer evenly and spoke without lowering his voice.

"I want to purchase a gun, please."

The dealer snorted and shook his head. His grin showed stained teeth and cracked lips. "You having a laugh?"

Unsmiling, Tom considered the man. "No," he said. "I'm not having a laugh. I want to purchase a small firearm. I want to purchase a gun."

It was loud in the Boar's Head. Aside from the raucous conversations that bellowed from every table, the jukebox had been turned up to eleven. Nine Inch Nails were going through *Closer* and the volume was so loud Tom could barely understand a syllable. He kept hearing the occasional *F*-word in the song, and he grimaced in distaste each time the expletive registered on his senses. But he tried not to let his discomfort be too obvious. He was anxious to blend in with the colour of this part of the local community.

He'd known of the pub and often, when he was patrolling the streets in his role as a lay preacher, complete with a sandwich board urging the wicked to repent, he paused outside the pub and wondered if there was any hope for the lost souls trapped within. But this was the first time he'd ever gone through the pub's doors and entered its inner sanctum.

He was not surprised to note that the Boar's Head lived down to expectations.

The pub had managed a brief claim to fame when it was used as the setting for a comparatively successful gangster movie a decade earlier. The success that had come with that celebrity status was short-lived and, after the surrounding streets had gained notoriety for a handful of sadistic murders, the Boar's Head had quickly been forgotten by anyone other than those who lived within walking distance. It saddened him to think that Etta had always been fond of the establishment.

Nowadays the pub had an unsavoury reputation as the 'hangout' for dealers, prostitutes and unrepentant cons. The arched beams over the bar were made from sturdy lengths of oak that reminded Tom of the crossbeam on which Christ had been crucified. But that was the only religious association his mind could make with the place. The air stank of sweat, stale beer and unhappiness. Glancing around the room from the seclusion of his corner booth, seeing that most of the clientele looked like untidy silhouettes and shiftless shadows, each one vague and menacing, Tom thought the pub's reputation for being unsavoury was well-earned.

He glared sharply at the dealer and, once again, said a silent prayer to gentle Jesus, asking his saviour to help him avoid unnecessary confrontation. He was doing godly work and, if it could be avoided, he didn't want to resort to violence.

"Can you get me a gun?"

The dealer sniffed and slipped into the booth on the bench facing Tom. "I can get you anything, bruv," he declared. He'd rested his elbows on the beer-spattered table between them. His hands moved in the lazy gestures of arrogant self-assuredness. "I can get you anything: weed, Charlie, Mandy. I can get you pussy or-"

"I want a gun." As he spoke, Tom pulled a screwdriver from his pocket.

It was a flat-blade, eight inches in length with a bulbous red, plastic handle. It was the sort of solid and reliable tool that gentle Jesus would have kept in his carpentry bag, if they'd had red plastic handles on flat-blades during the time of Christ. Tom tested the screwdriver's weight in his right hand and squinted at the tip. He wore the distracted expression of a careful artisan examining his tools. Repeating his words to the tip of the screwdriver, Tom said, "I want a gun."

"No, bruv," the dealer laughed.

There was a subtle stammer in his voice. The word 'bruv' came out as 'b-b-bruv'. It was only a small detail, but it convinced Tom he had been right to think that the man was using amphetamines. Stammering was a common symptom of amphetamine abuse.

"You don't want a g-gun."

"Can you get me a gun?"

"I can get you anything," the dealer insisted. "But, trust me on this, b-b-bruv. You don't want a gun."

"I'm sorry, Jesus," Tom muttered.

He acted swiftly. He grabbed one of the dealer's hands and pressed it flat against the booth's table. Using as much speed and power as he could muster, Tom raised the screwdriver high and then slammed the flat-blade tip hard through the back of the dealer's hand.

Tom's face was contorted into a grimace of hatred.

The blade of the screwdriver pushed between two of the phalanges on the back of the dealer's hand. If the man bothered to take his injury to the local A&E unit, Tom reckoned they would identify the point of trauma as being between the second and third metacarpals.

He missed the bones. Clearly gentle Jesus had been guiding his aim.

The screwdriver slipped through the flesh and thin muscles of the hand with such ease, Tom felt no resistance until the blade of the screwdriver was buried deep into the beer-spattered table.

The dealer stared at his hand and then stared at Tom. His mouth hung open. His John Lennon glasses sat slightly askew on his face.

"Good job you're stoned," Tom muttered. "Or that would hurt like billy-o."

"What the fuck, bruv?"

He tried to pull away from the table but his hand was fixed firm. He looked stupidly at Tom and then tried again to move. Again, his hand refused to be shifted from where it was impaled. A small puddle of blood began to swell around the base of the screwdriver. In the dim lighting of the Boar's Head, it was a black ichor.

"Do you have a gun on you?" Tom asked.

"What the fuck have you done to my hand, bruv?"

"Do you have a gun on you?"

"No. Why the fuck would I have a gun on me?"

Tom lowered his head and stared at the table for a moment to try and clear his thoughts. It was bad enough that Nine Inch Nails were screaming the F-word, but he knew they were only doing it because pop singers did that sort of thing to sell records. The dealer was spitting that foul language in Tom's face and, even though he'd just had his hand secured to the pub's table, Tom thought there was still no need for the man to be swearing in such a volatile fashion.

"You don't have a gun on you," he repeated. "But you can get me a gun?"

The dealer's eyes were now wide with justifiable fear. His lower jaw started to tremble, and Tom could see he was preparing to scream for assistance. Swiftly, he slapped the man across the face. He wondered if now would be the time to bring out his claw hammer, or if that would be more than the dealer needed to see.

"Take out your phone," Tom said eventually. "I want you to call your contact. Whoever it is you think can get you a gun, I want you to call him and I want you to place an order."

The dealer tugged again at his impaled hand. A slight wince of discomfort curled his upper lip, as though making a conscious decision to use his other hand, the dealer reached awkwardly into his jacket pocket with his left hand and retrieved a tatty-looking iPhone. The white plastic casing was battered. Dirt was ingrained in the many cracks. When the dealer swiped the battered screen alive it looked small and unimpressive.

"It's not easy dialling with my left hand."

Tom shrugged. "If I take the screwdriver out of your hand now, there'll be so much blood you won't bother making the call."

The dealer nodded his acceptance of this and then prodded a clumsy finger at the phone's screen. Once the connection was made he snatched the phone awkwardly from the table pushed it to his ear and held it there with his shoulder.

"Eh bruv," he began. "Can you get me a gatt?"

There was a pause as he listened to the person on the other end of the line.

"A gatt," the dealer repeated. "A piece. Don't make me spell it out. I'm in a busy pub, bruv."

He paused again, listening. Glancing sharply at Tom he asked, "What sort?"

"A Magnum." Tom said the words without thinking. He knew nothing about guns, but he remembered seeing Clint Eastwood use a Magnum in an old movie about a man called Harry. The weapon had looked memorably impressive.

"Magnum," the dealer repeated.

Whatever response he received it was enough to make him chortle. There was a moment's interaction between the dealer and his contact before Tom remembered something important.

"I want bullets," he said suddenly. He tapped the top of the screwdriver to make sure he had the dealer's attention. The impact clearly vibrated through the metal shaft because the dealer winced as though he had been stung. "A big box of bullets, please," Tom insisted.

"Bullets," the dealer repeated. He flicked Tom's hand away from the screwdriver. There was a frown of impatience creasing his brow.

Tom sat back in his seat and waited as the dealer continued to chat back and forth with his contact. The thump of music in the Boar's Head remained loud enough to obliterate every other sound. Nine Inch Nails had given way to Peaches who urged her listeners to *Fuck the Pain Away*. Tom grimaced each time he heard her sing the F-word. The movement within the pub was languid and, although he sensed an atmosphere of testosterone-fuelled hostility in the room, Tom knew none of the animosity was focused in his direction. Gentle Jesus was protecting him now, as he always had done – and as he always would.

The pool of blood at the back of the dealer's hand had stopped swelling and was now starting to look sticky. Idly, Tom wondered how long it would be until the dealer's body properly acknowledged the pain from that injury. He supposed, when the pain did set in, there would then be some animosity focused in his direction. He hoped, by that point in the evening, he would be a long way away from the dealer.

"Carlos can get you a piece, bruv," the dealer said. "It might not be a Magnum. It could just be a nine."

Tom shrugged. He didn't know what a nine was, but the brand didn't matter. He only needed something that had the power to put holes in those people he didn't like. He wasn't an expert, but he supposed most guns would have that capability.

"When can I get it?"

"It'll cost you a grand."

"When can I get it?"

"Carlos will have it by noon tomorrow."

Tom nodded and stood up. It was not an ideal solution but he was being assisted by a divine hand. Gentle Jesus wouldn't let him down. "Bring the gun and the bullets to this address," he said, handing over a business card. "I'll have the money waiting for you."

The dealer held up a finger. He still had the phone crushed between his ear and his shoulder. "Carlos says, if this is some sort of setup, a police sting or something, he'll make you sorry, bruv."

Tom considered this and then grabbed the screwdriver. Holding tight on the bulbous handle, he wrenched it from side to side until the blade was forced free from the table. The movement, the steel blade pushing hard against ripped tissue and tender metacarpals, was enough to make the dealer cry out in surprise.

"Try and think of some way to convince Carlos that I'm not the police," Tom said.

He wiped the screwdriver on the upholstery of the seat he'd been using and then placed the tool back into the inside pocket of his jacket. Unhurriedly, he sauntered out of the pub, confident that the gun and ammunition would be delivered tomorrow to Ben Haversham's London address.

#5

Ben awoke at 03.10. His wristwatch showed the time, luminous hands on a black dial. It took him a moment to remember where he was and why he was there. It took less time to realise a pair of eyes were staring at him.

A pair of eyes were staring at him.

He sat bolt upright in the bed. His hand scrambled at the bedside cabinet, trying to find the switch for the lamp. His heartbeat quickened. His fingers found nothing. The darkness continued to oppress him save for the glint of the staring, glaring eyes. He heard himself whimper.

Moonlight shone through the uncurtained bedroom window. He could see the sinister shape of the hilltop house standing tall and imposing against the night sky. From his position in the bed, sitting up, more fearful of things inside the room than outside, he thought it looked like there was a wagon parked beside the building and a bustle of nocturnal activity between the vehicle and the house.

But that was something, he told himself, he would think about later. For now, there were more important considerations. He could still feel the weight of those eyes glowering at him with cold, deadly malice. He renewed his blind and fumbling search for the bedside lamp.

His hand found the light switch. Ben didn't allow himself an instant to sigh with relief. He clicked the switch and the room was flooded with blinding, brilliant, beautiful light.

The eyes disappeared.

Anastasia was asleep at the foot of the bed, so he couldn't blame her for glaring at him. She shifted beneath the disturbance of the light, her shoulders shuffling in a considered stretch, but she didn't wake.

He released the breath he had been holding and took account of the room. With a light on it was impossible to see out of the window so his view of the hilltop house was no longer visible.

The colour scheme of the bedroom was an antiquated, dusky pink. The carpets and bedding were pink, as were the drapes and bed linen fitted around the four-poster. The only areas that weren't pink were the yellow-wood fixtures of dressing tables, shelves and bedside cabinets. He glanced at the wall to his left. The dusky pink wallpaper was hidden by the staring eye of the morose clown painting.

He didn't care for the painting.

The initials *CW* were scratched into the bottom corner in a flourish of black. For some reason he thought the initials seemed important and he wondered if the artist was someone famous. Not that he knew of many artists famous for painting sinister pictures of clowns.

The wall to his right was stacked with dolls. Ben figured that the unnerving idea of being stared at had come from them. Staying motionless on the bed, only moving his head so he could see the dolls, Ben turned to face them. Whilst it wasn't particularly comforting, the idea that his sleep had been disturbed by their sightless glares was the only explanation that made any sense.

"Which one of you creepy fuckers woke me?" he grumbled.

In the silence that followed he wanted to splutter a nervous giggle. He didn't know whether it was better to hear nothing, or if he would prefer to hear the whisper of one of the dolls responding. He imagined it would come in a voice that balanced between a childlike falsetto and a gravelly, demonic rasp.

The thought made him want to tremble.

He glanced again at his wristwatch and told himself he should be asleep.

He couldn't decide what had woken him but, in a way, he felt gratitude for the disruption. His dreams had not been pleasant since Etta's death. Too many times since her passing Ben had been treated to the sight of how he imagined Etta's last moments had passed, or images of her undergoing an autopsy. This evening had been a particularly vivid encounter with her memory and he was relieved to be away from those thoughts.

She had been talking to him about horror movies. He had an idea she'd been mentioning classic vampire films, although he couldn't recall which ones. Or why. Now that he was awake, the details were fading from his thoughts and leaving only the familiar sense of sadness that came from remembering she was no longer a part of his life. She was dead. The only detail he could clearly remember was her *EMPTY* tattoo and the words she had whispered to him as he was waking: "You need to kill her. It's going to be you or her. You need to kill Marion."

He shook the memory from his mind. It did no good remembering Etta in such circumstances. She had always been such an easy-going person, it was tantamount to sacrilege to think of her issuing fatwas from beyond the grave.

He stared at the wall of dolls, trying to return the ferocity of their communal glares with his own impatient gaze. He knew he was not going to win the confrontation. Only an idiot would enter a staring contest with a collection of dolls. He climbed out of the bed, shrugged on a bathrobe that he'd found in the bathroom and walked barefoot over to examine the collection.

They were not ugly or unpleasant. They were only dolls. Most of them had open eyes, the majority had pink hands, feet and faces. There was an occasional nod to diversity amongst the group with a brown or black doll, but these were less skilfully executed and made Ben think of racist white performers wearing blackface. The dolls were dressed in various fashions of baby clothes, from modern rompers and stretch suits through to tutus and baby-grows. A handful were wearing long, lace Victorian christening gowns. The blackface dolls wore bright and colourful swaddling.

But they were only dolls.

He seemed to recall that dolls had featured in his dream, although he wasn't wholly sure why.

Ben's objections to dolls, he decided, were based on the fact that he had never had dolls as a child. The idea of collecting replica babies, and then storing them on the shelves of a bedroom so that they stared out at whoever was sleeping there, struck him as being more sinister than any horrific notion he'd ever created in his own dark fiction.

He could see that each one was subtly individual. One of them, with its stern face and lacquered hair, reminded him of Hitler. Another, with a disturbingly large bald head, made him think of images he had seen begging for help in the posters published by children's cancer charities. There was a third, with angelic golden curls, that didn't seem quite right with its mismatched eyes of brown and blue. A dog breeder he'd known had once referred to this condition as being wall-eyed. Ben didn't know if that term still applied to humans, but he thought it would work for dolls and, at the back of his mind, he instantly christened the golden-haired doll as Wall-Eyed Wally.

This one, he recalled, had been in his dream. It had been running from its shelf to the mirror and trying to write a message on the mirror. One of the other dolls, he vaguely remembered it being the one he thought of as 'Al Jolson' had wiped the message away. That part of the dream, he recalled, had been made more vivid by the trundling of heavy doll footfalls on the bedroom's wooden floor.

The dolls smelled vaguely musty, although he had to concede that they looked scrupulously clean. Despite John's rude words about the cleaner, Ben thought the woman was doing a good job of keeping the cottage spotless.

He stepped back from the wall of dolls and decided there were more than thirty there. There were three shelves and it looked like there were a dozen or so on each shelf. Some were sitting, others were laid down, all the ones with open eyes stared at him with cold disinterest.

Ben didn't want to start counting them for fear it would become some nightmarish ritual that resembled the early onset of OCD. He could see himself counting dollies on the wall, night after night, and not being able to sleep until he'd reached the magic number of however many were supposed to be there.

He wondered if that would make an interesting scene for a story. A character stood in front of a wall of dolls counting their numbers repeatedly, always striving to get to a golden definitive total.

Thirty-five.

To Ben's frustration he found he had counted them all before he could stop himself. He supposed that thirty-five would probably work as an appropriate total in fiction. The character would appear panicked whenever the final figure came up one short. He would start to wonder where the missing doll might be lurking. Or, if the count came up one higher, the character would be puzzling over which figure was the new addition.

Ben could picture the story idea developing neatly. The character's lips shaping the numbers, smiling with satisfaction each time it reached thirty-five, and then, on a further count, that same character frowning on the finality of only thirty-four.

The idea inspired a delicious chill of panic.

Ben could imagine the character, in this as yet unwritten story, hurrying through the count again, and reaching the same unsatisfactory total. Under those circumstances the character would have to count again, but this time doing it more slowly, developing the narrative tension, allowing the narrator to describe each doll in meticulous, malevolent detail.

If the total still came up short…

He liked the concept as a potential short story. It would be awkward to frame the narrative so that a central character had to find himself in that position, but he didn't think that consideration was insurmountable. Admittedly, the idea was making the hairs on the back of his arms stand upright as he thought about it now, in such close proximity to the wall of dolls. But that response suggested the idea had potential as an eerie short story.

He stepped back from the wall and tried to decide what he should do with the dolls. He didn't fancy getting back into bed whilst they watched him. But he didn't yet feel so comfortable in John's cottage that he was ready to start packaging up a clearly treasured collection.

"Drink," he muttered to himself.

He stepped out of the room, visited the lavatory for a pee, and then shuffled down the stairs. He turned lights on wherever he walked, not yet sufficiently confident to walk around the cottage in the dark. Not yet sufficiently confident it would be safe. After making a swift trip to the kitchen to grab a mug of black coffee, he walked into the study and sat before the typewriter.

The room was cold but not too chilly.

He rolled a blank page into the typewriter and typed the words, CHAPTER ONE. After pressing the carriage return twice, then tabbing in on the first line, he sat back in his chair and began to sip at his coffee. It had been a year since he last produced anything. Quite why John thought that the isolation of a village cottage would help to vanquish a crushing case of writer's block was a puzzle that Ben didn't bother to contemplate. John seemed to think that Ben could put aside all the issues that stopped him from writing, the memories he didn't want to explore and the miseries he hadn't yet acknowledged, and simply churn out another story. If that was what John really expected, Ben thought, then the man didn't deserve his role as a well-respected editor.

He rested his fingers over the keys, sure he had an idea for a story. He ought to try and write that piece about the man staring at the wall of dolls and counting. He knew the idea was only a short story, there wasn't enough mileage to turn it into something bigger. But he felt sure it would be an interesting one.

He moved his fingers away from the typewriter, reminding himself that he was supposed to be writing a novel, not a short story.

Ben took a sip of coffee. Then he placed his fingers over the home keys as the perfect opening line trickled through his thoughts. Then he paused, changing his mind. He took another sip at his coffee, wondering if he was ever going to move past his writer's block.

Thirty seconds later he had drifted into a deep and dreamless sleep.

"Morning love."

He jolted upright at the sound of the voice. A motherly woman stood over him. She was broad on the hips with a suffocatingly ample bosom. He could see she was wearing too-tight jeans and a clingy T-shirt beneath a garish tabard. Her hair was a tangle of black wire that was somewhere between an obvious wig and an over-processed hair-colour. He shook the remnants of his sleep away with a twist of his head and tried to think of a way to introduce himself.

His fingers ached.

"You must be Mester John's writer. He said you'd be staying here for a few weeks."

Mester John's writer? Ben supposed he was. He also guessed this woman was the cleaner John had called Mrs Scum. He knew he couldn't call her that and tried to think of a way to find out her name.

"I'm Ben," he said, offering a hand as he stood up. He noticed a sheaf of typed papers by the side of the typewriter.

How the hell had they got there?

"You might want to fasten your dressing-gown, Ben," Mrs Scum said. She pointed at his groin. "The stable door is open and it looks like a sickly foal's been left behind."

Ben glanced down and realised his dick was hanging out of the robe. To make the embarrassment more acute, because he'd woken up needing a pee, he was also sporting a semi. He snatched the robe over himself and turned away, blushing. "I'm so sorry," he began.

"It's not the first pee-pee I've seen, Ben," Mrs Scum cackled. She picked up his cold coffee mug and took it away. Still laughing she added, "Hopefully it won't be the last one I ever see either. Do you want a cup of coffee and some breakfast?"

"Err. Coffee would be nice. Thanks."

His voice trailed off. He wondered if he should apologise again, or if protocol for this sort of situation allowed him to simply hurry up the stairs and get dressed and maybe hide in the bedroom until the woman had disappeared.

"I'll have it ready in a couple of minutes." Her voice drifted easily through the small house. "I'll do you a couple of slices of toast as well. You look like you could do with a bit of meat on your bones. Let's try and fatten you up whilst you're here, shall we?"

He processed the words but didn't know how to respond. She had a northern accent, all broad vowels and clumsy consonant clusters, which made it difficult to understand what she was saying. Even when he'd worked out the words she was articulating, he didn't know if the comment about meat and bones was a reference to his dick, or just something the locals said to each other in these parts.

Ben bolted up the stairs and lunged into the master bedroom.

It looked as though Mrs Scum had already been in there. The bed was made and the clothes he'd discarded on the floor were folded neatly on a chair in front of the window. He snatched a clean pair of shorts from his suitcase, stepped into the previous day's jeans and T-shirt, and then pulled on a pair of trainers.

His fingers throbbed with inexplicable discomfort. It was the sort of pain he imagined would come from a night of fighting. The skin on his knuckles was clean, unbruised and unbroken. But still, every joint was stiff and uncomfortable to move. The tips were a curious combination of numbness and ultra-sensitivity.

He promised himself a couple of painkillers if the pain persisted and then pushed the matter from his thoughts. After visiting the bathroom, he stumbled awkwardly down the stairs and went into the kitchen.

"Toast and coffee," Mrs Scum said, pointing to a plate and a mug at the head of the table. Beside the toast was a jar of jam, its lid covered with a disc of gingham fabric.

"Did you make the jam?"

She shook her head. "Mrs Morris from the WI makes that." She brightened and added, "I've put a tub of my home-made oattie shortbreads in the pantry for you. And I did that beef for you yesterday. Was it OK?"

Ben had no idea what a tub of oattie shortbreads were. He smiled through his ignorance and said, "The beef was delicious. Thank you."

She shrugged the compliment aside. "I can organise meals for you, if you like. The slow-cooker is no bother. That said, I've stocked up on frozen pizzas and burgers and the like, because I know you creative types will eat at all hours of the day and night."

"I'd be happier with something properly cooked," he admitted. Junk food bored him. It was always too sweet and came with an aftertaste of regret.

Mrs Scum cackled agreeably. "That's just what your predecessor said."

He chewed on a slice of delightfully crispy toast smothered with rich, sweet blackberry jam. The action of eating gave him a moment to consider the words she'd said and translate them into some semblance of sense.

"Predecessor?"

"That artist woman. Tina."

Ben shook his head. He had no idea who she meant.

"Mester John's put two or three of her pictures up in the house," Mrs Scum insisted. She made the statement as though that would help Ben better understand the woman's identity.

"The woman who painted the creepy clown's eye in the bedroom?" he asked.

"Is that what it is? I suppose it could be a clown's eye. It gives me the willies."

Ben was ready to admit that her response was similar to his own reaction to the painting. It was a sinister image, and the last thing he needed to have staring at him in the bedroom. He considered this thought for a moment and then remembered the wall of dolls. He decided the creepy clown's eye was possibly the next-to-last thing he needed to have staring at him before he drifted to sleep. The dolls were far more disturbing. Aloud he asked, "Which other paintings has she done?"

"She did that mural in the library," Mrs Scum said quickly. "She has a few exhibited in the doll museum. And, here in the cottage, there's the one in the study that shows Marion's Doll House."

Words from his dream came back to him. Etta had been whispering, "*You need to kill her. You need to kill Marion.*"

He shivered and shook his head to dispel the upset that came with the memories. Focusing on what had been said, he realised Mrs Scum's words made no sense. He didn't know anything about the local library. He hadn't seen any painting in the study and he had no idea who Marion was, or what her Doll House looked like. He wondered if the local library had a copy of a phrase book or translation guide for visitors.

"Tina left a shed load of other paintings in the conservatory," Mrs Scum went on. "I thought Mester John would have been taking them back to that London with him when he left last night."

Ben nodded as though he understood. He had yet to venture into the conservatory, and he suspected a visit there might help to provide an explanation that clarified the meaning behind Mrs Scum's words.

"I would have thought you knew who she was. Even Harry at the Mucky Duck had heard of her before she came here. She was a tiebreak answer to one of the pub quiz questions."

Ben sipped the coffee and nodded again. Etta had once downloaded a movie for them to watch. It was a pirate copy of some Hollywood blockbuster and part of the film was spoken in a foreign language. Ben couldn't remember whether the language was Elvish, or Klingon, or French but, he did recall it was foreign, because it was a pirate copy, the foreign language part had been missing subtitles. He and Etta had awkwardly sat through the important scenes where characters spoke, and spoke, and spoke in a language they were never going to understand.

Listening to Mrs Scum, Ben felt the same absence of comprehension.

He wondered if the cleaner was having the same difficulty understanding his accent. For some reason, and he couldn't understand why, he didn't think Mrs Scum was having any difficulty making sense of his university drawl. Surely, he thought, it would make sense for the lack of comprehension to work in both directions.

"Are there any other bits of shopping you need?" she asked.

He understood this question and remembered that Anastasia had shown no interest in sharing his beef the previous evening. "I could do with some cat food."

"Has that black moggy found its way back here?"

"I assumed the cat was a fixture of the house."

Mrs Scum shrugged. "The artist woman fed it. The writer we had up here before wasn't that partial to the thing. He boarded up the cat flap. Mean bastard laughed when it banged its head trying to get in."

Ben swigged a mouthful of coffee to cleanse his mouth of the last of the toast. "I'll pay for the cat food if that's an issue," he said. "Or I'll buy it myself if it's a problem."

"It's not a problem. This is John's house and he pays back every penny I spend on the shopping of his guests. Are you all right for all your writing equipment?"

Ben considered this and then nodded. "There's a typewriter and a couple of reams of paper," he admitted. "What else would I need?"

"Notepads? Pens? Pencils?"

Ben shook his head. He didn't like working with notepads. His handwriting always looked untidy and it seemed to diminish his creative aspirations. More importantly, he kept losing notepads and there were times when he wrote ideas down so quickly they were an illegible scrawl that he couldn't decipher their meaning when he later returned to them.

"You say there was an artist living here before me? When did she leave?"

Mrs Scum had been watching him savour his coffee. Now she looked away. A frown had crossed her brow that made him think this was a subject she didn't want to discuss. "The last time we saw her was about a month ago. She just upped and left in the middle of the night."

"How odd," Ben offered.

Mrs Scum shrugged. "It's not that odd. The writer before her did the same moonlight flit. Just disappeared in the middle of the night. He was seen taking his usual evening walk up to the Green Man on the Thursday night. And then, on the Friday morning, there was no trace of him. A similar story for the writer afore him. And for the painter before that one."

Ben sipped at the remnants of his coffee and tried to work out what he was hearing. He was about to ask Mrs Scum for the names of his predecessors and a brief description about who they were, but she chose that moment to stand up and say she was off to one of her other jobs.

"I'll get you one of the butcher's Barnsley chops for your slow-cooker," she said. "Albert might be up later to sort out the grounds if the weather stays fair. I can pick up the cat food and get your tea sorted in an hour or two."

Ben smiled as though he knew what a Barnsley chop was and had an idea who Albert might be. He couldn't fault the woman's geniality, but she seemed to think he shared her intimate knowledge of the village.

"I had a message from Mester John this morning," she added solemnly. "He asked if you could get some writing done and switch your phone on."

Ben nodded. He thanked the woman, watched her go, and didn't bother moving from his seat at the kitchen table until long after he'd heard the front door close behind her. He only shifted from his seat in the kitchen when Anastasia came padding into the room. Snatching a saucer from the collection of crockery Mrs Scum had left drying beside the sink, he poured a splash of milk for the cat and watched as the creature lapped greedily at its breakfast.

"Mrs Scum will be back later with some real food for you," he told the cat.

Anastasia didn't bother glancing in his direction.

Ben considered doing himself another coffee and then decided he wasn't that thirsty. He glanced into the conservatory. It was a spacious room, brightly lit from the chill autumn day outside. Although the furniture was sparse, the room was cluttered with artistic paraphernalia. There were a couple of easels and a handful of canvases. He recognised the same dull colour palette and bold strokes he'd seen on the creepy clown's eye. Curious, he stepped closer to examine the artwork.

There were pictures of clowns and dolls.

Ben recognised the doll that shared Hitler's hairstyle and the angelic curls of Wall-Eyed Wally, the doll with the mismatched eyes. But there were others as well and the artist had captured them in poses of an intensity that was almost lifelike. He suppressed the urge to shiver as he studied them. He had thought it would be a relief to discover that not every picture showed an image of the sinister clown but the well-realised pictures of dolls were equally unsettling.

Some of the paintings were of the local area, offering him glimpses of things he had briefly noted on his journey through the village to John's cottage. They included the library, the police station, and the cemetery-fringed churchyard. The paintings were well done and realistic, even though the palette was grim and earthy. Each one was signed with the *CW* scribble of the artist's signature and he wondered again why that seemed vaguely familiar.

As he walked back into the kitchen, Anastasia sauntered past him and leapt through the cat flap. He guessed the cat was heading out for its morning constitutional, or whatever the polite term was for when cats went outside to crap.

He stepped through to the study and settled himself behind the typewriter.

It wasn't a comfy seat, he thought. It had been sufficiently comfortable so that he'd had been able to spend the night there the previous evening. Considering it was a wooden chair with the thinnest cushion, he supposed that was quite surprising.

Distantly, he heard the creak of the cat flap. The sound was far enough away so that he didn't bother to consider what he was hearing. Instead, he found himself looking at the typewriter and considering the pages by its side.

He remembered rolling a blank sheet into the platen the night before. He had typed the words *CHAPTER ONE* at the head of the page and then he had fallen asleep.

Except he was no longer sure that that was what happened.

There was a stack of typed pages next to the typewriter. Rolled around the platen was a sheet that was blank save for the words, *CHAPTER FIVE*. He picked up the sheaf of typed pages, maybe forty in total, and leafed slowly through them.

"What the...?" he muttered. "I've been sleep-writing?"

Anastasia leapt onto the table. The unexpected appearance of the cat startled him so much that he almost dropped the pages he held. When his racing heartbeat had calmed down Ben composed himself and shook his head as he tried to make sense of what he was holding.

He knew it was a stupid idea. Nobody could sleep-write a sheaf of pages. That was the sort of impossible idea that made no sense whatsoever. But he could think of no other explanation. He read the opening sentence beneath the words *CHAPTER ONE*.

'I killed Etta.'

"Holy fuck."

#7

Tom wrinkled his nose in disgust as he wandered around Ben's apartment. The air was stale with memories of beer and, he suspected, either tobacco, marijuana, or dirt. Any of the scents should have soured his mood but, because he knew it was important to remain in control of his emotions for this meeting, Tom refused to let his anger develop. It was only when he came across a framed photograph on Ben's desk that Tom finally snapped. He studied the image of Ben and the blonde woman for a long moment before hurling the picture across the room.

It was Etta.

She was smiling.

She had an arm around the worthless writer.

The framed picture shattered against the wall and the silence of the apartment was momentarily fractured by the brittle tinkle of glass shards dancing against each other. He blinked his eyes dry and shook his anger away.

Gentle Jesus would not condone such an irrational response.

"He's going to pay," Tom grumbled.

The PC on the desk had been booting. The monitor came to life and the screen waited expectantly for a password. Tom scoured through the Post-it notes and pages on the desk trying to find some clue that might give him access to the contents of the machine. He saw nothing that he thought might be the machine's password.

"Fiddlesticks."

He snatched a Post-it note from the side of the monitor. This one said, 'Alice' and was followed by a mobile phone number. It was beside a second Post-it note labelled 'John' and, beneath the telephone number on that one was the message 'always call Alice first.'

Ben's agent was called John. Tom wondered if the message meant that Alice might be John's secretary. He didn't know if that was likely but he thought it would be prudent to keep hold of both numbers. He glanced again at the computer screen and wondered if it would be possible to guess Ben's password. In films and novels, the hero always managed to guess passwords. In reality, Tom thought there was as much chance of guessing next week's lottery numbers.

He had expected to find a brimming ashtray on the desk, empty tins of lager and other signs of substance misuse. Despite the fusty smell of the apartment, and a clutter of papers that looked like half-read books and strategically open magazines, the home was not particularly untidy. Instead of making him feel any sympathy or compassion for Ben Haversham, the ordinariness of the place made Tom feel sure the writer was trying to hide something.

The bedroom looked relatively neat. The bathroom had mildew growing in one corner of the shower unit but, otherwise, it was unremarkable. The kitchen was uncluttered. There were three bottles of Beck's lager stored in the fridge alongside a half empty tub of margarine.

Tom took one of the bottles of lager, opened it and drank.

"Haversham? You in there?"

Someone was knocking on the door.

Tom walked cautiously towards the spyhole in the centre of the door and peered out at a pair of men that could most kindly be described as suspicious. He recognised the dealer from the pub. The man was in the same clothes he had worn the previous evening: a dirty grey hoodie, skinny jeans and scuffed trainers. His injured hand was bandaged with what looked like a grubby T-shirt.

The man who was knocking was undoubtedly Carlos. He had a swarthy complexion, dark hair, and large brown eyes that suited the name. He glared angrily at the spyhole. Over one shoulder he rested a baseball bat. Black lettering on the pale wood of the bat spelt out the words '*Louisville Slugger*'.

"Haversham?" Carlos called as he thumped the side of his fist on the door.

They thought he was Ben Haversham, Tom realised. Because he had given the dealer a card with Haversham's name and address, they assumed he was Haversham. Whilst Tom didn't approve of duplicity and deception, he figured he could use that misunderstanding to his advantage.

Carlos banged on the door again. "Are you in there, Haversham? We've got the nine you ordered."

Tom nodded to himself as he looked at the baseball bat on Carlos' shoulder. He had expected this would likely be a violent encounter. He had hoped it would be a simple exchange of goods for cash. However, he wasn't wholly disappointed that there would be a chance to vent his anger on someone deserving. In truth, he was looking forward to acting as the scourge that gentle Jesus needed.

He waited until Carlos was raising his fist to hammer on the door again.

Then Tom pulled the door wide open.

Carlos was caught in the act of throwing his fist where the door had been. He almost stumbled into the hallway of Ben's home. There was an expression of stupid surprise on his face as he struggled to maintain his balance.

Tom snatched the baseball bat from Carlos' grip. He slammed the handle hard at the man's face. The weight of the bat caught him fully on the nose. Tom heard a groan of discomfort as Carlos staggered back. He clutched at his broken nose and Tom saw twin spurts of blood erupt from the man's nostrils.

Tom kicked him hard in the ankle.

Carlos was already uncertain on his feet and this blow was enough to trip him. He fell heavily to the floor and spat out a string of furious curse words.

"Stay down there," Tom told him, pointing the baseball bat at Carlos. "Stay down there and don't give me a reason to hurt you."

"Who the fuck are you?"

Tom kicked him sharply in the face. It was a vicious blow, landing over Carlos' eye and knocking his head back to an unnatural angle. Carlos moaned with pain and raised a hand to protect himself. Tom kicked again, this time crushing two fingers between the toe of his boot and Carlos' skull.

"Don't swear," Tom said absently. "Gentle Jesus doesn't like swearing. I don't like swearing. There's no need for such language."

"Do as he says, b-bruv," insisted the dealer. He raised his bandaged hand ruefully, almost as though he was saluting respect to Tom. "You don't want to mess with this guy," the dealer told Carlos.

Tom glanced at the dealer. He stood outside the doorway and it was clear he would be making no effort to help Carlos. He looked nervous and anxious to leave.

"Did you bring me the gun I requested?" Tom asked.

"Carlos has got it."

Tom turned to Carlos. The man looked like he was trying to lever himself up from the floor. He had one hand planted on the carpet and the other was reaching into his jacket pocket. His face was flushed an angry red, although Tom conceded, that could have been caused by the kicking he had just received.

Tom stamped on Carlos' hand.

He put a lot of effort into the action. His boot was raised high. Then he slammed it down hard, driving it into the knuckles of Carlos' spread fingers.

Tom felt bones cracking under the weight of his foot.

Carlos howled. He crashed back to the floor with a cry of pained dismay.

Tom turned to face the dealer. He pointed at him with the baseball bat and said, "Have you genuinely brought me the gun I ordered?"

"It's in his pocket, b-bruv," the dealer stammered. "He was just reaching for it."

"Get it out of his pocket," Tom told the dealer. "Kneel down on the floor. Do this slowly, and you might get out of this without anyone getting hurt."

Carlos chose that moment to groan. He held up his hand and Tom saw that two of the man's fingers were bending at unusual angles.

"Well," Tom amended. "You might get out of this without anyone getting hurt any further." He flashed a smile that could have been mistaken for an apology. Then he gestured with his baseball bat, urging the dealer to hurry up and retrieve the gun.

The dealer was obedient. He passed the gun to Tom with shaking fingers.

"There you go, bruv," he said, trying to make it sound as though he was doing Tom a favour. "This is just what you asked for, isn't it?"

Tom did not reply immediately. This gun was not the massive piece of hardware that he had been expecting. Admittedly it was heavy. The weight, in his hand, made Tom realise he was wielding something that had the potential to be deadly. He struggled to suppress a smile as he held the gun, knowing he now had the power to become the avenging scourge that gentle Jesus needed. He only stopped smiling when he caught a glimpse of his reflection in one of Haversham's mirrors and saw that the expression made him look like a lunatic.

"Does it have bullets?"

He pointed the gun at Carlos' face and pulled the trigger twice. The hammer snapped against an empty chamber each time. It made a clicking sound that resounded hollowly in the confines of the apartment.

Carlos sobbed.

Tears poured from his bloodshot eyes.

"He's got the bullets in his other pocket, b-bruv," the dealer explained. "Let me get them."

Carlos tried to pull away, but the dealer was swift. He dragged a small box of bullets from Carlos' pocket and tossed them at Tom's feet. "Here, bruv. These are what you need. Take them and let us-"

Tom stopped listening. Instead of the word *MAGNUM*, as he had wanted, this gun was labelled with the word '*RUGER*'. He supposed it wasn't an important detail. He plucked the box of bullets from the floor and began to slide them individually into the chambers of the gun's cylinder. He'd never loaded a gun before but he thought it seemed fairly obvious. So long as he loaded the bullets with the pointy ends facing away from the handle, he figured it would be safe. The catch for the cylinder release had been easy enough to find. The weight of the gun, so impressively heavy and alien at first, now felt perfect in his hand. He wondered if this was another sign that gentle Jesus was guiding him.

"You'll pay for this, Haversham," Carlos grunted. He was spitting the words between clenched teeth. There was a spittle of blood on his lower lip. "You'll fucking pay for this."

Tom pointed the Ruger at him. He considered warning the man about his potty mouth but he realised there would be no point. To men like Carlos, swearing was such a common part of their everyday life that they barely realised they were doing it. They heard it in pop music songs like those he had heard in the Boar's Head the previous evening. And they used swearing to colour their every utterance, whether the profanity was needed or not. Instead of telling Carlos not to use such naughty words, Tom asked, "Do either of you gentlemen know how to hack a password?"

Ben rushed out of the house. It took him a couple of minutes to run down the driveway. It was darkly overhung by low-reaching branches that snatched and scratched at his head and shoulders. He suspected the trees were willows, but he wasn't particularly confident about identifying them and simply pushed them away from his face with his forearms. It didn't matter what the trees were. All that mattered was getting out of the house and getting away from the confession.

The day outside the tunnel of trees was gloomy and overcast.

Crunchy autumn leaves covered the driveway and made a satisfying, if unacknowledged, accompaniment to his footfalls. Once away from cottage's driveway he thought of trying to find a newsagent or some shop that would sell him a packet of cigarettes. It would probably be a tobacconist in this provincial little hellhole, he thought. The idea of having to interact with any aspect of the village's antiquated charm made him feel irritated. It wasn't that he wanted to start smoking again anyway, he told himself. But there were some things that required a cigarette and the discovery that he had typed forty pages of murder confession in his sleep was enough to make him feel that tobacco, at the very least, would be a good starting point.

I killed Etta.

He didn't know where he was walking. The shadow of the spooky old house remained above him as he walked. Glancing at a pair of gates that shielded a driveway leading up the hill to the door of the house, he saw a sign saying 'Doll House.' Stepping closer, anxious to read anything that didn't look like his own murder confession, he studied the text beneath the sign.

'Doll House
Sandalwood's celebrated museum of dolls
and their history in the village.
Proprietor Ms Marion Papusa.'

"*You need to kill her,*" he remembered hearing Etta whisper the words. "*You need to kill Marion.*" He pushed that idea from his thoughts and re-read the sign. The Doll House was a museum? He remembered that Mrs Scum had referred to the building as Marion's Doll House.

Glancing up at the spooky old building he tried to make sense of what he was seeing. For an instant it had looked as though a clown was standing outside the doorway. He knew little about clowns, this one was dressed all in white, save for the huge black, pom-pom-like buttons that ran down its jacket. The face was deathly white. The pants were deathly white. Even the cone-shaped hat on its awkwardly-tilted head was white.

"Jesus fucking Christ," he gasped.

He blinked and tried peering at the doorway, only to note that the clown had disappeared. Ben wondered if it had been a figment of his imagination. He considered walking up to the museum and maybe taking a tour in the hope the distraction would allow him to collect his thoughts. Then he decided that was a stupid idea. He'd been woken from his sleep because of the creepy doll collection. He was still recoiling from an unnerving and likely supernatural encounter. A trip around a fucking doll museum was not going to help soothe his frazzled nerves. Angry at himself for even contemplating such a fatuous idea, Ben stormed past the gates and headed into the centre of the village.

I killed Etta.

It didn't make any sense. He wasn't sure how the pages came to have been typed. He couldn't bring himself to think that he was responsible for them even though there was no other explanation.

He paused halfway up a hill and took brief stock of his surroundings. He had no idea where he was. All the yellow stone houses with their slick, black roofs looked identical. He supposed, if he retraced his steps now, he could maybe find his way back to the entrance of the Doll House and then find his way back to John's cottage. But that idea held no appeal.

Suppose Mrs Scum had deposited the pages there when she arrived that morning? He hadn't seen her do any such thing, and he could think of no reason to motivate her to play such a prank. But it would certainly be a way to explain how the pages had ended up on his desk this morning.

Except…

The more he thought about it, the more he felt that was unlikely.

The pages had been on the desk when he blinked his eyes open. Thinking back to the moment he was now sure that was the case.

The cleaner had woken him by shouting a cheery 'morning love' as she walked into the room. There had been no time for the woman to make the exchange whilst he was coming to his senses from a night sleeping in an uncomfortable office chair.

Trying to rationalise the idea, he wondered if Mrs Scum might have crept into the room, placed the pages on his desk, and then crept out to return a moment later and pretend that she had only just arrived.

Except that didn't seem likely either.

He had typed the words *CHAPTER ONE* at the heading of the page he began the previous evening. The sheet he'd typed on had not been in the typewriter. There had been a fresh sheet headed *CHAPTER FIVE* and there was no way Mrs Scum could have swapped those pages without waking him. The noise of the typewriter would have broken his sleep. He didn't think someone had been in the room with him, typing, because even the noise of the platen rolling out a fresh sheet would have been enough to stir him from his slumber.

I killed Etta.

He wondered if that was why his fingers ached: because he had been hammering away through the night on an old typewriter. If that was true, then it made sense that his fingers ached. That would also explain the numb/sensitivity on the tips of his fingers and the throbbing stiffness at the small of his back.

I killed Etta.

"I typed a confession in my sleep," he muttered.

He said the words as he passed a harried looking young woman. She frowned and hurried on past him. Ben ignored her.

He thought, if Mrs Scum was playing a joke on him, it was an elaborate construct and it was in pretty poor taste. The poor taste suggested John was possibly involved because the agent was renowned for his questionable sense of decency and off-colour humour. But, even though this all looked like the sort of thing John would do for a prank, Ben could see no real way of how the pages had been typed and placed by his side.

He stood outside the entrance to the Doll House.

How the hell had he ended up back here? He'd been walking up the hill. The entrance had been at the bottom of the hill. Had he walked down without noticing?

He thought again about visiting the museum, partly to satisfy his own curiosity about dolls and partly to ask if it was likely that he had really seen a whiteface clown outside the doors. He stopped himself from pushing through the gates because he knew such an action would just be delaying the inevitable. He needed to get back to the cottage and read the confession. Whether the typed pages were a malicious prank orchestrated between John and Mrs Scum, or a product from his own troubled subconscious, he needed to see what had been written so he could start to make sense of the situation.

"Are you John's writer?"

He hadn't seen the approach of the woman. She was small and, although she looked elderly, he got the impression that she remained physically capable. Her face was framed by tight, greying-brown curls. Her features were weathered and tanned to a sepia colour. Looking at her slender waist, and her deceptively quick way of moving, he wondered if she had previously been a dancer.

"Yes," he admitted. "Ben Haversham."

"John mentioned you." She had a voice that clearly didn't belong in the village. She spoke with the crystal-clear pronunciation of someone who was educated at a prestigious finishing school. Her welcoming smile and easy manner made her seem successful, accomplished, approachable and easy to like.

Ben decided he didn't trust the woman.

Why the hell would someone successful be hiding in a northern village?

"How are you settling in?" she asked.

"Who are you?"

She laughed and offered a hand. "I should have introduced myself before. My name's Marion, darling. I'm an old friend of John's and I keep an eye on his cottage whilst he's away in London."

"You need to kill her. You need to kill Marion."

The fingers he held were spindly and cold. He was conscious of the hard bones in her grip. It didn't feel like a human hand. It felt like mechanical fingers inside a thin skin glove.

"I saw you reading the sign to the museum earlier," she smiled. "Do you fancy the tour?"

Marion, he thought. This was Marion Papusa. The proprietor of the doll museum according to the sign he had read. And she was offering to take him on a tour of her doll museum.

"It's very kind," he said. "But I should get back to my…"

"Your writing," she interjected. "Of course. John says there's a tight deadline on this title."

John had said that to her, had he? How much had John told this woman about his writing? He thought of asking her, and wondered if he should also mention the clown. Before he got a chance to voice any thoughts, Marion was talking over him.

"I'll let you get back to your work," she said. "But it would be lovely to have you over for a meal one evening."

"A meal?"

"I always enjoy talking with authors," Marion explained. "And I'd imagine it will only take a day or two before the isolation up here drives you insane."

"That's very kind of you," Ben began. "But…"

"I'll let your cleaner know what night I'm expecting you," Marion said. "I can see you need to get back to the cottage now. I suspect you've just had some genius idea for what to do with that cunning little story of yours, so I'll let you get on, Mr Haversham."

She gave him a cheery smile and headed through the gates that led up to the museum. He glanced up at the doorway to the Doll House, but there was no clown there now. Bewildered by the exchange he had shared with Marion Papusa, Ben sauntered across the road and returned to the cottage.

#9

He didn't go straight to the study. Instead he went through to the kitchen. Anastasia was sitting on the table staring at the fridge. Absently, he splashed milk into a saucer for the cat and then boiled the kettle and poured himself a coffee. If he'd been back in London, he would have wanted something stronger. If he didn't have access to any serious tablets or a decent high, then he would have needed a scotch or a vodka. At the very minimum he would have wanted a beer and a fag.

But here, he could see, he was having to make do with a coffee and maybe a couple of Mrs Scum's oattie shortbreads. He examined the biscuits in their metal, airtight tin and sniffed one doubtfully. They were brown and lumpy with rugged bits of oatmeal sticking out from their sides.

They did not look appetising and yet, after nibbling on one, he conceded that they were slightly more addictive than crack. A year ago he had used chemical assistance to help address every problem. Now he was resigned to having a strong coffee and a biscuit that looked like it had already been digested.

"Look on my works ye mighty and despair," he muttered.

Anastasia made a loud meowing sound and pushed her body against his legs.

Feeling as though the cat was encouraging him to go into the study and face the issue, Ben made his way out of the kitchen and through the hall.

The grandfather clock ticked ominously as he stepped past it. The regular, unrelenting *tick-tick-tick-tick-tick* only seemed to change as the clock was girding its loins to chime out the hour. Then, seemingly struggling to continue, the sound of the ticking was lost beneath the multiple knells of the hour chiming.

Ben stepped into the study as the clock sounded eleven chimes.

The typed pages were exactly where he had left them, beside the old Silver Reed typewriter. He had half-hoped that there might be nothing there on his return. The pages could have been a figment of his imagination and it would have been better to think he had suffered some sort of episode. Unresolved grief, an active imagination, and a lifetime of substance abuse had to have some sort of effect on a person's psyche and, he figured, imagining a handful of typewritten pages would not be beyond the realms of possibility.

But the pages remained waiting for him.

He settled himself in the chair that faced the typewriter and placed down his coffee and biscuits. Picking up the first sheet he read the opening sentence again and wanted to swoon with relief.

I killed Ella.

It said *Ella*. Not *Etta*.

Ella was the name of one of the central characters in the trilogy he was writing. Etta was the name of his best friend who had died twelve months earlier. He felt chilled by the wave of relief sweeping through his body as he realised this wasn't a murder confession. It was genuinely the first pages of the final book in the trilogy he was supposed to be writing.

He wasn't sure how he'd managed to write the words whilst he was asleep.

He hadn't believed such things were possible. The technicalities of that achievement were something he knew he would have to ponder on later. But he couldn't argue with the facts that were facing him. And, the most important detail of all was the knowledge that he had written the start of a novel and not some damning and personal murder confession.

He had written forty pages of his next book.

Miaow.

Anastasia was standing between him and the typewriter. He stroked the cat without thinking about the gesture. It seemed natural to pet the creature whilst he read and, if not for the distraction of the text, Ben would likely have decided that he needed to have a cat living with him in his London home. But, instead of thinking about the companionship of cats, his thoughts were torn between the peculiarity of him having sleep-written a manuscript, and the anomaly of the content he was reading. His hand was still trembling when the second realisation struck him.

He turned curiously back to the opening pages.

Ella was dead? And his narrator had killed her?

Book One of the trilogy had been an embarrassingly autobiographical piece of fiction that was often referred to as being part of the confessional genre. It had been the story of a young writer, Bill, who went through the usual traumas of trying to get his work noticed by publishers. Once Bill got his work noticed by publishers the story documented his attempts to get reviewed and become successful. The story had been a rags-to-riches loosely-based-on-Ben's-own-life-story yarn that concluded with Bill's title sitting on a bestseller list.

Book Two had been the reverse side of the writer's coin. It had been similarly autobiographical but, in *Book Two* Bill had suffered miserably with fame. He had cut himself off from friends. He had overindulged in too many pleasures: chemical and physical. He had lived life to an unnecessary and unhappy excess. The core of the story had been a focus on Bill's relationship with his best friend and occasional fuck-buddy, Ella. The sexual side of things had stopped when Ella developed a steady relationship with a lay preacher called Timmy. And then, when Ella broke up with Timmy, she had borrowed money from Bill to go on an all-night binge to banish her upset. *Book Two* ended with Ella in an A & E ward, suffering respiratory failure due to an overdose.

He sipped his coffee and considered the opening pages of the story.

I killed Ella. I didn't pump the poison into her system, or flick the switch on the life-support machine. But, instead of giving her the money for those drugs, I might just as well have slit her throat and watched the blood pump from her veins.

It was a tad more violent than his usual style of writing and darker in its tone too. But, Ben conceded, his central character had endured a lot and had probably earned that level of darkness. He settled back in the chair and read carefully through the pages.

Miaow.

At some point he realised he had stopped stroking Anastasia.

The creature pushed its head against the pages in his hand and almost made him lose his place. He grumbled an absent, "For fuck's sake," and then stroked the cat with one hand whilst holding the pages with the other.

It was a compelling start to the story. Rather than beginning with Ella in A & E, the story seemed to be starting with the build-up to how Ella had ended up dead. He wasn't usually a writer who enjoyed delivering hard chunks of backstory, but this way into Ella's story seemed appropriate for the conclusion of the trilogy.

As he flicked through the pages, Ben didn't know what should have impressed him the most: the quality of the writing, or the fact that the pages seemed to have appeared without him making any conscious effort to put words on the page. The fact that he had yet to find any typos in the manuscript was surprising. He didn't usually produce anything on a first draft that wasn't filled with spelling mistakes, tense shifts or too many adverbs. But this read like a surprisingly clean copy. It was at a standard he would have been happy to submit to an editor. In truth, it was a standard he would have been happy to receive back from an editor.

The story also seemed like a logical development from what had happened before. Bill, mortified over the death of Ella, had spent a miserable year suffering the twin blows of writer's block and substance addiction. Bill's gruff-but-kindly agent had taken him out of the city and set him up in isolated accommodation in the middle of nowhere. The nowhere seemed somewhat gothic and sinister, Ben thought. The subsidiary characters seemed dark, and unpleasant, and potentially dangerous. But, from the way the story was now developing, Ben thought such characters were probably appropriate for this novel.

His only issue with the story was the lingering presence of Ella's violent ex-boyfriend, Timmy. The character seemed to bridge two worlds that should have been separate and Ben didn't think he fitted into the story for the third book. He also thought the character took the novel away from its biographical aspect because the person he was based on, Etta's real boyfriend, was currently in a secure mental health facility, or whatever name it was people now used to be politically correct when discussing lunatic asylums.

"That's your only issue?" he muttered.

Saying the words aloud did not seem irrational or indicative of his dwindling grasp on reality. Saying the words aloud simply reminded him of the unnatural phenomena he was trying to comprehend. He had vanquished his writer's block. He had written the first few thousand words of a story that he thought could potentially satisfy John's demands. And he had managed it all, literally, whilst he slept. If the only aspect of the novel was that he didn't like the presence of a particular character, it was a small drawback he could learn to live with. At worst, it was a detail he might want to remove in the final edit.

The front door creaked open. The sound made him stiffen in his chair.

Anastasia glanced towards the doorway.

For an instant Ben feared it would be Etta's boyfriend, standing tall and broad and with his hands clenched into powerful fists. He knew that it was the story that had made him think about that non-existent danger from Tom the God-botherer, but the image was so powerful it was almost unshakeable.

"Cooee. Mr Haversham?"

It was Mrs Scum's voice.

He breathed a wavering sigh of relief.

"Are you decent?" she called. "I've just come back to set up your Barnsley chop in the slow-cooker."

#10

I killed Ella. I didn't pump the poison into her system, or flick the switch on the life-support machine. But, instead of giving her the money for those drugs, I might just as well have slit her throat and watched the blood pump from her veins.

I should have noticed that she needed help when she came home with the tattoo. It was eleven in the morning. She was staggering on too-tall heels and her make-up had been fucked to a smudged memory. The tattoo was wrapped in clingfilm like a piece of cut-price meat.

"What the fuck is that?"

"It's a tattoo."

She sounded defensive. She tried turning her body away so that I couldn't see the stylised lettering. I placed a hand on her shoulder and pulled her with more force than was probably necessary. She pouted and grudgingly showed me her arm.

It was a raised mess of horrific black ink on the underside of her slender, pale forearm. Bold letters, vaguely calligraphic, seemed to blend into each other to make a pointless statement.

"I can see it's a tattoo. It's a word, isn't it? What does it say?"

"Can't you read it?"

"I can read the word EMPTY. Is that what it is? You've got a tattoo of the word EMPTY? What the hell does that mean?"

She pulled away from me and stormed into the kitchen.

"Have you got a couple of spare quid?" she called.

"For drugs?"

I'd followed her. I watched her open cupboards, scowl at the bare shelves, and then slam the doors closed with obvious frustration. The only thing she retrieved was an old box of paracetamol. After popping the final four pills from the strip she opened the fridge and took a bottle of Beck's.

"Is that what you want money for?" I repeated. "For drugs?"

"I want something to take the edge off," she insisted. She snapped the lid from the Beck's and then used the drink to swallow down the four tablets. "The painkillers aren't helping," she said, gesturing towards her freshly tattooed arm. "I'm feeling pretty bummed that my best friend can't think of anything nice to say about the body art I've invested in."

She fixed me with a sour scowl that I tried to ignore.

"And I just need a little something," she whispered. Her words were close to a sob. "I need a little something to dull the day's sharp corners."

I glared at her, annoyed to be hearing poetry come from her when she was in this frame of mind. "Dulling the day's sharp corners? That's a good turn of phrase."

She shrugged. "I think I heard you use that line the other night when you were off your tits."

I blinked, pleasantly surprised. A part of my mind wondered if she was simply saying that to win me over, but I think the arrogance that is my Achilles' heel wanted to believe I had originally made the cool comment. I made a mental note that the phrase 'dulling the day's sharp corners' would appear in the next story I wrote. Always assuming I could write another story.

She sipped at more of her beer and gestured to the tattoo again.

For the first time I noticed it was not as clumsy or as brutal as I'd imagined. The lettering was reminiscent of Olde English fonts with thick black-letter bars contrasted against delicate, intricate serifs. It was dark and looked red raw against her pale skin. But it was not the atrocity I'd first imagined.

"What do you think?" she asked. "Honestly. Tell me what you think."

I understood the subtext to the question. Ella was fond of the word EMPTY. She used it to describe people she thought were shallow. She used it to describe any situation that struck her as unsatisfying. She used it frequently.

I answered without letting my brain filter the thoughts. "It looks like a tattoo to promote self-harming."

Her brows narrowed.

"Did you go for the word EMPTY because ATTENTION SEEKING EMO would have cost too much?"

"For fuck's sake, Bill," she exploded. "Who pissed on your cornflakes this morning?"

We glared at each other for a lingering moment. I could see she was angry but there was no point in trying to recant what I'd said. The tattoo did look like a self-indulgent cry for help. I wasn't going to lie to her and say I thought it looked like a bold expression of nihilism.

She lit a cigarette, knowing that I hate it when anyone smokes in the apartment. Almost as an afterthought she walked to the open window and blew the smoke outside. I could see that the hand holding her cigarette was shaking. It was difficult to tell if her shivering came from cold, the pain of her tattoo or something else. The narrowing of her brows and the way her attention was fixed on the end of her cigarette suggested that she was no longer in a mood to talk about her upset.

"Your boss called."

She fixed me with a sidelong glance. "What did he want?"

"He wanted me to tell you you're fired."

She sucked hard on her cigarette. With a determined effort she shrugged as though trying to assure me the matter was of no consequence.

"Tell me you weren't with that weirdo Timmy last night."

She sucked harder on her cigarette. "Timmy's not a weirdo."

"So you were with him?"

"No. Timmy's got the same issues with fun that are making you such a miserable fucker this morning."

I shook my head in exasperation. It annoyed me to think that Timmy and I had something in common. One of the reasons I thought Ella was with Timmy was because he was the exact opposite of me. He was deeply religious and bereft of humour or positive qualities. I squandered my weekdays sitting in front of a computer trying to cram words into a novel that refused to be written. Timmy spent his weekdays parading around the town centre wearing a sandwich board that urged the godless to repent. Timmy spent Sunday mornings in church with his God, whilst I spent them in bed with a hangover.

But now, it seemed, Ella was pointing out that Timmy and I shared a common belief: we both thought she was overindulging.

It was probably that notion of sharing something with Timmy that made me act. There was no way I was going to be likened to Timmy and just accept the comparison without challenging it. Rummaging in the depths of my jeans pocket I pulled out a note that had been crammed in there. I expected it to be a fiver. It was a lazy habit to stuff notes into my pockets and eventually retrieve a crumpled bundle and place them neat and flat in my wallet. I seldom had more than a fiver crumpled in the bottom of my pocket. Rarely it might be a fiver and a tenner tangled together.

But this time I produced a twenty.

I wasn't happy with the idea of giving Ella a twenty. But, because she had seen it in my fingers, and because she had clearly noticed the distinctive purple colour, I could see no way to refuse her the money.

I tossed it to her and tried to make the gesture look generous and casual rather than angry and resentful.

"It's as much as I've got at the minute," I told her.

She snatched it out of the air and grinned. "It's as much as I need for now." She was halfway towards the door and there was a triumphant grin on her lips.

"Call me later," I told her. "Let me know that you're OK."

"Yeah."

I wanted to say something more, something that would retract the hurtful things I had said about the tattoo or the unpleasant names I'd used. Whilst I was still thinking of how to phrase apologies and retractions, so I didn't look like I was admitting fault, the door slammed.

I never got a chance to say those apologies whilst she was alive.

#11

Tom watched Alice fingering her crucifix. It was a small shard of silver dangling from her plump, maternal throat. He suspected the touching was a habit, a nervous gesture that had been acquired over the years, rather than a genuine sign of devotion. Nevertheless, a small smile crept across her lips, as though gentle Jesus was giving her the strength and reassurance she needed during this difficult conversation.

"I need to speak with Ben Haversham," he said again. "It's important. It's very important."

Alice shook her head. She let her fingers fall away from the crucifix and settle back onto the home keys of her computer keyboard. Her smiled disappeared into a determined frown. "I'm sorry," she said without any trace of genuine contrition. "I'm not allowed to supply contact information for any of the agency's clients."

"It's important," Tom assured her.

Alice shook her head again. Her determined frown fluttered with the briefest suggestion of sympathy. Tom suspected her sympathy was as false as the reverence she had for the crucifix around her neck. But he didn't bother to say that much. He could see no point in having an angry exchange with the woman.

It had not been a productive morning.

Neither Carlos nor the dealer had known how to get past the computer's password protection. Given that they couldn't seem to produce a sentence without spitting out a barrage of swearing, Tom wasn't surprised by their lack of skills with words. Even when Tom had pointed his newly acquired gun in Carlos' face, demanding the man hack the computer or take a bullet to the eye, the man had refused to help.

He had simply sobbed for mercy, said the *C*-word repeatedly, and eventually pissed himself.

Tom had allowed Carlos and the dealer to leave after that. It was obvious that they were both intent on revenge and Tom suspected that Carlos planned to return one night and set fire to Haversham's home. Although Tom didn't condone violence, he found himself smiling at the idea of Ben's flat being razed to the ground. It was no more than the bastard deserved.

With a spirit of defiant optimism, Tom told himself that he didn't need to hack Haversham's stupid computer to make progress on his investigation. He had the address for John, Ben's agent, and it was only a short walk from Haversham's home to visit John's offices. The premises were in a part of the city he had often passed on his way to church. As he had walked there from Ben's flat, he had recognised familiar sights, including the agent's neighbour: a company Tom remembered with the striking name of Raven and Skull.

However, before he could get to see the agent, it seemed he had to get through John's secretary, Alice. And Alice, occasionally fingering her crucifix and constantly frowning with the zealous determination of an impassable administrator, was proving to be an effective barricade.

The office was surprisingly classy.

A converted townhouse, the reception area was a shiny expanse of minimalist furnishings and glossy surfaces. There were a handful of framed pictures, album covers and certificates on the walls. One that caught his eye was a book cover called *The Demon of Sandalwood* by the author Nick Fallow. Tom remembered the name of Nick Fallow as an investigative journalist who had gone missing a year or so earlier. Fallow had written books about dangerous religious cults in the city and crazy non-Christian practices in various locations throughout the country. Tom had been a fan of Fallow's writing and knew *The Demon of Sandalwood* was the last book he had published before his mysterious disappearance.

The idea that a writer, as respected as Nick Fallow, had been represented by an agent who would deal with someone as reprehensible as Ben Haversham, told Tom that the world was a confusing place.

He shook his head to clear that idea from his thoughts. There would be no hope of successful negotiations with Alice if he was approaching the conversation with such a negative mindset.

The waiting room chairs, angular leather and steel combinations, looked sophisticated even if they didn't look comfortable. Tom was pleased to see that none of the framed pictures on the walls demonstrated the spurious achievements of Ben Haversham. It would have been difficult to retain his composure if he'd been faced with such an abomination. But it was still difficult to remain calm given the disturbing nature of some of the materials on the walls. He didn't care for the sinister-looking clowns in the paintings that were signed *CW*. There was something ungodly about the way painted faces glowered into the room. Similarly, he didn't particularly like the book covers that were from some writer named Jason Connor. The cover art showed images of desolate houses, and the titles, *Scourge* and *Vengeance*, looked as though they had been written in blood.

It made Tom wonder what sort of godless reprobates were represented by Haversham's agent, and whether he had been wrong to revere Nick Fallow. He drew a deep breath and tried to exercise a diplomatic smile.

"You don't understand," he said stiffly. He was trying hard not to let his anger appear too obvious. "I'm a good friend of Ben's and I need to see him urgently."

Alice shook her head.

"If you give me a contact number," she said, "I can have John pass on your details the next time he communicates with Mr Haversham. But I can't give you a client's number or tell you where he is. That's confidential information and at this agency we do respect client confidentiality."

Tom thought of pulling out the gun and pushing it in her face. He wasn't sure he could act in such an aggressive way to someone wearing a crucifix. He chewed on his lower lip, torn between needing the information on Haversham's whereabouts but reluctant to do something that would go against the wishes of gentle Jesus.

Alice continued to study him. He could see her smile was faltering, as though her patience was on the verge of evaporating. She glanced past him and, for the first time, Tom realised there was someone standing behind him, another person waiting for Alice's attention. From the corner of his eye, he saw it was a tall man in a powder-blue suit.

"Alice," the man said cheerfully. "I see John's keeping you busy."

"John's always keeping me busy," Alice told him. "I don't think I've had a two-minute reprieve since the day I first started working for him."

Tom coughed importantly. When Alice glanced at him, raising an eyebrow, he fixed her with an imperious frown. "I believe you were in the process of attending to my request," he reminded her. "I'd prefer it if you could resolve my query before you start to deal with people who are in the queue *behind* me."

Alice rolled her eyes. Her smile was weary. She flashed a sympathetic nod in the direction of the newcomer and then turned to face Tom. "I'm not sure I can offer any further help for your query," she told him. "It seems we've reached an impasse. I'm not going to give you Mr Haversham's contact numbers. You're not going to give your information to me. So, if we're not going to help each other, perhaps you should leave?"

Tom considered this in silence for a moment. He was on the verge of nodding agreement, ready to acquiesce that she was correct and they had reached some form of standoff, when the newcomer placed a hand on his shoulder.

"It might be an idea to follow the lady's advice," he began.

Tom wasn't even sure that the man got that far into his sentence. He was sure he had heard the first five words. But he suspected the remainder of the sentence wasn't something he heard: it was something he guessed the man was about to say.

Tom grabbed the man's hand by the wrist. Snapping it backwards with a sharp and violent movement, he made the man scream before driving him to his knees.

"Jesus Christ," gasped Alice.

Tom rounded on her. "Don't you dare take the Lord's name in vain." He fixed her with a warning finger, intending to remind her that she should be acting like a woman who wore a crucifix, and not some gutter-mouthed harridan. His voice thundered with a menacing boom. "Don't you dare take the Lord's name in vain."

"My fucking wrist," groaned the newcomer.

He was writhing on the floor, hitching the words between startled, gargantuan sobs. He held his hand with protective dismay, wrenching his gaze from Tom to the twisted join between his hand and his arm. "It's fucking broken," he gasped.

Tom ignored him.

He wanted to take the man to task and tell him to keep his vocabulary clean but he knew that would be a distraction. He kicked the newcomer into silence and, still pointing at Alice, he said, "I want to know how to find Haversham."

"Bloody hell!" she exclaimed. "Are you going to kill me?"

It was only when she asked the question and stepped back from the desk that he realised he had drawn the gun. He wasn't sure how it had moved from his pocket to his hand. He supposed it could even have been the divine intervention of gentle Jesus. Ultimately, he reasoned, it didn't matter how the weapon had made that movement. He was holding it, pointing at her chest and, when she then called him a fucking lunatic, it felt natural to squeeze the trigger.

The gunshot from the Ruger was deafening. The retort rattled up his arm and left the muscles in his bicep tingling. Sound was blistered in the confines of the reception room and Tom felt as though he was hearing everything from the bottom of a swimming pool. His nostrils caught the metallic stench of cordite and the burnt stench of something on the verge of burning.

"What the fuck?" muttered the newcomer.

Tom shot him.

A spray of blood made the room stink of wet copper. The metallic tang was so powerful it filled Tom's nostrils. It was disturbing to think there were so many people on the planet who were happy to curse and blaspheme. Didn't they know that gentle Jesus had died for their sins? What was the point of their Lord making such a monumental sacrifice if these ingrates were going to belittle his magnificence with their potty-mouths?

He shot the newcomer a second time for good measure.

The man's body twitched.

Tom was on the verge of walking out of the office, suddenly worried that there might be a danger that his actions could be perceived as falling foul of the law. For some reason he couldn't fathom, the law didn't make allowances for those guided by spiritual authority. He stopped when he saw that there was a diary on Alice's desk. Hurriedly, he began to flick through the pages.

On the Friday, John was scheduled to attend an award ceremony. The entry was flagged with a large warning: 'NB – DON'T DRINK. YOU'RE DRIVING TO SANDALWOOD FOR SATURDAY.' Sandalwood, he remembered: the village Nick Fallow had written about in *Demon of Sandalwood*. Saturday was flagged with an appointment for the evening: '*MP and BH at the Doll House.*'

BH, Tom noted. He guessed the initials stood for Ben Haversham. And, if Ben Haversham was scheduled for an evening appointment with John on the Saturday, that suggested the bastard could now be found in the village of Sandalwood.

His smile tightened into a beam of triumph.

The expression collapsed when Alice placed a pair of cold hands around his throat and began to choke him. He shot her three more times, but the impact of the bullets didn't seem to have any effect, other than to make her cold, dead eyes glower with darker malevolence.

#12

It transpired that a Barnsley chop was a double-sided loin cut of lamb. It was a huge slab of obscenely pink flesh. If not for the thick, blood-caked bone, Ben could have believed he was being offered a freshly skinned baby. But he didn't think a freshly skinned baby would contain such a massive bone. He thought it looked like enough meat to feed a small-but-very-hungry family, yet Mrs Scum assured him the meat was all for him and she said something about fattening him up which made his thoughts turn again to notions of cannibalism. She seasoned the chop with various herbs and some spices he didn't recognise and then put the meat onto cook. She also produced a box of dry cat food, a fresh carton of milk, and a tub of double cream that she said was for the cat.

He was surprised by her thoughtfulness but she brushed his thanks aside with one of her indecipherable remarks.

"I've allus gotten time foran animal lower."

He nodded as though the words made sense. "I was thinking of going out for a pint this evening," he told her. "Can you recommend a pub?"

"There's two here in Sandalwood. If you fancy a lively night you can always try the Mucky Duck. It's Monday night so there'll just be karaoke and a pub quiz."

"The Mucky Duck," Ben repeated. The prospect of a pleasant pint seemed unlikely if it was coupled with an environment that included karaoke and a pub quiz. It made him think there would be some availability of recreational drugs because he didn't think an entire community could tolerate evenings of karaoke and quizzes without something to dull the sharp edges.

"Or, if you want something a bit more sophisticated, the Green Man has the occasional poetry night. You'll like that, being a writer."

Given the options of a poetry evening, or hammering rusty nails through his scrotum, Ben figured he would have to sit down and think about the choice. He tried to think of a polite way to say that he wasn't a great lover of poetry. If it was a choice of village poetry or karaoke and a pub quiz, he thought sobriety and solitude had never before looked so desirable. Mrs Scum's revelations about the local nightlife were certainly taking some of the sheen off his romantic ideas about being an isolated writer in a small village community.

"I'll sort out some Cumberland sausage for your dinner on Wednesday," Mrs Scum told him. "But Marion tells me you'll be eating at the Doll House tomorrow evening."

He stared at her for a long moment, trying to work out what she'd said. When understanding clicked into place he immediately shook his head, sure that he hadn't agreed to Marion's invitation. He thought he'd hedged his way around giving a response and avoided making such a commitment. Whilst he wanted to say as much, he could see from the thin set of Mrs Scum's lips that the matter wasn't up for discussion. It was clear that Marion invariably got her own way in Sandalwood. Keeping the resigned sigh to himself he said, "You work for her as well as John?"

"I've worked for Marion all my adult life," Mrs Scum confided. Her smile brightened as she added, "Marion has her peculiar ways but she's an easy-going employer and she takes good care after those in her employ. She takes very good care."

Peculiar ways? Taking care of people? Weren't these the euphemistic sentiments people bandied when they were talking about serial killers or kiddie fiddlers after the revelation of a big news story? Ben pushed the matter from his thoughts. Whether he liked it or not, he was going out to eat with a creepy stranger tomorrow evening. A creepy stranger who knew too much about him. A creepy stranger with a grip like a mechanical hand inside a thin skin glove. Uncomfortable with the prospect, and hoping a way to side-step the invitation would present itself, he figured it would be best to concentrate on matters of greater importance.

"How do I get to these pubs you mentioned?"

Mrs Scum frowned. "How do you mean?"

"I went for a walk earlier and I just ended up back at the main gates of that doll museum."

Mrs Scum laughed.

It was a musical cackle that reminded him of the joy he often heard behind the camera on prank videos. This was the laughter that would accompany someone breaking a leg or suffering a serious and disfiguring injury.

"You're like the artist woman," she admonished. "She had the same problems finding her way around the village. I reckon she was lost without one of those satellite navigator contraptions."

Ben smiled as though he was sharing the cleaner's amusement. In truth he was more impressed to hear someone describe a satnav as a satellite navigator contraption.

"Could you draw me a map?"

Mrs Scum chuckled as though they were sharing a joke. "You don't need a map for Sandalwood. It's nobbut two roads and a set of traffic lights. If you fancy the Green Man you turn right out of the bottom of the driveway and walk up the hill *before* you get to the Doll House gates. If you fancy the Mucky Duck you turn right out of the bottom of the driveway and walk up the hill *after* the Doll House."

Ben considered these directions and thanked her. He wasn't sure they would be helpful, but he figured turning right out of the driveway would lead him to one of the pubs she had mentioned.

"Have you charged up your phone yet?"

He grinned shamefacedly and muttered an apology.

"You should do that now," she told him. "John will be livid if you haven't done it soon. He was on at me to remind you to do that earlier."

John had been on at her earlier? Did that mean John phoned the cleaner? Ben wondered if she was just a cleaner/housekeeper or whether was she employed with a more sinister purpose. Did John use her to spy on him? He shifted uncomfortably in his seat, not sure he liked the idea of being the sole resident in John's version of the Big Brother house.

"You'd best go and do it now," she said. "He'll be mithering me again if you don't."

Ben nodded and, seeing that Mrs Scum wasn't going to let the matter drop, he sauntered off to the study to find the box containing the phone. He opened the packaging and found himself staring at a small, basic flip phone in Captain Scarlet red. It looked cheap and nasty: the sort of thing he imagined an errant Saturday-dad would buy as a last-minute gift for a teenage daughter he didn't particularly like. Ben guessed that John had deliberately bought a phone that offered the fewest features. This one could be used to send and receive calls, send and receive texts, take pictures, play the radio or even be used as a torch.

The iPhone he'd left behind in London included a satnav, three separate e-book readers and apps for all of his email and social media. Comparing that against this bright red flip-phone was, he thought, akin to comparing his Mac and word-processing software to the Silver Reed in the study. Or like comparing Sandalwood to London.

After flicking through the instruction manual he plugged the charger into a mains socket and then attached the phone to the charger. According to the manual it would be ready for use within eight hours. The typewriter held no appeal for him. He considered going to bed for a leisurely nap, and then remembered he would have to do that under the watchful gaze of the doll collection. The grandfather clock in the hall began to chime the hour and he was surprised to hear it strike three o'clock. He hadn't realised the day was already so far gone.

"I'll get off to the pub," he told Mrs Scum.

She nodded. "Your chop will be ready for about eight o'clock. It'll still be edible if you don't get back in until midnight."

Ben checked his wallet, said goodbye, walked down the driveway and turned right.

#13

He awoke at exactly 03.10. The weight from a pair of eyes glaring at him was almost unbearable. He knew, if he got to the lamp switch soon enough, he would be able to flood the room with light and find out what or who was glaring at him in the dark.

But it seemed he was wrong.

His fingers found the switch and he pressed it immediately.

Sallow light shone weakly through the gloom.

And he saw there was nothing staring at him. Anastasia was at the foot of the bed curled into a foetal ball. He guessed the cat had already decided this was her spot whilst he was in residence at John's house. He wondered if that had always been the cat's spot regardless of who was living there. The thought, making him appreciate the cat with renewed fondness, helped to banish the natural unease that came from being the only person awake in the house.

The platinum blonde he had brought back from the pub was asleep, snoring lightly, and faced away from him. She seemed to like facing away from him, he remembered. She'd had a penchant for doggy-style that, given the delicious curves of her rear, he'd found extremely stimulating.

He turned away from her, realising it was not her gaze that had woken him.

The only eyes in the room that were fixed in his direction were the eyes of the creepy clown in the painting and those of the thirty-five dolls on the wall beside the door.

He slipped out of bed and shivered in the night's cool, autumnal chill. The floorboards creaked beneath his bare feet as he shuffled over the bedroom's rug. He wrapped a bathrobe around his slender frame and went to stand in front of the dolls.

He didn't want to stand in front of the dolls. Memories of the dream he'd had on the first night, the dream where the wall-eyed doll was writing messages for him to flee, and Al Jolson was removing those messages, still lingered at the back of his thoughts. The dolls unnerved him, and the idea of getting so close to them in the near-darkness was more than a little disquieting. He wasn't sure what he expected them to do. Even if they had been animated he didn't know whether he feared that they would be fitted with tiny little razor-sharp teeth inside their mouths, or talon-like claws on the ends of their tiny fingers. He wouldn't let his thoughts brood on the possibilities because he knew that such speculation would only make it more difficult to sleep alone with the collection.

But he knew, if he didn't force himself to stand confidently in front of them and pretend he wasn't afraid, he would start to be controlled by his fear. He took a deep breath as he scanned his gaze over the rows of dolls. Baby Adolf continued to glare at him. Wall-Eyed Wally stared over his shoulder. The one he had christened Luke, because it looked like it was stricken with Leukaemia, met his gaze in an unflinching challenge. Al Jolson sat on the lowest shelf, near the corner. He tried to remember if Al Jolson had always sat in that same spot.

Ben squared his shoulders. "Which of you creepy bastards woke me up?"

None of the dolls replied.

The platinum blonde stirred slightly behind him but Ben ignored her. He continued to study the dolls for a moment longer and then stepped away from them. He was wide awake and could see no point in going back to bed. He would likely disturb the blonde and that would mean some awkward post-coital conversation. Walking quietly, trying not to make the boards beneath his feet creak, he peered out of the window.

The sinister old house, Marion's Doll House, was again a hive of middle-of-the-night activity. Yellow lights, the colour of nicotine stains, lit the windows. A bustle of dark and bulky vehicles remained parked in front of the building. He could see shadowy figures making their way to and from a doorway at the rear: a garage he guessed. All the figures he could see seemed to be carrying large packages and struggling beneath the weight.

"What the fuck is going on there?" he wondered.

"Are you sleepwalking, Bill?"

"Ben," he corrected her absently. He didn't mind that she'd got his name wrong. He didn't feel quite so bad for forgetting what she was called. "And no, I'm not sleepwalking. I'm just getting familiar with my surroundings."

It wasn't technically true. It was a bedroom and he already knew the location of the door, walls and the windows. If he was being honest with himself, Ben knew he was boldly trying to defy those things in the bedroom that most unsettled him. He didn't like the dolls on the wall, so he steeled himself to stand in front of them and endure their blind stares. He wasn't happy that his bedroom window was overlooked by the eerie silhouette of the doll museum, so he was standing in the window and silently watching the building, in the way that he felt the building was watching him.

Beneath the silver glow of moonlight, the bustle of activity continued outside the doll museum. But, aside from it being either a rush of deliveries or dispatches, he could see nothing to better help him understand what he was witnessing. He yawned, pleased that he had confronted another fear, and walked idly over to the painting of the creepy clown's eye.

"Could this place be any more unnatural?"

"Are you talking to the walls?" The platinum blonde's voice was groggy with sleep. Her curiosity sounded as though it was tempered by enormous weariness.

"I'm not talking to the walls," he assured her. Even though they'd only known one another for a few hours, he didn't want her to think he was crazy. "I was just talking to the paintings and the dollies."

This seemed to appease her. A moment later he heard the dull rasp of her light snores. As he stared into the massive, bloodshot eye of the clown, he could have imagined he was listening to the faraway growl of a dangerous wild animal. The thought was sufficiently disconcerting to make him shiver. It didn't help that the eye he was studying was rich in detail. There was the reflection of a pale figure on the iris. Ben puzzled over this detail for a moment until he realised the clown was looking at another clown. The pale one reminded him of the whiteface figure he had seen outside the Doll House. It was painted in such convincing detail he glanced back over his shoulder, suddenly fearful that the clown would be in the room with him.

Aside from the platinum blonde, the room was mercifully empty.

The scleral veining on the painting was obscenely well realised. He could pick out the dewy film that lubricated the eyeball. It was so convincing he was almost prepared to see the eyeball blink.

That idea made him step back uneasily.

Eager to find a reason not to stare into the large eye, sure that he had done enough in this one evening to overcome his fears, Ben quietly left the room. He left the door ajar so Anastasia could join him if she wanted. He didn't suppose the cat would mind sharing a bedroom with the blonde. But he didn't want the creature to feel as though it had been trapped. He made his way down the stairs and into the kitchen, boiling the kettle for a coffee and pouring out a saucer of cream for Anastasia, in case she decided to follow.

As he waited for the kettle to boil, he shuffled impatiently from one foot to the other. It seemed insane to admit it, but he was looking forward to getting back to the study and sleep-writing the next part of his novel.

The scurrying of footsteps overhead made him wonder if the blonde was now awake. He would have called out to her if he had been able to remember her name. He thought it was either Sharon, or Shirley, or Shelley, but he couldn't be absolutely sure. He couldn't imagine she would be impressed if he shouted, "Hey, blonde, are you awake?" Cocking his head into the hallway he heard no further sounds and decided the noise had been a figment of his imagination.

The kettle boiled and he made his coffee. A swirl of instant granules in a gingham-patterned mug. Taking the mug into the study, he settled himself in the chair at the head of the desk and studied the page that was already rolled into the platen. The only words that remained there were the ones he had seen the previous morning: *CHAPTER FIVE.*

The telephone charger was blinking to tell him that it could now be disconnected. He disconnected it from the wall and fumbled with the keypad to switch it on. It took two minutes and the phone then spat out a series of large and tuneless beeps. Ben guessed the thing was announcing that it had received text messages.

John was clearly anxious to make communication.

Ben didn't bother reading the messages.

He turned the phone off and stared at the blank page. After having a sip at his coffee, and succumbing to a moment's doubt as to whether or not he would be able to produce any pages this night, he slumped in the chair and was fast asleep.

#14

Tom came slowly back to consciousness. There was an unpleasant taste at the back of his throat, a medicinal flavour that he did not recall ingesting. His breathing hurt and his head throbbed like the walls of Jericho. He started to groan and then stopped himself as the pain struck his larynx and rekindled a wealth of unwanted memories. When he swallowed, his throat blistered with pain.

That mental bitch, Alice, had been choking him.

He recalled squeezing the trigger on his gun and shooting her repeatedly. He then remembered that she had seemed unmoved by the gunshots. No. That wasn't entirely true. She hadn't been unmoved. She had flinched with every impact. But she hadn't been slowed. If anything, the gunshots had made her choke him harder. The gunshots had made her angry. She seemed distressed that there were holes in her blouse.

"That God-bothering bastard is awake."

He sat up straighter and squinted his eyes to get used to the new surroundings. The room was unfamiliar, dimly lit and seemingly bereft of windows. There were a series of workbenches around him, each looking ancient but tidy. On the workbench in front of him he could make out a handful of items, but the gloom was too intense for him to see what he was looking at. They seemed like vaguely familiar shapes but his eyes refused to focus on any individual piece. Beyond the workbench he could make out the shape of a rolled-up rug.

"Why is he coming round?"

"I have a use for him."

He was not alone. A slender, elderly woman sat at the other end of the room and she was stooped over another figure. With a jolt of dismay he recognised the other figure as Alice. Alice had been the one who had first spoken. She had been the one who called him 'a God-bothering bastard'. She was clearly disappointed that he was coming round.

He stiffened his posture and tried to climb out of his chair. His muscles refused to obey. He was struck by the worry that he had forgotten how to stand up. He couldn't remember which muscles he was supposed to use. Dwelling on the subject, he wasn't sure he'd ever known which muscles were needed to shift his body from sitting to standing. It crossed his mind that he might be paralysed, and a knot of fear tightened in his stomach. Helplessly, he remained in a sitting posture staring at the two women.

"Kill him, Marion," Alice insisted. "Or, better yet, let me kill him. That blouse I was wearing was a Stella McCartney."

She reached up to finger her crucifix.

The woman called Marion slapped Alice's hand away. "He'll meet his maker soon enough," Marion promised. "But, for now, I have a use for him."

Tom peered at the pair and was disconcerted to see that Alice was topless. Her plump old woman's breasts, sagging heavily, were exposed to the room. He could see the ugly dark shape of her areolae and the thrust of her fat old woman nipples. It was a disquieting sight and one that he knew he should never have witnessed.

Marion appeared to be working on the woman's chest with needle and thread. She was frowning industriously as she sewed up the gunshot holes. Tom wasn't an expert, and he was too far away from the two women to be sure, but he thought it looked like she was using twine and a darning needle.

"Where am I?" he demanded.

"You're in a lovely little village called Sandalwood." Marion spoke in a matter-of-fact tone. "It's a bit further up north than where you were yesterday-"

"Sandalwood?" He remembered reading that name in the diary that had been on Alice's desk. "Am I near Haversham?"

Alice and Marion exchanged a glance.

"The author Ben Haversham is currently residing in this village," Marion said carefully. "Although I'm not sure you'll get to see him."

Tom struggled again to get out of his seat. He had managed to shift into a position that suggested a readiness to stand up, but now his body seemed unable to move any further. He thrust his feet hard against the floor and forced his fists against the seat of the couch as he tried to push himself into an upright position. But his body was having none of it.

"Stay there, Tom," Marion warned him.

Tom ignored her and continued to struggle.

"He's not listening," Alice complained.

Marion shrugged. She hadn't bothered looking up from her needlework on Alice's chest. "I don't suppose it matters," she admitted. "The spell is holding him in place sufficiently well."

Spell? Tom scowled at the word. *Was he in the presence of ungodly witches?*

Marion pressed her mouth close to Alice's breast. Tom wondered if he was witnessing some elderly act of lesbian intimacy. Of all the atrocities he could be forced to witness, this was one that he thought would be most disquieting. It was only when he heard Alice wince, and watched Marion's head snap back swiftly, that he realised Marion had bitten off the thread she was using.

The slender old woman stood and walked behind Alice.

"The holes are pretty bad back here," Marion frowned. "The exit wounds are always larger but these seem enormous. I'll pack them, but we might have to remodel your shoulder-blades."

Alice glared at Tom. "Do you hear that, you God-bothering bastard?" She reached for the crucifix at her throat and began to tug on it. "Do you hear what you've done to my body, you shit?"

"You shouldn't use language like that whilst you're touching your cross," Tom warned her. It hurt to say the words, and he could hear them coming out in a raspy drawl. But still he forced out every syllable. He wanted to say more and tell her that gentle Jesus wouldn't approve, but the scowl on her face told him that she wouldn't be moved by such an observation.

Marion rummaged through a bag of fluffy white fibre. She was standing behind Alice, so Tom couldn't see what she was doing. If he had been prone to flights of fancy, he could have imagined that she was forcing wads of the fibre into the holes in Alice's back. But that idea seemed ridiculous. He kept his flights of fancy reserved for practical demonstrations of the impossible, such as evidence of God's goodness in the world, and genuine miracles. The notion of one old woman pushing stuffing into the back of another seemed too farfetched to consider.

"Ignore him," Marion said. "Ignore him and hold still whilst I assess the damage."

She was bent over Alice's back and it looked like she was again working with a needle and thread. Tom tried to process what was happening but it made little sense. He didn't know how Alice had managed to survive four gunshot wounds to the chest. He suspected the gun he had been given wasn't as effective as the guns he had seen people using in movies. Either that or Alice was a lot hardier than any old woman had a right to be. Even so, even if she had a physical constitution that bordered on the superhuman, he would have thought it would make more sense to take Alice to a hospital for appropriate medical care, rather than transporting her and her assailant a few hundred miles up the country to undergo the ministrations of an elderly seamstress. The facts made so little sense he knew he was missing something obvious. Silently, Tom prayed to gentle Jesus for guidance and understanding. He dearly hoped the answers he received would have nothing to do with sorcery or witchcraft.

Alice grimaced and hissed as Marion worked on her back.

Tom kept casting a glance towards the two women but, because he could see Alice's breasts, he wouldn't allow his gaze to linger. He didn't approve of female nudity, particularly when it was someone as repulsive and old as Alice. But, at the back of his mind, there was the nagging suspicion that watching the two women would likely give him the best clue as to what had happened.

"Who are you?" he demanded. The words came out in a hoarse croak. "Who are you? And why am I here?"

Alice said, "I think he's talking to you, Marion."

"Yes," Tom said stiffly. "I am. The one called Marion. Who are you? Why am I here? And what have you done to me so I can't move?"

"He asks a lot of questions," Marion observed. She sounded distracted, as though her attention was somewhere else. "His throat must be killing him, and yet still he's asking all those questions. I think he must be some sort of masochist." She smiled thinly and said, "Religious types are usually masochists, I find. They get pleasure from the pain. I've never known a single religious type who didn't enjoy a good flogging or gratuitous beating."

She released a lascivious chuckle and, in that moment, Tom hated her.

"What are you going to do with him?" Alice asked.

Marion paused in her sewing and stood up. She stretched out an ache from her hunched shoulders and glanced in Tom's direction. Tom watched her guardedly, wondering if she was going to give away any clue as to how she intended his fate to develop.

Stepping towards Tom she fixed him with a gaze that reminded him of soulless snakes on nature documentaries, or cruel reptilian predators on the verge of catching and devouring hapless prey. The humour in her expression didn't reach her eyes. "My name is

Marion Papusa," she told him. "I run the village of Sandalwood. I run the museum and factory that the locals call the Doll House. And, from today onwards, I'll be the person controlling you."

"I doubt that very much," Tom sniffed.

He stiffened the muscles in his arm and made an attempt to reach into his jacket pocket. He didn't know if the gun was still there. He hoped it was, but he suspected Marion and Alice would have removed the weapon when they had been transporting him up to Sandalwood.

His arm refused to move. He could feel every muscle in his body straining with the tension of trying to retrieve the gun. He could even feel his knees locking with tension as he struggled to reach the gun. But he didn't move. He remained motionless on the couch.

"Are you looking for this?" Marion asked.

She reached onto the workbench and picked up his gun.

Tom glowered at her. "Give that back."

She shook her head and dropped the gun back onto the bench before him. From a pocket she removed a small, badly made doll and held it in front of his face.

"Do you know what this is?"

He pulled his head back so he could see it clearly. The doll looked as though it had been fashioned from strips of corn husk and twine. The face, if it could be called a face, was deathly white with blood-red lips. The head was topped with a knot of hair that looked like it had been cut from his head. He would have thought it was some sort of effigy, if not for the fact that this handmade doll was dressed in the costume of a clown.

"Aren't you a little old for dollies?"

Her smile thinned. "This isn't a dolly," she said tightly. "This is an effigy. This is what controls you."

He laughed at her.

Her smile disappeared. She stroked one hand over the handmade clown doll, her eyelids fluttering in a momentary paroxysm of concentration. Then her smile returned and her eyes shone with a glittering wickedness.

"Grab hold of the screwdriver," she told him.

He acted without thinking. He leant forward to the workbench and picked up the screwdriver that was beside his gun. He recognised it as the one he usually carried in his jacket pocket. It was flat bladed and had a bulbous round plastic handle. There were remnants of dried blood on the sturdy, aluminium shaft.

Tom wondered why he had reached for the screwdriver when he could have easily snatched up the gun instead. He also wondered why he was no longer wearing the clothes he had been wearing when he started the day. His eyes wouldn't take it all in but it seemed he was wearing some gaudy red-and-gold clown's costume.

"What the…?"

He stopped himself from swearing but it was a close moment. A million questions rushed through his thoughts. He had no idea why he was wearing the clown costume and he couldn't understand how someone had managed to put him into the clothes without him being aware of the change.

"What's going on?" he croaked.

Marion ignored the question. She was staring at the screwdriver in his hand and unconsciously squeezing tighter on the effigy.

"Stab yourself in the leg," she told him.

He stared at her as though she was insane. "Do you really think I'm going to-"

He didn't get to finish the question. Instead his hand slammed the screwdriver down swift and hard. The blade pushed through the leg of his clown-suit trousers and plunged into the meaty flesh of his thigh. The pain was sudden and sharp, his throat locked around a scream.

Alice chuckled.

"Do it again," Marion said quietly.

Tom stared at his treacherous hand as it lifted up and then slammed back down with the same unyielding force it had used before. His eyes opened wide with disbelief. The pain that spread through his thigh was enormous. He watched and waited for a patch of blood to start spreading through the fabric. Mercifully, he saw that he hadn't plunged the screwdriver so deep as to draw blood, even though it felt as though the blade had scratched against the bone of his femur.

"Make him do it again," Alice called. "Make him do it and then twist the blade whilst it's in there." She seemed to sparkle with malicious glee. "Marion's controlling you with that effigy and the tonic that she made you drink before you woke up."

Tom remembered the unnatural taste that had been at the back of his throat when he awoke. He'd been forced to drink some sort of potion? His heartbeat raced.

"Make him stab himself again," Alice insisted. "Make him wriggle the blade around whilst it's in his leg."

"Don't," Tom called. He spat the word with panicked urgency. "Please don't do that."

Marion's laugh was so soft it was almost gentle. "Of course I won't do that," she assured him. "That would be cruel."

Alice sighed unhappily.

Tom released a grateful groan of gratitude.

Marion said, "Now stab yourself in the groin."

#15

"Morning love," Mrs Scum said cheerfully. She slammed the mug of coffee down on the desk beside him. "I see you had company last night."

He blinked himself awake and pulled the robe over his groin for fear of exposing himself to the cleaner again. He processed her words and tried to make sense of what she was saying. "Company?"

"There were two plates in the kitchen," Mrs Scum told him. "Two glasses in the sink. You had company, didn't you?"

The platinum blonde, he remembered. The obliging blonde who'd had a penchant for doggy-style. It was impossible to stop the smile from spreading across his lips. "There's not much that gets past you, is there?"

She chuckled. "It was Deborah Argyle from the Green Man, wasn't it?"

Ben frowned. He'd thought she was called Sharon, Shirley, or Shelley. He wasn't sure how he could have got the woman's name so drastically wrong but he remembered they *had* met at the Green Man and the name, *Deborah*, did not seem unfamiliar. He wondered if she was still in the house or if she'd left to take the walk of shame back to her home in the centre of Sandalwood.

The childish red casing of the phone caught his attention.

He glanced beyond the phone to see that there were sheets of freshly typed paper sitting by the side of the typewriter. The story was continuing.

He almost swooned with relief. Once again, it seemed, he'd been sleep-writing. He wondered how the story was progressing. It took an act of enormous willpower not to reach for the fresh pages and begin to flick through them to see what was happening in the story. He managed to resist because he did not want to read the story and have the narrative interrupted by Mrs Scum's constant chatter.

"I haven't done your bedroom this morning," Mrs Scum said. "If Deborah was still there, I didn't want to embarrass her. The same if the room was awash with condoms or bondage gear, or whips and chains, dildos and butt plugs. I'd prefer to save us both the embarrassment of my knowing about the perversions and depravities you've brought up here from that London."

Ben considered her and tried to decide if she was joking. Whether she was mocking him, or expressing her serious prejudices against Londoners, he couldn't think of an appropriate way to respond other than to flex a diplomatic smile. He switched on the mobile phone and began to read through the texts that John had sent.

'CALL ME WHEN YOU GET THIS MESSAGE.'
'WHERE THE FUCK ARE YOU?'
'BEN – IT'S JOHN. I NEED TO TALK WITH YOU URGENTLY.'
'FFS. HAVE YOU SWITCHED THAT PHONE ON YET?'
'MRS SCUM SAID SHE PASSED ON MY MESSAGE. CALL ME.'
'IF I DON'T HEAR FROM YOU BY END OF PLAY TODAY YOU'RE FIRED.'

Ben grinned tightly at the final message and texted a swift response.

'SORRY FOR THE DELAY IN RESPONDING. I'VE BEEN BUSY WRITING YOUR NOVEL.'

John's response came back an instant later.

'KEEP YOUR MOBILE SWITCHED ON AT ALL TIMES. I NEED TO BE ABLE TO TALK TO YOU WHEN IT SUITS ME. HOW'S THE NOVEL GOING?'

Ben smiled at the question and tried not to feel smug as he typed his response.

'IT'S WRITING ITSELF.'

Still chuckling at that, he flicked through the typewritten pages and realised his productivity had increased. There looked to be another fifty pages of story waiting for him to read. He saw a smear of brown on one of the pages and wondered if it was chocolate or something less savoury.
He supposed it was best not to know.
He was sleep-writing, and that could mean he was either binging on Mrs Scum's chocolate oattie biscuits. Or it could mean he was sleep-dumping and not washing his hands properly afterwards. He

could even see a situation where the brown smear had been deposited by Anastasia, his farting feline companion. He shook his head, not sure why his thoughts had taken such a coarse and scatological diversion this morning.

"How was your Barnsley chop?"

Ben tried to remember. He recalled staggering back into the house with the platinum blonde, Deborah, late in the evening. The house had been homely with the scent of the lamb and, although he and his companion had both been hungry for other things, Ben had made a point of sitting down and sharing the meal with her. She had found tinned vegetables in the pantry and a frozen pack of oven chips in the freezer. Between them, they had managed to serve a surprisingly accomplished meal.

"It tasted delicious," Ben told Mrs Scum. "Thank you."

"Did Deborah eat some?"

"Yes. That wasn't a problem, was it?"

Mrs Scum was scowling, and Ben guessed it was a problem, but she was being too polite to concede the point. "Of course not," she said. "When I saw she'd been here I reckoned she might have had some."

He noted that her smile was forced and he wondered what the issue might be. The meal had meant he had been forced to wait for a couple of hours to coax the woman into bed. Not that Deborah had needed much coaxing. She had been as eager for him to scratch her itch as he had been to scratch it for her. Admittedly, a part of him had been desperate to slake his arousal but a larger part had needed to devour Mrs Scum's cooking.

If he'd been in a similar situation back in London, Ben knew he would have ignored the food and gone straight to taking the woman to bed. He didn't think his priorities had shifted that much in the last couple of days but he couldn't argue with the fact that Mrs Scum knew how to prepare an irresistible joint of meat.

And it wasn't as though the meal had spoilt the evening. If anything it had allowed him a chance to sober up slightly before the sex, and he knew that was always a good thing. He could have tried lying to himself and saying it had given him a chance to better get to know his partner for the evening but, as he hadn't been able to remember the woman's name until Mrs Scum reminded him, he figured there was no point pretending the delay was anything other than a fortuitous break that had allowed him to shrug off some of the alcohol and build up a little stamina for the main event. Being honest with himself, he distinctly recalled thinking that her chatter was banal, her life story was dull and uninteresting, and he had hoped she was better at fucking than she was at talking. He remembered being thrilled that she wanted him to take her in the doggy-style because that meant he didn't have to stare into her face whilst he was enjoying the sex.

Classy, he chided himself. *Deborah really found her Prince Charming in you, Haversham, didn't she?*

"I'll not be cooking you a meal today because you're visiting Marion," Mrs Scum reminded him. "Have you got a suit or do you want me to bring you one?"

"Marion?" *Was that today?* He didn't remember agreeing to visit the woman. "A suit?"

"She's very formal is Marion."

"I don't own… I mean, I haven't brought a suit with me."

Mrs Scum placed a hand on his. Her smile was sympathetic and comforting. "I'll get something brought over for you this afternoon."

He wanted to tell her there was no need but she was already standing, taking away the clutter of his empty coffee cup and heading towards the kitchen. He wondered if this might be a convenient deal-breaker to excuse him from having dinner with the woman. If she insisted on him wearing a suit, and he didn't have a suit, surely that meant he could send his apologies and dodge the invitation.

"I'll do you a slice of toast before I leave and I'll be back around five with your suit."

"There's no need," he spluttered.

She wasn't listening. And, because his bladder was now on the verge of bursting, he decided to take himself up the stairs to visit the loo.

The door to his bedroom was closed. Pushing it quietly open he was only a little disappointed to see that the blonde was no longer there. The bed was made, the room seemed as tidy as if Mrs Scum had already gone through her morning routine. But there was no sign to suggest anyone had spent the night in the bed.

He frowned, wondering if the quilt cover looked different from the one he had seen the previous night. He scratched thoughtfully at the scrub of beard that coated his throat and tried to work out why something didn't seem quite right.

Was it possible the blonde, Deborah he reminded himself, her name was Deborah, had decided to change the sheets and quilt cover after their night of drunken passion? If that was the case, he decided he needed to have more one-night stands with village blondes. The women didn't just fuck well, they also cooked and tidied.

As he walked to the lavatory he noticed the door to the linen closest hadn't been properly closed. It made him think that his first guess was correct and the woman had gone to the trouble of changing the sheets.

He walked over to the linen closet and tried to push the door shut. When it wouldn't close properly he pulled the door open wide so he could see what was stopping it. On the middle shelf sat Deborah's severed head.

… #16

A rising tide of nausea rushed through his body. The desire to vomit was fighting with a scream of terror and he didn't know which would be first to burst from his lips. He slammed the closet door shut. It closed with only a little resistance and he was aware of a vague popping sound that made him think of unripened berries being crushed.

Then he was hurrying to the lavatory.

Closing the door behind himself Ben fell to his knees in front of the toilet and began to heave. The oily black residue of the coffee he'd just finished came blasting out of his mouth. The partially digested remnants of biscuits, bile, and vegetables sluiced into the white basin. He closed his eyes so he didn't have to witness the disgusting flow, but that didn't help. The stench of his stomach contents, bitter, dark, and unnatural, assailed his nostrils.

Worse, with his eyes closed tight his imagination presented him with a still image of all that he'd seen when he had discovered the woman's severed head.

The eyes had been taken out.

Her empty eye sockets had stared up at him, the hollow holes showing him a glimpse into the darkly pink interior of her head. That had not been the worst of it. In the instant he had studied the linen closet, he had seen more than he ever wanted to see. He had seen that her severed hands were rested, one on top of the other, to the left of her face. Her arms, long, clean, waxy, and bent at the elbows, were on the same shelf to the right of her face. There was her limbless torso on the shelf below. The bared breasts and exposed sex looked obscenely unarousing. On the shelf above, her legs rested length-ways. Her severed feet stood before them like shoes waiting to be polished. Worst of all, and this was the part that kept making him dry heave long after he'd emptied the contents of his stomach into the lavatory, was the single round blue eye that he'd seen staring up at him from the floor of the linen closet.

When he took the time to wonder why there was only one eye staring up at him, he remembered the unripened popping sound the door had made when he slammed it shut. He had slammed the closet door and burst an eyeball.

His stomach muscles clenched tight and another spasm of pain rattled up his oesophagus. Nothing came out of his mouth except for a string of viscous brown drool. He could feel tears squirting from the corners of his eyes and wondered if he was crying from distress, shock, or simply from the exertion of vomiting so hard.

He knew it was the woman he had bedded the previous evening. It was Deborah. He recognised the platinum curls of her blonde hair.

How the hell had it happened?

His stomach continued trying to retch but it was empty. There was no longer anything to drag up and dump in the toilet and he flushed away the foul-stinking mess he had deposited there. His fingers were shaking as he pulled the handle. His palm was clammy with perspiration.

Who the hell had killed her?

Had Mrs Scum done it? It seemed unlikely, but the woman had access to the house. She was clearly strong and capable. She had a key and could have slipped in whilst he was asleep in the study. It might have been an easy matter to simply kill the blonde and then remove her eyeballs, dismember her and store her severed limbs in the airing closet.

Another wave of nausea threatened to rush through him. He held himself still over the lavatory bowl, holding his breath and praying that the desire to vomit would pass without incident. His brow was sweating so profusely he could feel each bead of clammy sweat growing fatter on his forehead.

Grudgingly he decided that Mrs Scum was not likely to be responsible. She'd bought cat food for Anastasia. A person couldn't buy cat food and be a murderer, could they? He supposed he was oversimplifying things a little there. But Mrs Scum had cooked and cleaned for him. Surely that meant she couldn't also murder and dismember?

Had he done it?

Ben thought that seemed even more unlikely. He had been asleep. Not only had he been asleep, but he'd been asleep in the study downstairs and he'd been busy sleep-writing fifty pages of his latest novel.

Well that sounds like the most airtight alibi I ever heard, he told himself. He straightened up, his knees hurting from the prolonged impact with the bathroom floor. *You couldn't have murdered the woman because you were busy being asleep and writing.* Flushing the toilet again he tried to shake his head clear and better understand what had happened. His stomach rippled through a series of spasms. When he stepped outside the bathroom he hurried past the closet.

Ben staggered quickly down the stairs, his thoughts still chaotic as he tried to work out what he should do and how best he should handle the situation. The house was empty, no sign of Mrs Scum in the kitchen and only a cooling mug of coffee and a slice of toast on the kitchen table to suggest she'd been there a few moments earlier.

He stumbled into the study and picked up the mobile phone.

Then he stopped himself.

Was that the best course of action? Was he intending to phone the police or John? He could think of no other option. If he'd had access to a computer, he would have Googled the question: *who should I call when I find severed body parts in the linen closet?*

Collapsing into the chair he rubbed a hand through his hair and groaned.

If he called the police he would be arrested and held on suspicion of murder. It would be a fairly reasonable suspicion, he supposed. He didn't think he'd killed the woman but his only excuse was that he'd been in the room below her writing a novel whilst he slept. As far as excuses went, he didn't think that one would tolerate much scrutiny.

But he did think that worked as an alibi to settle his own mind to the question.

He glanced at the fifty freshly typed pages. On a good day, back when he had been writing, Ben could produce twenty pages of scruffy copy. More typically he had churned out ten to fifteen pages of poor first draft during his most industrious periods. But here, between roughly 3.30 in the morning and twelve o'clock noon when Mrs Scum woke him, he was churning out forty to fifty pages of decent text. Was it feasible that he had time to bang out three or four times his usual output and murder a woman, drain her body of blood and neatly dissect her corpse into component pieces?

His stomach clenched hard as though it wanted to vomit again.

For an instant his mind's eye had been revisiting the scene of the open closet door. He had noticed that the severed limbs looked surprisingly bloodless. The stumps looked like something laid out neatly in a butcher's shop window.

He shook his head.

Taking the writing out of the equation, Ben knew he didn't have the skills to drain a corpse of blood or sever the limbs with such clinical neatness. He wanted to tell himself that he didn't have the ability to murder someone, but he wasn't sure he believed that. A part of him was still convinced that he had been the one who murdered Etta. As far as results went, there seemed little difference between giving someone enough money to fuel a suicidal overdose and murdering someone and then hacking their limbs from their torso. It struck him as being nothing more than a matter of degrees.

But, even though he felt sure he hadn't, and couldn't have committed this murder, he doubted the police would so easily accept his innocence. He'd be arrested and imprisoned. There would be charges and the whole situation with Etta would be dredged up in the media.

He slammed the phone down on the desk. His hand was still shaking. His fingers hovered over the mobile as he considered picking it up again.

Would it be best to call John? And say what? Some blonde he'd fucked the previous night was now dead, dissected and sitting in the linen closet? He didn't know how to start such a conversation and he couldn't imagine where it would possibly go.

If John was a decent person, and Ben had no reason to think otherwise, the agent would contact the police and John would find himself facing the arrest, imprisonment and the media circus he had feared would result from his own call to the police. If John was not a decent person, he would likely help Ben conceal the murder and dispose of the body parts. And, whilst that didn't sound like the worst of the two options, Ben wasn't sure he wanted to become an accessory to a murder he didn't remember committing.

He groaned and dragged himself out of the room.

Going into the kitchen he saw that Anastasia was nibbling at the toast that had been left for him. He turned away from her and rushed up the stairs to the bedroom.

He wouldn't allow himself to glance at the door for the linen closet. It was disquieting enough to know there was a dismembered corpse hidden there. He didn't want to dwell on the concept any longer than was needed.

Snatching his jeans and T-shirt from where they had been folded on the dressing table, he stepped into a pair of trainers and grabbed his wallet. He couldn't phone the police. He couldn't call his agent. He didn't want to be a party to the murder and he didn't want to suffer the blame for a crime he was sure he hadn't committed.

He paused momentarily on the landing and glanced at the linen closet.

At the bottom of the door he noticed something wet was oozing onto the floorboard from where the door met the jamb. He remembered the popping sound he had heard. It was enough motivation to have him hurrying out of the house with a vow never to return.

"You should feel honoured," Marion chided. "You've been chosen as a woodsman."

Tom glared at her. He did not feel particularly honoured.

In truth, because of the place where she had made him stab the screwdriver, he only felt hurt, violated and angry. He also felt a little bit disconcerted because, after he'd shoved the screwdriver hard into his groin, so hard he had felt the screwdriver puncture one of his gonads, he had still not managed to make himself bleed. Not that he wanted to bleed. But, given that the tip had gone inside him, given that the tip had gone so deep there had been one point where he could feel the blade scratching against the underside of his pelvis, he would have expected some bleeding. It still hurt sorely. Every movement reminded him there was now a hole in his groin. But the absence of blood suggested something was amiss.

Not sure he wanted to address this point with Marion, he asked, "What's a woodsman?"

"Stand up," she insisted.

He stood.

"Grab that," she said, pointing at the rolled-up rug. She pulled a shovel from one corner of the room and, without waiting to see whether or not he obeyed, she said, "I'll carry this."

Tom told himself he should be resisting her orders, that he had no need to be doing her bidding. At the back of his mind he knew it would be a simple matter, now he was standing, to lunge for the gun and shoot her. It wouldn't matter whether he shot her in the back or in the face, just so long as he shot her and ended the unnatural control she was wielding over him.

Shoot her? he thought dourly. *The way you shot Alice? Remember how well that worked?*

Those doubts were not the only reason why he didn't reach for the gun. Even if he hadn't been thinking about his lack of success in shooting Alice, and even if his groin had not been in throbbing agony, Tom knew he would be unable to defy Marion's instructions. Whatever command she gave, his body was instantly obeying, even when he didn't want it to.

He bent to pick up the rug from the floor.

It was heavy. So heavy he knew it was not only a rug he was picking up. His first thoughts were that it concealed a corpse. He made no complaint about the weight. Lugging the roll over one shoulder, trying not to grimace from the exertion, he stared at Marion and waited for his next command.

The weight was enough to make his back bend.

"Aren't you good and strong?" Marion said with condescending approval. She studied him with a sly smile and said, "You know, the way you're coping with that weight, it reminds me of Jesus carrying his cross."

Dull rage flared within him. He tried to ball his hands into fists and discovered they would not obey the impulse. "You're a witch," he spat. "You're not fit to say the name of gentle Jesus."

Marion stiffened.

Alice muttered something he didn't hear. The words sounded uneasy. From the corner of his eye, Tom could see the woman make a superstitious sign, as though she was summoning the protection from an evil eye.

"Put the rug down," Marion told him.

Tom obeyed. It was a relief to have the burden away from his shoulder but he suspected the relief was not going to be long-lived.

"Make a fist," Marion told him.

Tom obeyed.

She fixed him with a glare of absolute disgust. Her loathing was so obvious that, even though she was a witch, or a sorceress, or some other living proof that godless creatures existed, he still felt uncomfortable beneath the ferocity of her scowl.

"Clench that fist tight," Marion insisted. "Get ready to punch really hard."

His fingers strained beneath the exertion. He could see the knuckles had turned white and bloodless. He was prepared to deliver the most punishing blow he could manage.

"Now," she whispered. She spoke with a firmness that suggested she was articulating every word so that there was no danger of being misheard or misunderstood. "Each time you mention Jesus-"

He opened his mouth to tell her that she should not be using the Lord's name.

Marion spoke over him. "Each time you mention Jesus, you'll have the irresistible urge to punch yourself in the jaw." Her eyes flared brightly as she fixed him with a scowl. "Understand?"

He met her scowl with a look of defiance. Shaking his head, feeling confident that the witch needed to be challenged appropriately, he said, "You're not fit to say the name of gentle Jesus."

The punch came out of nowhere. He'd been aware that his hand was held in a tight fist. He'd heard her ridiculous command. But he'd not expected his own body to respond like a traitor and do her bidding. The punch was hard enough to make his teeth smash together. Stars flashed at the periphery of his vision and the room momentarily swayed in and out of focus. If the force of the blow had been any harder, Tom suspected he would have been knocked off his feet.

Marion continued to scowl at him although he thought he saw the flicker of a smile on her lips.

"Every time you say the name Jesus," she murmured, "you'll punch yourself hard in the jaw." Her scowl finally softened as she asked, "Do you want to say it again?"

Tom stared at her with stone cold fury. His hand was already formed into an impotent fist but it was not because he had intentions of striking himself.

"Do you want to say it again?" she taunted.

Slowly, deliberately, exerting a mammoth control over his fist so it wasn't going to catch him again, Tom spoke with grim defiance as he said, "You're not fit to say the name of gentle Jesus."

The second punch was harder than the first. This time he could feel the pain rushing through his knuckles as well as his jaw. He swayed on his feet and felt his eyes growing wet with tears. He didn't know if the tears were coming from embarrassment or pain, or the unhappiness at not being able to say the name of gentle…

…at not being able to say that name.

"Do you want to say it again?" Marion pressed.

He stared at her for an age, sure he had never hated anyone more in his entire life. Even the murderous loathing he felt for Ben Haversham, a murderous loathing that he felt was justified given that Haversham was responsible for Etta's death, paled beneath the overwhelming contempt he had for this sorceress.

"Do you want to say it again?" Marion repeated. "Because, if I didn't have dinner plans this evening, I could watch you punch yourself senseless for the rest of the day. It's very entertaining."

Reluctantly, he shook his head. His jaw ached, and his knuckles felt bruised, but the real pain came from knowing he was under the control of a witch. The Bible said, 'Thou shalt not suffer a witch to live.' That was somewhere in Exodus, he remembered. But, instead of killing the witch who now stood before him, he was obeying her instructions. He told himself that he had to find some way of doing as the Bible insisted. He promised himself he would find a way to defy her commands. But he knew that defiance would not come in the next few moments.

"Do you want to say it again?" Marion asked.

Tom shook his head.

She nodded, satisfied. Turning her back on him and heading to the door she said, "Pick up that rug and follow me."

"I can't believe you're using him as a woodsman," Alice scowled.

Marion walked past the woman without acknowledging her words. Tom followed and tried to fix Alice with a glare. It was difficult to challenge her with his eyes. She was still topless, and his gaze was drawn to the freshly stitched wounds on her chest. The skin was puckered into bloodless blanket-stitched seams. It didn't seem right that she could–

"Stop looking at my titties," Alice said. Her hand went to the crucifix at her throat. "Stop looking at my titties."

Tom wanted to tell her that she shouldn't be touching gentle Jesus and saying the word 'titties'. He kept the thought to himself because he realised he needed all his strength, concentration and effort to carry the enormous weight of the rolled-rug and its contents. He also knew what would happen if he said the name of his saviour aloud.

"This way," Marion called.

She opened a door and hit a light switch, Tom realised she was leading them up a flight of stairs. As an afterthought he realised he had awoken in a basement and he understood that was why there had been no windows. He lumbered slowly after Marion, trying to understand why his body was obeying her commands and wondering if there was some way he could defy her. He would have asked her how she had managed to exert such a control over him but there was only one question that came from his lips.

"Why am I dressed like a clown?"

"You're not dressed like a clown," she called over her shoulder. "You're dressed like one of the Sandalwood woodsman."

They made it to the top of the narrow stairway and Tom marvelled that he had managed such a steep climb whilst coping with such an onerous weight. They were standing in a prestigious hallway, a black and white marble floor beneath his feet, a double staircase at one end, and creepy looking pictures of clowns on the walls.

"Are those clowns or woodsmen?" he asked peevishly.

"Those are Sandalwood's woodsmen."

"They look like clowns."

"The first of the woodsmen were clowns," she said blithely. She spoke as though this was a conversation she had often had before, and she knew her lines with practised ease. "They came here, with a travelling circus and they had need to perform the duties of woodsmen." As she spoke she led him across the black and white hallway to the imposing main double doors.

It was daylight outside. A light rain fell and quickly soaked the clown costume. A part of him worried someone would see him in the ridiculous clothes and mock him for the way he was dressed. But, because he was under the hypnotic spell of a madwoman, and because he was close to collapsing from the weight of the rug and whatever was wrapped inside its centre, Tom figured that such considerations weren't worthy of his worry.

He simply followed as Marion led.

A glance over his shoulder told him that they were walking out of a large house that seemed to sit on the top of an imposing hill. He didn't dare look for long. A quick glance was enough to tell him it looked like a sinister building. And then he was staring at her back as Marion led him downward, towards a junction of three roads.

The roads in each direction were lined with trees and lush, verdant greenery. He thought he saw wrought-iron fencing and gates being swallowed by one leafy hedge, but that was in the periphery of his vision.

Tom couldn't recall the last time he had seen so much nature. He was used to life in the city with buildings, pavements, roads, street lamps, churches and traffic. This empty wilderness, looking like something from the set of a zombie apocalypse movie, struck him as alien and potentially threatening.

Marion seemed oblivious to his consternation. "The first of the woodsmen came here more than two centuries ago," she said. "He was a clown in a travelling circus, Arlecchino, the Harlequin, from their production of the *Commedia dell'arte*."

Her tone was assured and suggested Tom would understand the cultural references. He had no idea what she was talking about.

With a nod back to the building she said, "Their circus camped on the top of this hill."

Tom said nothing. It hurt to talk and with the exertion of lifting and walking, he was unable to find the breath he would have needed to form words. He wondered how much hope he had of surviving the afternoon and told himself not to brood on the idea. He was adamant he wouldn't be vanquished by a sorceress.

"There was a love interest and a rival," Marion said. She made the remark as though there was always a love interest and a rival. "Harsh words were exchanged. Violence ensued. And then Arlecchino found himself standing over a freshly made corpse."

"He killed the rival?" Tom didn't want to be intrigued but it was easy to imagine the scene she was painting. He could almost see the clown she was talking about standing over a corpse. Tom was wearing the gaily patterned costume of the Harlequin and, in his mind's eye, he could picture the detail of splashes of blood on Arlecchino's white face paint.

"Not the rival," Marion said quietly. "The lover. She'd tried to intervene. Neither of the two combatants had noticed. And she ended up with a knife in her heart."

Tom said nothing.

"It was very much like the conclusion to *I Pagliacci*," Marion said blithely. "Only with the roles of the *Pierrot* and the *Harlequin* reversed."

"I'll bet it was," Tom said. He still had no idea what she was talking about. He suspected *I Pagliacci* was the title of some foreign language film he had never seen.

Marion seemed to sense his ignorance because, when she next spoke, her voice was hurried. "I suspect this is why we usually end up with a pair of woodsmen," she declared. "The *Pierrot* and the *Harlequin* worked as a team that evening. They wrapped her body into a roll of spare awning and carried her out into the centre of the woods. These woods."

He hadn't noticed that they were now walking through a thickening forest until she said the words. Then he realised the rain was no longer a constant mist on his face and the quality of the light had changed to an eerie, green-dappled twilight. His nostrils caught the fresh tang of damp wood and moist earth. He wrinkled his nose, worried he would start to sneeze with some hay-fever-esque reaction.

"They dug a hole for the woman," Marion went on. She seemed to be enjoying her role as storyteller. "They dropped the body in the hole. And then they resumed their quarrel." She chuckled softly and said, "Only one of those woodsmen walked out of the woods that night."

"What does any of this have to do with me?"

Marion turned around and slammed her shovel into the earth. Fixing him with a solemn expression she said, "I was giving you a little background history on your new job as Sandalwood's latest woodsman. That's what it's got to do with you."

He shook his head. "I don't want the job."

"Too bad," she snarled. She pointed at a gaping hole in the ground and said, "You've got the role and your first job is to start covering him."

Tom glanced into the grave and saw that a stranger lay at the bottom. He wasn't sure if it was a corpse or something barely alive. Fortunately, shadows were cloaking the body. But he could make out the distinctive pattern of the clown costume that covered the creature's frame. It was a Harlequin costume that matched the one he was wearing. "Who is he?"

"He's no one now."

"Who was he?"

Her smile was cold and merciless. "He was your predecessor. He was the village's previous woodsman."

Tom stiffened with the urge to vomit.

Marion seemed oblivious to his discomfort. "Once you've finished burying him, I want you to dispose of that body." She pointed at the roll of carpet he had dropped on to the floor of the woods.

Tom strained to find words of defiance in his vocabulary but he knew that he wasn't going to refuse. As soon as she'd given the instruction he knew he would do exactly as she'd demanded. There was something in her tone that he knew would be impossible to deny.

"And, once you've finished burying that body, I want you back at the Doll House ready to obey my next command."

He stiffened and glared at her and longed to tell her he would never obey her commands. But he knew it wouldn't matter what she demanded of him, Tom knew he would obey.

#18

Fat Jay snorted the line and savoured the buzz. It was one of the clearest hits he could recall experiencing: a buzz of magnificent proportions. He considered himself an aficionado of many things, clothes, rap and pussy, but he was a motherfucking expert when it came to recognising quality coke and this was the motherfucking bomb.

"What d'you say, b-bruv?" the dealer asked. "Is that the shit or w-what?"

The Boar's Head dealer was wearing a dirty grey hoodie that was decorated with a marijuana leaf on the back. His jeans were skinny and slung low at the crotch and his trainers were scuffed. His jaw was unshaven and his eyes, peeping above the rims of John Lennon shades, were bloodshot, watery orbs swimming in a face of uncooked dough.

Fat Jay wasn't listening to him. When you savoured a good line you didn't need some stuttering dealer, who stank like an unwiped arse, trying to tell you it was good. Breathing deep, basking in the rush of adrenaline that seemed to course like icy liquid silver through his veins, Fat Jay smiled and quietly celebrated the moment.

It was one hell of a hit. And this batch had come from an unexpected source. Normally he supplied to the Boar's Head dealer. He had been trading with the scruffy, unwashed wannabe for the past decade. The trade supply usually came in the form of Fat Jay providing the dealer with small quantities of weed, pills and powder, depending on the man's needs.

But this time trade was coming in the other direction. This time the dealer was trying to sell Fat Jay half a kilo of pure coke. And Fat Jay was determined to make sure he got himself a bargain.

"Where did it come from?"

"There's a new g-guy in town," the dealer explained. "He's a foreigner. Name of Carlos."

"What does he want?"

The dealer seemed to think about this for a moment before shrugging. "I reckon he wants to party with respected dealers like you and me."

Fat Jay groaned inwardly. He could feel the comedown hitting him too quickly. As all the pleasure bleached from his body he realised he was still sitting in the dealer's booth at the Boar's Head. The pub was a shabby stain on the local area and Fat Jay had never liked being there. The seats were damp and, on a good day, they were sticky enough to cling to clothing and only stank of piss. He supposed he could say something similar about a lot of the clientele. Those who weren't incontinent or marinated in alcoholism still looked genuinely unsavoury.

Every time he visited the Boar's Head, Fat Jay knew he looked out of place.

Everyone else there, with very few exceptions, was dressed in dirty jeans and wash-weary T-shirts. Those few who wore something else were invariably sporting shapeless Primark tracksuits and knock-off Fila-footwear. Fat Jay, by way of contrast, was wearing designer brands: a crimson Nike hybrid, Ray Ban wayfarers and Giuseppe Zanotti leather and velvet mid-tops. He guessed, to an outside observer, it was like seeing a thoroughbred standing in a stable filled with seaside donkeys. With that thought he opened his eyes and tried not to let his disgust with his surroundings show.

"That's what I reckon," the dealer repeated. "I reckon this Carlos guy wants to party with us respected dealers."

Fat Jay made a mental note that the dealer was a moron. It seemed obvious that this Carlos was trying to take over their territory and the Boar's Head dealer was too dumb to understand.

"It's uncut," the dealer explained. "Uncut and a very decent price." He wiped nervously at his nose and added, "I reckon, if we start to deal this guy's shit, we could see a lot more trade."

Fat Jay pulled a brightly coloured pack from his jacket and slammed it in front of the dealer. The packaging had open panes that showed a fine white powder. The whole bag looked roughly the same size and shape as a bag of sugar. The same size and shape as the bag of uncut coke. "Cut it with that," Fat Jay said. "And make sure everyone knows that the new product comes from this Carlos."

"What the fuck's that, b-bruv?"

Fat Jay smiled. "That's profit," he said easily. "That's profit and a way to get rid of this Carlos before he becomes a problem."

The skank chose that moment to speak up.

"That's not profit," she said quietly. "It's levamisole."

Fat Jay had seen her sitting beside the dealer. She looked so totally zoned he had wondered if she had some sort of medical syndrome:

too many or too few chromosomes. She was a dirty blonde who'd sat next to them with a crumpled twenty and an ugly fresh tattoo on the inside of her forearm. He'd tried not to breathe in when she was walking past him because he suspected she would stink of the last blowjob she'd given. He'd felt comfortable talking in front of her because, like most doped-out users, she looked to be lost in the world of her own internal magical concerns rather than being troubled by his personal reality.

Now, he wondered if he'd made a serious error of judgement. The way she had identified his product, and articulated the key chemical component so eloquently, made his stomach tighten with mistrust. Could she be with the police?

"L-lever-what-now?" the dealer asked. He picked up the pack and tried to shape the words as he read the label on the front of the pack. His brows knotted together with the furious concentration that came from trying to make sense of the words.

"Levamisole," the blonde said quietly. "It's a medication used to treat parasitic worm infections in animals. There was a big news buzz about it a couple of years ago because a handful of people started to get huge sores when it had been cut into their coke." She fixed Fat Jay with a challenging glare. "Am I right?"

"It wasn't even a handful of people," he said. "There were maybe two or three cases-"

"Reported cases," the blonde interrupted.

His lips tightened into a frown. Had she just corrected him? No one corrected Fat Jay, especially not some doped-up skank with a hankering for twenty quid's worth of junk. He had to physically restrain himself from reaching across the table and fattening her lip.

The dealer was studying him with idle curiosity.

The rest of the Boar's Head seemed oblivious to their afternoon deal. Dull conversations continued, and glasses clattered laconically against one another.

"Reported cases," Fat Jay conceded. He tried to quell the irritation that the skank inspired. "What makes you such an expert?" he asked. "How come you're so knowledgeable on the subject of levamisole?"

"She used to fuck a writer," the dealer explained. He gave a dismissive wave of his hand and said, "She knows everything." Tapping the bag of levamisole, he asked, "What's it for?"

"What do you think it's for?" Fat Jay sneered.

"He wants you to cut it with the coke," the blonde explained. "Levamisole is great for cutting with coke because it's a fine white *powder of the same consistency. The mixing process is fairly easy and, unlike some of the other substances that can be used as additives, levamisole doesn't leave a residue."*

Understanding washed over the dealer's face. He nodded eagerly and told the blonde, "And he wants Carlos' name attached to this so that everyone thinks Carlos is peddling diluted merchandise."

The skank seemed to consider this for a nanosecond and then nodded in agreement.

"How come your friend knows so much about the industry?" Fat Jay asked the dealer softly. The good mood from the line he had snorted was fading to a distant memory. It was being replaced by a paranoid rush of antagonism for the skanky blonde with the bad tattoo and the busy mouth that needed shutting. "How come she knows so much about this?" He turned to glare at her and said, "You're not the filth, are you?"

He was pleased to see the dealer shift uneasily away from the blonde when he suggested that she might be with the police.

"Ella's not with the filth," the dealer muttered.

Despite the conviction in the dealer's argument, Fat Jay could hear a thick line of doubt underscoring the man's words.

"If she's not with the filth, how come she knows so much about our business?"

"I know so much about it because I read newspapers," she explained in a prissy, pissed-off voice. "I might be dumb enough to shove this shit up my nose," she said. "But that doesn't mean I don't do a little reading to keep myself informed." She had been holding the crumpled twenty in her fist. Her fingers tightened around the money and she pushed it into one cup of her bra. "Honestly," she said with haughty exasperation. "If you're cutting it with that shit, I'm taking my business elsewhere."

She started to get up, but Fat Jay placed a hand around her wrist and held her tight. Slowly, he shook his head. "Sit down," he told her. "You're not going anywhere."

She glared a warning at him but it was impotent and they both knew as much. Even if she decided to kick up a fuss, screaming and shouting for help, no one would come to her assistance in a hovel like the Boar's Head. He kept his hand on her wrist, the fingers squeezing so hard he could feel the thin, bird-like bones grinding together.

She looked pained but she didn't make a sound. Her eyes were narrowed with defiance. "I'm not with the filth," she insisted.

"Maybe not," Fat Jay conceded. "But you seem to know more about my business than is proper, and I want to find out why. I think we should have a discussion about all this somewhere a little more private."

Her eyes had been narrowed before. Now they widened. The cocky defiance fled from her posture and she shook her head, as though she had read his thoughts. "I just want a twenty-quid line of something that's not cut with something that's going to rot off my face," she insisted. "I'm not with the filth."

Fat Jay tightened his grip on her wrist and nodded at the dealer. Coming to a terminal decision, he said, "Let's discuss this back at my place."

"Afternoon, Mester Writer."

The man on the porch looked to be on the wrong side of seventy. His face was wrinkled. His eyes were shadowed beneath bushy, grey eyebrows. He was dressed like a vagrant in a shapeless jacket and saggy, brown pants that were worn to beige at the knees and cuffs. Over one shoulder rested a large, silver-bladed shovel. Ben was reminded of the *shovel-in-the-moonlight* painting on the wall in John's bedroom.

He almost stumbled back, fearing the old man was there to attack him. Kill him. Bury him. How would that be for a demise? He could see it as a tabloid headline: Writer bludgeoned to death by a geriatric shovel-wielding maniac. His heart raced. He struggled not to raise his hands to fend off the old man.

"Marion asked me to call over and tidy up the driveway and grounds."

His accent was thick with northern vowels and missing consonants. When Ben had finally worked out what the man was saying, the words stirred a vague sense of recollection. Mrs Scum had mentioned that a gardener might visit at the behest of the woman from the Doll House. She had said his name was Alfred or Albert. He couldn't remember which. Given that the man was employed by someone else, and Ben had no real reason to interact with him, he didn't suppose the man's name mattered that much. It was enough to know he was a gardener and not some homicidal, shovel-wielding maniac.

"Marion said Mester John would be coming up this weekend."

"Yeah," Ben agreed. He didn't bother feigning interest or politeness. Shouldering his way past the man he stumbled onto the driveway and said, "I'm going."

"Very good, Mester Writer," the gardener called after him. "I know where all the tools are kept."

Ben didn't bother acknowledging this. He waved a dismissal at the gardener and rushed into the tunnel of trees that sheltered the driveway. An autumn wind was rustling through the leaves above his head. The light beneath the canopy of branches was a preternatural dusk of unfamiliar colours and shifting shadows. Fallen leaves crunched crisply beneath his trainers as he quickened his pace to reach the bottom of the drive.

He didn't like the driveway.

The air beneath the trees held an aroma of earthy nature. He supposed, having spent his life living in the city, he didn't trust the smell. It made him think of things that were rotten and mouldering and left to decay. The cold chill, the alien sounds of winds chittering through branches, and the untidiness of twigs and leaves on the floor, all conspired to make him feel as though he was dealing with a very unfamiliar world.

His brisk pace had practically turned into a trot by the time he reached the bottom of the driveway. The light outside the canopy of trees was marginally brighter, although the overcast afternoon threatened another downpour. *Did it do anything other than rain in the north?* The clouds were heavy, low and the colour of fresh bruises.

Ben stepped through the gates that secured John's property. He crossed the road and turned right past the entranceway to the doll museum's estate. Glancing up at the gates to the Doll House, he saw a figure in a white clown suit staring down at him. The figure's head was tilted unnaturally to one side. Although there was a substantial distance separating him from the figure, Ben thought he could see cold, glassy eyes staring at him from within the depths of the makeup.

A large droplet of rain splashed on his brow. He brushed it from his head and continued marching away from the cottage with renewed purpose. It was a slow and arduous uphill trek. His muscles seemed to resist the effort but he pushed on regardless. He had come to a decision about how it would be best to deal with the situation and he was determined to act on that decision.

He was going to run away.

He was going to leave the village and maybe get a minimum wage job in a factory or a shop, and he was going to give up on the idea of being a writer and he was going to pretend that Ben Haversham never existed.

The rain fell heavier.

The fat droplets were cool on his skin.

He didn't care.

He grew short of breath from the exertion of marching away from the cottage, but somehow that sense of weariness was liberating. He was finally doing something to escape his miserable existence. He would no longer be a prisoner in John's cottage. This was his chance to make a new start.

Ben didn't know if his idea to run away and start afresh was truly feasible but he figured it would be easier than people usually pretended. He could work as a cleaner. The labour seemed simple enough and, even though he couldn't recall when he had last cleaned anything, he thought the work would be well within his abilities. It only involved operating a cloth, a mop and a toilet brush, didn't it? Working as a cleaner would give him enough money to exist and he felt sure no one was really bothered about the identity of cleaners.

He frowned as he remembered the last time he had seen a cleaner before arriving at Sandalwood. It had been someone who was part of a contracted cleaning group. They had been dressed in a corporate polo shirt and wearing a laminated ID badge on a corporate lanyard. Didn't contracted cleaning groups usually mean references, identification checks and the other nuisances of real life? Did that mean there were no real jobs for cleaners anymore? No real jobs that could be taken up by those disenfranchised writers who wanted to drop below society's radar? Mrs Scum was a cleaner, working for at least two separate clients, although Ben suspected she had a lifetime's legacy of trust built up in the village of Sandalwood.

His frown deepened and he shook his head again to clear his thoughts.

If he couldn't be a cleaner, then he could get a job working as a labourer or gardener like Alfred/Albert. He doubted anyone worried about the National Insurance numbers or official documentation for unskilled labourers or casual gardeners. He could make a fresh start with his life and forget all about Etta's death, his writer's block, and the shock of finding Deborah's dissected corpse in his linen closet.

The memory of that discovery flashed painfully across his thoughts. He could see every detail of the unsettling surprise. The pale and bloodless limbs, as well as the severed head, stood clearly in his mind's eye. Unconsciously, he placed a hand over his mouth to suppress the urge to vomit. He stood still for a moment, trying to quell his nausea.

He was momentarily distracted by the familiarity of his surroundings.

He was standing outside the doll museum.

Ben glanced back over his shoulder, sure he had stormed past the Doll House on his way up the hill as he tried to escape the village.

There was nothing familiar in the road behind him. He glanced again at the sign for the doll museum and his mouth worked soundlessly for a moment.

He could see the front gates for John's cottage.

Alfred/Albert stood at the gateway waving amicably at him. The man no longer had his shovel with him but, other than that, he looked exactly the same as when Ben had last seen him.

"Are you alright there, Mester Writer?" he called.

Ben shook his head and lurched off in the opposite direction.

The rain was now falling in heavier droplets and it seemed to be coming harder and faster. His face was slick with rain and his hair was plastered to his scalp. His hoodie and jeans stuck to his damp flesh and a shiver of cold rippled through his arms. He wasn't sure what had happened to make him lose his bearings, but he put it down to the fact that he was feeling panicked following the memory of discovering the body. He also reasoned that his decision to flee and make a new life was clouding his judgement of where he was going and what he was seeing.

Determined, he marched up the hill and passed the sign for the Green Man pub. He had passed the same thing when he went out the previous evening. He felt an uneasy sense of guilt when he remembered walking out of the place arm-in-arm with the blonde as he took her back to the cottage. The blonde, Deborah, was now dead and dismembered and, if she hadn't left the pub with him, she would likely still be alive. With those thoughts still lurking at the back of his mind, he passed the police station, the library and a row of yellow stone, slate-topped houses.

He closed his eyes to blink away a mist of rain that now clouded his vision.

And then he was standing again outside the entrance to the driveway that led up to the doll museum.

Alfred/Albert waved at him again from the driveway of John's cottage. Alfred/Albert stood beneath the protective canopy of the driveway's trees. He looked comparatively dry, even though the floor at his feet was dark and glossy with fresh rainwater.

"This is insanity," Ben muttered.

From the top of the hill he could see a short, slender figure stepping from the doorway of the museum. The white-faced, white-costumed clown was, thankfully, no longer standing there. There was only the spindly woman closing the doorway of the Doll House. She was far away, almost too far for him to see clearly, but he guessed it was Marion Papusa and he had no desire to speak with her. He ignored the gardener who was still waving, and he stormed off in a third direction.

This was the way that Mrs Scum had said would lead to the pub called the Mucky Duck. It was an uphill walk and his legs began to strain from the effort. He could feel oily sweat slathering his chest, warming the rain-soaked cotton of his hoodie. From behind him he could hear someone shouting his name but he didn't bother turning around. He was determined to walk on and find some way to make his escape from the damned village.

The sights he encountered were no different than every other thing he had seen in Sandalwood that afternoon.

He passed yellow cottages with black roofs. He passed bland shops that didn't seem to sell anything and looked like they might have been there since before the days of Queen Victoria. He could see a pub sign, a swinging board above the entrance to a mock-Tudor building. It showed a picture of a tranquil summer's day with a distinctive bird floating in the middle of the lake. Instead of mentioning mucky ducks, the sign identified the pub as *The Black Swan*. Ben considered stopping in the pub and asking for directions on how best to leave the village, but he didn't think it would be a good idea. He had come out of the Green Man with a woman who was now dismembered. He didn't want to run the risk of causing another death. Shaking his head, he walked briskly past the pub and moved on past the cemetery-fringed churchyard.

A pair of old women stood in the shelter of the lychgate before the churchyard. They were involved in an animated discussion with the local vicar, a burly man wearing a long black frock coat and a high white clerical collar. All three of them stopped to stare at Ben as he trudged past.

Ben could feel himself blushing beneath their scrutiny.

He wondered if they all knew about the dead woman in his closet, and then shut that thought from his mind as it threatened to make him shriek with hysterical laughter.

The silent accusation of their stares followed him as he walked past. He didn't want to be intimidated by their curiosity but it was difficult to feign indifference.

The lychgate was a typical wooden frame construction, offering shelter at the entranceway to the churchyard. He had looked into church architecture for his first novel, and that was where he had first encountered the terminology '*lychgate*'. The word *lych* came from an Old English noun, either *lic* or *lichama*, his sources hadn't been explicit, meaning *corpse*. According to tradition, the first part of a burial ceremony usually took place under the gate's shelter, which was why it was named for the corpse.

A shiver rippled down his spine as he realised he was standing in the rain, staring at sinister strangers and thinking about all the hundreds of corpses that had historically passed through that shelter.

He hurried his pace away from them until the churchyard was far behind him.

"Mister Haversham," Marion called cheerfully.

He was again outside the doll museum. How the hell had that happened? He stared back at the way that he'd come but the route offered no clues. He could no longer see the churchyard, the lychgate or the Black Swan. The route was lined only with yellow stone cottages that squatted beneath rain-slick black slate roofs.

And the clown, he noted uneasily. The white-faced clown, with the unnatural tilt of its head, was staring down at him from the road he had just walked. Ben wrenched his gaze away from the figure and tried not to shiver with disgust. Was there no escaping this fucking village?

"Did the cleaner tell you about our dinner date this evening?"

Ben ignored the question. He glanced around and tried to decide which routes he had already tried to use to leave the village. Three roads converged outside the gateway to the doll museum. He felt sure he had tried walking along each of them. But all three had brought him back to this spot. How was that even possible?

"Which way did I come from?"

"I don't know, darling," Marion purred. "I wasn't paying that much attention."

"I..." He paused and pointed up the road that led to the Green Man. Then he glanced at the road that led to the Black Swan. The white-faced clown was no longer there. Shaking his head, sure that wasn't the right way to start, he pointed up the road that led away from the other two. "I..."

"You look like you've had a busy time with your writing," Marion told him.

She seemed indifferent to his distraction. She had a black umbrella above her head and it seemed to protect her desiccated features from the elements. Ben could hear the heavy *plop-plop-plop* of quickening fat droplets spattering onto the canopy of her brolly.

"Are you involved with a particularly exciting plot?" she asked. "I don't know how you writers manage to separate fantasy and reality with the stories you write. There must be times when it feels as though you're living in the dark places that your imagination creates."

He glanced back towards John's property. Alfred/Albert was pruning back overhanging branches. The sky looked darker than he could recall seeing before. The rain was falling heavier and the light seemed to have been squeezed from the day.

"I was trying to leave the village."

"Oh! No! You can't leave the village just now. You're expected for dinner at mine in about an hour. My staff have been working so hard on preparing something nice for you."

It was automatic to glance at his wristwatch.

An hour?

He vaguely remembered Mrs Scum saying the meal was meant to be around six thirty but there was no way he had been out walking for so long.

His watch said it was five o'clock. He suddenly noticed the cold. His limbs ached as though they were being stung by the pain of too much exercise. He worked his mouth soundlessly and tried to decide what he needed to do for the best.

"Why don't you get yourself back to the cottage and get yourself washed and changed?" Marion suggested. "I'll see you at six thirty and we can chat properly then, darling."

He nodded dumbly and stumbled back across the road to the cottage.

#20

Marion's words came back to him as he stepped inside the house. "*I don't know how you writers manage to separate fantasy and reality with the stories you write. There must be times when it feels as though you're living in the dark places that your imagination creates.*"

He would love to have bought into that idea. Wouldn't it be wonderful if, instead of finding a drained and dissected corpse in the linen closet, he had just imagined a scene from a story he had yet to write? Admittedly, a disturbingly sinister story, darker and more twisted than the confessional fiction he normally penned. But, of all the possible outcomes available from this nightmare scenario, Ben knew this would be the best.

But he didn't hold a lot of hope for that being the case.

He had seen the severed parts. He had heard the squish of an eyeball popping when it got caught between the door and the jamb. He could still recall the meaty stench of the corpse's parts, the scent intermingling obscenely with the sweetly dusty fragrance of freshly laundered linen. The idea that the body had been a figment of his imagination was a tempting fantasy that he couldn't afford to entertain because he knew it wasn't true.

He closed the door behind himself and tried to think what he should now do to address the problem. He knew, given the enormity of the situation, he had to do something. Authorities would need to be involved and he couldn't afford to let himself be distracted from taking positive action.

There was a suit hanging on the kitchen door.

Pale grey and of a style that didn't look too unattractive, Ben felt surprised that Mrs Scum had such a good eye for what he found sartorially pleasing. The suit was hung with an ironed white shirt and a cobalt-blue tie, he thought the ensemble looked like the sort of clothing he would have picked for himself if he'd been trying to impress someone.

There was a note pinned to the breast pocket of the jacket.

'I've put a pair of polished shoes beside your bed. X'

The woman thought of everything. If he hadn't been feeling so anxious because of the way the day was developing, he would have smiled. Instead he glanced nervously up at the ceiling. He wasn't wholly sure of the floor layout upstairs but he imagined his gaze was fixed in the right direction for the cupboard where he had seen Deborah's dissected body.

He boiled the kettle and noisily shook a generous handful of dry cat nibbles onto Anastasia's saucer. The cat made no attempt to come running into the kitchen and he suspected it was either asleep or outside. He poured himself a coffee and stared warily again at the ceiling.

The kitchen was spotlessly tidy.

He splashed a drink of milk into Anastasia's other saucer, then took his coffee and the suit into the study. The grandfather clock in the hall tocked solemnly as he stepped past it. He shivered a little at the sound but refused to let it ruffle his composure.

He was not going to succumb to panic.

He was not going to let himself brood on the idea that he was trapped in an inescapable village and alone in a house with a disassembled corpse. With that thought his gaze immediately went up to the ceiling.

The pages that he had typed in the night were exactly where he had left them. He remembered his excitement, shortly after three that morning, when he had settled down in front of the typewriter. At the time he had been wondering where his story would go whilst he wrote and slept. The excitement had returned when he woke but he had resisted the temptation to read the pages then because Mrs Scum had been lurking nearby and he hadn't wanted the pleasure of reading spoilt by the interruption of her chatter.

Now the idea of reading the pages seemed pointless and irrelevant.

He stared at the walls and, for the first time noticed the painting that hung in the study.

It was a picture of Marion's doll museum.

He remembered Mrs Scum mentioning the painting. She had said it was an original from the artist woman, Tina. He studied the picture and saw it was the same image he had seen each night when he awoke at 03:10. It was the image from his bedroom window that showed the darkened old building sitting high on its hilltop with nicotine-yellow light pissing from its windows. It struck him that there had been times whilst he was sitting in the study when he must have glanced at the painting and thought he was looking through a window and up to the sinister gloom that was the Doll House. He couldn't decide whether that meant the painting was a particularly vivid image, or if he was a particularly unobservant individual.

The letters *CW* were scratched in the bottom corner of the painting.

He wondered why he had never noticed the painting before. Or, at least, why he hadn't realised it was a painting. It was large, dominating one wall, and it was very striking. But his mind seemed to have misled him, until now.

He stepped closer to see how the artist had developed the image.

The spooky house was the central focus of the picture but there was much more detail visible when he stepped closer. He could see the shape of the vehicles parked outside the old building. There were a couple of large vans and a handful of modern, expensive cars. He recognised the BMW and Mercedes logos on a couple of the bonnets as he stepped closer and he figured they were there to suggest prestige and affluence. He could even see one car that looked like it had the flying *D* hood ornament that he'd seen on John's Daimler.

CW was clearly a competent artist.

The foreground of the painting looked black from a distance but now, standing with his nose almost brushing the oiled surface of the canvas, Ben could see it portrayed a shadowy hive of frenetic activity. There were figures in the darkness. Some of them were dressed in hooded robes, the cowls covering their faces. They looked as though they were part of some sort of satanic cult.

There were others. They were naked, muddied by filth, hidden by shadows, and writhing together in positions of salacious abandon.

"What the fuck?"

His voice trailed off as he realised the images were obscenely carnal. There was a woman sucking on two swollen erections. There was a man being taken roughly from behind by another man. One of these figures reminded Ben of the vicar he had seen whilst he was out walking earlier. Other familiar faces struck him and he recognised Alfred/Albert, the barmaid from the Green Man, and Mrs Scum.

"What the actual fuck?"

The grandfather clock chimed the hour. The noise was so loud, sudden and unexpected, Ben almost shrieked with surprise. As his hammering heartbeat began to subside he realised he had thirty minutes to get himself ready to visit Marion's doll museum. More importantly, he had to brace himself to look in the closet again and decide how to deal with what he found there. Gingerly, he left the study, snatched the phone from the desk, and began to climb the stairs.

The decision had come with the chiming of the clock.

He was going to go to the linen closet and take a picture of the disassembled corpse. He was then going to send a copy of the picture to John and wait for his advice.

The rationalisation was relatively simple. John was his agent. An agent's job was to take care of unpleasant things on behalf of a client. It seemed like a logical solution to let John deal with the problem.

His heartbeat pounded from the exertion of climbing the stairs.

He fumbled with the phone, trying to open the camera app and hoping he could work out how to take a picture and then send it to John. Guardedly, he opened the closet door.

The shelves only held towels and bed linen.

The body, if it had ever been there, was now gone.

No.

With a rush of sudden insight he understood the body had never been there. Marion's words had been prescient. *"I don't know how you writers manage to separate fantasy and reality with the stories you write. There must be times when it feels as though you're living in the dark places that your imagination creates."* That had to be the explanation, he told himself. The fear that he had found severed and drained body parts was nothing more than a figment of his imagination.

Ben closed his eyes and resisted the urge to cry with relief. He lowered the camera and, even though he still felt as though something amiss had happened in the house, he assured himself that he had almost certainly not found a dissected corpse in the linen closet.

#21

Burying the corpse in the clown suit was not a pleasant experience. Tom stood over the thing for a long, long moment and considered it solemnly. The face was rotted to a stained skull, bubbled with blemishes of green-grey skin. The costume, identical to the one he wore, was an incongruously cheerful sight at the bottom of the grave, wrapped around a mouldering corpse. There was a sprinkling of fallen autumn leaves on the body that shifted occasionally. Tom told himself it was the light breeze that made the leaves shift because there was no way a creature in such an advanced state of decomposition could still be alive.

No way at all.

He told himself that he didn't see any movement in the bony fingers. There was no suggestion that the lifeless figure was reaching out for assistance. And he was absolutely certain he didn't see the lipless mouth of the skull move as though it was trying to form a plea for help.

Hurriedly, and not allowing himself the luxury of thinking any further, Tom began to shovel dirt into the grave. It was not easy work. The exertion pulled at the muscles in his shoulders and down his back. Whilst that pain was uncomfortable, he knew that the alternative, waiting and watching and trying to convince himself the thing was still not moving, would be all the more unbearable.

The sorceress, Marion, had called the creature a woodsman. She had said it was his predecessor and, he suspected, the fate that had been dealt to this sad creature was the same one that awaited him when he was no longer of any use to her. The thought made his stomach muscles tighten with a band of nausea. If the thing in that shallow grave was still alive, and he desperately hoped it wasn't still alive, then he imagined she one day would intend for him to be disposed of in the same fashion.

The idea of being buried beneath an inescapable weight of soil, and then locked in the limbo of eternal, claustrophobic darkness, struck Tom as the cruellest fate imaginable. As he worked, he fervently prayed that his Lord would save him from such an ignoble end.

It took him the best part of an hour and, when he was finished, Tom was slathered with oily sweat. His face burnt from exertion and every muscle in his body begged for rest.

But, instead of resting he turned to address the next chore.

Marion's instructions had been explicit and they had not allowed for rest.

As soon as he finished patting the final sod onto the filled grave, Tom put down the shovel and turned to the roll of carpet. He unfurled it in one brusque gesture, pulling the stiff remnant of carpet aside, trying to see what he had to deal with. It came as no surprise to discover he was expected to bury another body.

Tom vaguely recognised this corpse.

It was the man he had shot in the offices of Ben's agent. Tom remembered that the man had been wearing a powder-blue suit. It was a distinctive colour, too summery in his opinion for the glumness of the autumn they were currently enduring. For some reason that he couldn't fathom, this man in the powder-blue suit had died from his gunshot wound whereas Alice had proved immune to gunshots.

And the clown you just buried seemed to have survived death and decomposition, a voice at the back of his mind taunted. *How do you explain that?*

Tom shut those thoughts off, focusing on the body. He did not want to think about the corpse in the clown suit. He did not want to think that such a fate most likely awaited him.

The man in the powder-blue suit was tall and, if not for the hole in his face, would likely have been handsome. Tom didn't recognise the remnants of the man's face but he did recognise the distinctive suit. Aside from the shock of blood he had encountered at the agent's office, the suit had proved a memorable colour. *Who, in heaven's name, wore powder-blue in autumn?* The shoulders of the suit were now black with dried blood. The blood had faded to streaks of dark crimson around the lapels, but the pants and waistcoat seemed not to have been dirtied in the trauma of the shooting.

Tom swallowed down the bilious taste of revulsion.

It was still raining and his clown costume was sticking clammily to his skin. Grave-digging had proved to be surprisingly challenging work and, despite the chill of the weather, he was sweating profusely. He also ached with a ferocity that made him wonder if he had seriously injured some part of his anatomy. His spine throbbed and the muscles in his shoulders and biceps burnt as though they were on fire.

Before reaching for the shovel, for the briefest moment, Tom considered resisting Marion's commands. He had a mission that he knew was governed by a divine power. He was sworn to avenge Etta's death – that was what his saviour wanted from him. He did not have time to be dressed as a clown, or a Harlequin or a woodsman, or however it was that Marion had described his role. And he certainly didn't have time to be standing in a forest and burying bodies. He was a scourge and he had his own wrongs to right.

In a momentary spirit of defiance, he pushed the shovel away.

A flash of bright pain skewered through his skull.

The intensity was strong enough to make his stomach fold with nausea. Tom was driven to his knees. He groaned. The sound was soft but it carried like the growl of an injured animal through the woods. Bloody tears began to trail from his left eye. He noticed their disconcerting colour when he wiped the back of one dirty hand against his cheek. For some reason, he couldn't bring himself to be concerned about this development. It was the first spot of blood he'd seen on himself since waking in the sorceress' basement. Blood hadn't come from the wounds Marion had made him inflict. Nor had it come from any other injury. But now it was pouring from his eyes like tears. Yet he knew there was no time to brood on this development. The pain in his skull was sufficient to make him want to weep. Knowing that he had to do Marion's bidding, or his condition would most surely worsen, Tom reached for the shovel.

The pain stopped immediately.

The relief was so sudden he could have swooned with gratitude. If he hadn't thought that swooning might be construed as defiance he would have given into the impulse. Another tear trailed down his cheek as he realised he was no longer able to exercise his free will. He was being controlled and the idea that he was following instructions from a stranger, some ignorant sorceress who mocked his belief, was sickening. But, no matter how much he wanted to resist her commands, he dreaded the resurgence of pain that he knew would come from such defiance.

Dutifully, he began to dig the grave.

He told himself this was a chore he would have had to do anyway. The corpse in the powder-blue suit was his responsibility. He had been the one who shot it in the face and ended the person's life. And it was his Christian duty to accept and take care of his responsibilities.

It was what gentle…

It was what his saviour would have wanted from him.

Tom got the grave down to just a little over a metre in depth and figured that would suffice. Thrusting the shovel into a mound of displaced earth, he reached for the corpse's feet and tugged it towards the grave.

A twinge of pain in his back made him stop.

He was panting heavily. His hands were blistered from the exertion of digging. His face was greasy with bloody tears as well as dirt and perspiration. He ached more than he could ever recall aching before and he desperately wanted to defy the will of the woman controlling him.

Don't bury the body, he urged himself.

It was only a single thought, accompanied by a sharpening of the ache in his lower back, but he wondered if it would be possible to defy her instruction. If he could defy one of her instructions that would suggest it was possible to defy all of them. The idea was exciting because such an act of defiance would mean he was not under her absolute control. His temple throbbed with the quickening of a headache. The pounding pulse over his left eye darkened his vision. He could feel a fresh tear of blood slipping from his eye socket.

Don't bury the body, he urged himself again.

If he could manage that single act of defiance, Tom knew he would be able to defy all Marion's commands.

A sting of fresh pain speared his eye. He wiped his hand against the tear and saw it was blood-red. The pain in his lower back throbbed more ferociously than ever. His hands pulsed with the effort of holding onto the shovel, and he could see that his little finger was almost hanging from his hand.

No blood came from the wound. But the finger hung away from him like a loose thread on a cheap garment.

Bloody tears trailed from below his left eye as he studied this injury.

He puzzled over the anomaly of parts of his body not bleeding when they ought to have, and other parts bleeding when they shouldn't, when he saw that he had almost finished covering the body.

"When did that happen?" he muttered.

He wasn't sure what his mind had been doing whilst he went through the actions of burying the second corpse. He had thought he was simply standing by the impromptu graveside and fighting an internal struggle. But it seemed, rather than standing idle, whilst his thoughts had been preoccupied, his body had slipped into some automatic mode and treacherously done the bidding of the sorceress.

His fingers curled into a fist. His hatred for the woman intensified. His desire to defy her was so strong he could taste it in the coppery tang that came when he chewed angrily on his lower lip.

"Gentle Jesus," he began.

The prayer got no further.

Tom silenced himself with a punch to the jaw.

He groaned in frustration and fell to his knees. Staring up at the awning of trees above his head, praying silently and hoping his Lord could hear him, Tom wondered if it would be possible to defy that cruellest instruction she had given.

Remaining on his knees, tensing every muscle in his body with determination, he turned both hands into fists and pressed them against the hard-packed soil of the grave he had just made. A confused worm touched against his bruised and hyper-sensitive knuckles. The cool wetness of recently turned earth was a balm against his aching skin.

"Blessed be the God and father of our Lord, gentle Jesus Christ."

He stiffened, willing himself not to deliver the punch, but unable to stop himself expecting the pain. His arm throbbed from the act of resistance. His shoulders ached from the exertion. Another bloody tear slipped from his left eye.

But this time, there was no punch.

His heartbeat quickened with hope.

He remembered a passage from Romans and urged himself to recite it as a part of his prayer. "For I am sure that neither death, nor life, nor angels, nor rulers, nor things to come, nor powers, nor height nor depth, nor anything else in all creation, will be able to separate us from the love of God." He paused before reciting the conclusion to the passage and steeled himself for another display of willpower. "In Christ, gentle Jesus. Our Lord."

His fists remained pressed to the soil. He realised he was holding his breath and he released the air with a sigh that was close to being a sob of relief. Pulling himself into a standing position, determined that he would deal with the witch who had held him under her evil control, he grabbed the shovel and started out of the woods.

"Gentle Jesus is going to make you pay for your wickedness," he mumbled.

His hand tightened its grip around the shovel but, again, there was no attempt to punch himself in the face. His smile tightened as he pushed through the woods and stepped out into the dreary autumn rain. Ignoring the weather, striding purposefully forward, he pushed through the gates to the Doll House and climbed the hill to Marion's home.

"Gentle Jesus will make you sorry for your sacrilegious ways," he growled. The words were spoken with the laboured rhythm of his footfalls as he climbed the steep incline. When he reached the doorway of her home he pushed his way inside without knocking and headed purposefully towards the basement.

It had changed since he was there.

He could see more than a dozen people crowded into the room. Each was bent over a workstation and Tom was struck by a moment's horrific revulsion as he saw they were all handling small body parts. A scream of disgust threatened to leap from his throat as he saw them holding tiny arms, baby legs, and severed heads.

When he realised the parts were doll limbs the rush of relief was dizzying.

These workers were Marion's employees, he guessed. This was her basement workshop where she assembled dolls. His relief was so strong that he didn't realise that none of the staff had looked up as he blundered into the workshop. They each kept their heads dutifully lowered and concentrated intently on the task of painting and assembling the kits that rested before them.

Tom marched into the gloom of the basement and got his bearings. The workstation where he had awoken was still empty. Alice remained in the room and, thankfully, she was now covering her ugly breasts. Marion stood talking to the woman, her stiff posture suggesting she was delivering instructions. She had changed clothes from earlier and now stood in a snug skirt and loose blouse. She was wearing stockings and high heels. Her face was painted with the harlot red lips of a much younger woman.

"Witch," Tom bellowed.

He made to point at her and discovered he still held the shovel. It looked like some powerful weapon of accusation in his hand. The broad blade quivered as an extension of his trembling arm.

Alice and Marion turned to stare at him.

Alice's eyes were wide with apprehension but Marion seemed calm and unperturbed. The staff continued painting and assembling the dolls on their workstations. Not one of them bothered to glance in Tom's direction. For the first time it struck him as odd that none of them were looking at him.

Marion slowly turned to face her accuser. She tilted her jaw defiantly.

"Witch," Tom roared again. "You held me in your thrall but I've broken your spell. I'm no longer your puppet. And I shall have my vengeance."

"Really?" Marion smiled. "You think you've escaped my hold over you?"

He stormed across the basement and towered over her. Tossing the shovel to the floor, where it landed with a loud clatter, he said, "The Bible tells us we should not suffer a witch to live." Originally, he knew, the Bible had said 'Thou shalt not suffer a sorceress to live'. But he figured the new translation of *witch* was equally accurate. He balled his hand into a fist and said, "Witch, I'm going to purge you and your evil from this world now. And I'm going to do it in the name of gentle Jesus."

His own treacherous fist slammed hard into his cheek.

The impact was so harsh he heard bone break and a spike of pain made him want to wail. The only thing that stopped him from releasing any sound was the uncertainty of not knowing whether the cry would be borne from pain or disappointment. He staggered on his feet, close to falling, and he glared at Marion with glassy eyes.

"You're entertaining," Marion mused. "I like that you're trying so hard to maintain your independence. But there's no time for this silliness now. I have a job for you."

He was shaking at the thought of his hard-fought defiance being described as 'silliness'. And yet, all he could do was stand dutifully in front of her and wait to hear her commands.

"I want you to drive Alice back to London this evening," Marion told him. "Then you'll come back here, do you understand?"

Sullenly, Tom nodded.

She handed him a set of car keys and nodded at Alice as though confirming previously delivered instructions. "Now get out of my home," she snapped. "I have an important evening ahead of me and I don't want you to be seen by my visitor."

Visitor? He frowned and struggled to think why she would be worried about him being seen by anyone in the village of

Sandalwood. He had never travelled this far north in his life before and he didn't think there was anyone in the village who would know him.

Except for one person, he remembered sullenly. In that moment he knew that Marion would be entertaining the hateful Ben Haversham that evening.

A single bloody tear trickled down his cheek.

#22

"Welcome to the Doll House," Marion cried cheerfully.

Ben smiled and offered her a bottle of red wine he had found under the sink in the cottage. He suspected it was one of those bottles of wine that had been repeatedly given but would never be consumed. He had handled cases of them in his time – last minute gifts for and from people he barely considered gift-worthy.

"Thank you for… inviting me," he said cordially. He hesitated over the word 'inviting'. It would be more truthful, he knew, to say he had been summoned to the Doll House. But he could see no reason to complain about this point and spoil the mood of the evening at the onset.

"Come inside, come inside." Marion took him into an embrace that seemed overly familiar yet somehow appropriate for her personality. He could smell the dusty fragrance of her perfume and an underlying scent that made him think of rot and decay. "Come inside, come inside."

He managed to maintain his smile when the embrace was broken and he acquiesced to her urging and stepped into the building.

The hallway was grand in its black and white majesty and splendour. The ceiling was a mile away and decorated by a huge, glittering chandelier. The light it threw onto the dark panelled walls below seemed, somehow, not quite bright enough for the room. The pictures that decorated the walls didn't seem properly lit and the images they showed seemed to be lurking in perpetual shadows. He caught a glimpse of a menacing looking clown, a figure that he thought might have been Rigoletto, Ronald McDonald or John Wayne Gacy. A shiver of unease tickled up his spine. He couldn't understand why anyone would want a picture of any of those figures on their wall. But, if he was being truthful with himself, he had never subscribed to the idea of displaying regular artwork in any of the flats where he had lived. As far as preferences for artwork went, he thought plates of fruit, flowers, and bottles of wine besides cheese were equally unappealing subjects for artwork, but he had to admit they were a lot less sinister than pictures of clowns.

There was a triptych of clown paintings to his right. The first showed a huge clown holding a small clown doll. The clown doll was an exact replica of the large clown. They were both dressed in garish Harlequin costumes, diamonds of red and gold on a white background with matching jester's hats. The jester's hats even had jangly bells hanging from their tails.

The faces, Ben thought, were unsettling. They each wore deathly white make-up and had lips as red as bloody murder. Their eyes were circled with dark smudgy shadows and they glared out at the viewer with glowers that were cold, hard, and devoid of emotion. Their smiles were threatening grimaces vaguely hidden beneath a smear of greasepaint.

The second image showed a pair of clowns dancing together. This time it was the large, colourful Harlequin from the first picture dancing with a black and white Pierrot. The Pierrot, with his pasty-pale face, tall pointy hat, and the big black buttons on his smock, looked comically thin against the rotund bulk of the colourful Harlequin. But, although they were clowns and they were being comical, Ben did not smile at the painting.

He had no idea why the clowns would be dancing, or what the dance was supposed to signify. He suspected the scene was meant to convey symbolism of control, or asymmetry, or some sort of balance but he wasn't wholly sure. Despite not knowing what the picture represented, not liking it, he found himself drawn to something in the image. He supposed it was his favourite of the three.

The third image was the most disquieting.

The Harlequin and the Pierrot stood back to back over a mound in the earth. There was a shovel buried in the earth, a shovel that reminded Ben of the shovel he had seen in the painting in John's bedroom. The clowns were staring out at the viewer as though posing to have their image captured after they had completed a night's nefarious work.

He stopped himself from frowning too hard at the painting, sure that his unease would be apparent in the sneer of contempt he was wearing. He could vaguely see a relationship between the paintings and the doll museum. The Harlequin was being depicted with a doll in each image: a copy of itself exact in every detail except size. But he couldn't see any other reason for the paintings, unless the museum's policy was to instil nightmares in everyone who walked through the entrance hall. He felt sure, if he did dream this evening, the dream would be haunted by the spectral figures of controlling clowns and moonlit burial mounds. And there would likely be the smell of Marion's fusty perfume.

"You'll have to forgive the layout of the place, darling," she purred. "We do a lot here. This is my family home, but the Doll House is also a doll museum and it's an operating workshop."

"A workshop?"

"We make dolls."

For the first time he noticed her outfit. It was a smart, dark business suit with a short hem to the skirt that showed off a pair of slender, stocking-clad legs. The jacket was figure hugging, accentuating her slender waist and brushing over the absence of her breasts. Her stiletto heels clipped on the wooden floor as she led him into the house.

She's dressed to get laid.

The thought was disquieting and almost soured his good mood. Since he had discovered that there was no body in the linen closet Ben had been riding a high of relief. He was not the sleepwalking killer he had feared he had become and he didn't have to worry about the repercussions of having discovered a dead body in his linen closet. He had even found himself looking forward to the distraction of visiting Marion and her quirky doll museum. But, if the woman was going to try and fuck him, he reckoned it might make for an awkward evening as he refused her. She was old enough to be his mother. Maybe even his grandmother. He had nothing against any woman of any age wanting to get her chimney swept. But he didn't want to be brought in as the brush.

"Would you like to start at the top and work your way down?" Marion asked. She laughed and paused and linked her arm in his when he caught up to her side. "You'll have to forgive me if I sometimes say things that are occasionally rude," she told him. "I have a deep love for *double entendre* and flirtation."

Her bony fingers squeezed tight against his bicep.

A mechanical hand inside a skin glove.

Ben hid his grimace as she led him up the flight of stairs at the end of the entrance hall. The stairs branched in two directions, but one way was partitioned off with a red rope barrier. It reminded Ben of the barriers he had seen outside theatres to help patrons form orderly queues.

Marion unhooked the rope and urged him to go through.

"This is the private tour," she explained. "You'll get to see those special places that I don't make available for everyone."

They went up another flight of stairs and she told him this was where she kept her offices. "The offices work for the museum, the workshop and *my other affairs.*"

He nodded as though he understood.

Or cared.

She said 'affairs' as though she was thinking about clandestine liaisons between beautiful people unable to contain their mutual lusts. He imagined she read a lot of raunchy romances.

Taking him up a further flight she said, "This is the top floor of the museum, but not the top floor of the building." Guiding him up a rickety, spiral staircase she said, "This is the top floor of the building. This is my personal recreation area."

He had to concede it was impressive. The floor space was as large as the whole of the house's footprint. Aside from five or six supports, which he guessed were holding the roof of the building in place, the room was completely open. Even the supports, glossy with mirrors, seemed almost invisible on his first glance around the room. The fact that the space was so large, and had windows going from the floor to the ceiling, gave an overpowering sense of openness. The room made the building seem far more modern than the *Scooby-Doo* mansion that cast its shadow over the village.

"This is incredible."

"I can see any part of the village I desire," she explained.

She took his arm and led him to one window. He noticed, as they were walking, that the floorboards were marked with chalk circles. He glanced curiously down at them and realised they had the look of pagan inscriptions. He knew little about such markings, but he had seen pentagrams within circles whilst watching TV shows where witchcraft was mentioned. He was thinking particularly of *Charmed* and the Willow-heavy episodes of *Buffy the Vampire Slayer*. These markings looked similar to those. Somehow, Ben suspected, these markings seemed more likely to have real magical power – if such a thing existed.

Walking him slowly around the room, Marion pointed out various landmarks. "You can see our library over there," she explained. "Have you seen the Christina White in the foyer?"

He shook his head. She could have been speaking in a foreign language.

"Did you know the library carries all your books?"

He smiled and tried to think of a response that would show he cared.

"That's our local church, Saint Genesius'. And over there is the Green Man. And over there's the Black Swan."

He nodded. Whilst he had no interest in Sandalwood or its local landmarks, he did like seeing the village from this elevated perspective. It reminded him of the days in his childhood when he'd been playing trains sets and creating the first toy-populated worlds of his imagination. Dusk was skulking to its place beyond the horizon and street lamps sparkled in the quickening gloom.

"There's John's cottage," she said, pointing down at the building at the foot of the museum's driveway. "I see you've left your bedroom light on," she chuckled. "Is that in case you take anyone back there this evening?"

Ben hadn't realised he'd left the bedroom light on but he supposed Marion knew the details of the village better than he knew them. He tried to think of a way to avoid addressing her question and asked, "Which is the road out of Sandalwood?"

The bony fingers gripped tighter at his arm. "Are you still wanting to leave?"

"It's not so much that I want to leave. I'm just curious to know how I missed finding the exit roads earlier today."

She pointed over the rise of a crop of towering poplars. He could see the tail-lights of a Mercedes sliding along the road. "That way will take you to the motorway. I can't remember the number. The M6 probably. Or maybe the M60-something." Walking him to the other side of the room, her heels clicking against the ancient markings scratched onto the floorboards, she said, "That way will take you to our nearest neighbouring village, Carleton. But, trust me, you'll be happier staying in Sandalwood than trying to abandon us."

The night outside the windows was becoming a glossy black. He could see speckles of dim lights in house windows breaking through the shadows. An occasional car's headlamps illuminated the darkness but, although the scene was dark, Ben thought it looked picturesque and almost pretty.

"This is a lovely view," he said eventually. "Did you say you use this room for recreation?"

"Yes."

"What sort of recreation?"

She laughed. "I'm a very spiritual creature, darling. I come up here to practice my witchcraft and pay homage to my gods in a sky-clad haven." She pushed her lips close to his ear and said, "That means

I'm naked." Treating him to the sound of her sultry laughter she added, "Perhaps you'd care to join me with my celebration one evening, Ben?"

"I'm not much of a worshipper," he said tactfully. "To any religion."

"Then you could just turn up here naked and I'd do the worshipping."

He remained rigid and said nothing.

She squeezed his bicep again. "You're so easy to tease, darling. You blush whenever you think you're being propositioned. I'm going to enjoy having your company here this evening."

I look forward to amusing you, he thought bitterly. Aloud he said, "It was very kind of you to invite me."

She took him down the stairs and showed him around the upper floor of the museum. There were exhibits of ancient porcelain dolls, most of them looking ancient, dusty and unnatural. They chilled him with their staring eyes and the peeling pigmentation of their cheeks. They looked antiquated and out of time, and he could understand no reason for anyone collecting such eerie examples of outdated histories and dead childhoods.

He didn't voice his thoughts. He maintained a grin of polite interest and nodded every time Marion explained another tedious aspect of dolly history that he had never previously known. She said that dolls had been part of prehistoric cultures. Dolls had been discovered in Egyptian graves dating back to 2000 BC. And the majority of her museum exhibits were seventeenth, eighteenth and nineteenth century dolls.

Ben suppressed the urge to yawn. He nodded his head and made noises that sounded like expressions of interest and enthusiasm. He was still nodding when she took him through to the display of dolls from the twentieth and twenty-first century. He even believed he was acting like a man who understood the purpose of the museum.

Not that he could properly understand the dolls. They were happy-faced with wide staring eyes. An obscene stench of talcum powder assaulted his nostrils. Aside from being fake examples of happy, smiling genuine babies, he was appalled to learn that some of them also made noises.

"This one giggles when you hold her," Marion explained.

The room was filled the sound of a child's burbling laughter when she squeezed its stomach. Standing with Marion in an otherwise deserted museum, Ben thought the sound of carefree childish laughter was one of the most disconcerting noises he had ever heard. Surely that was a horror-film staple, wasn't it? Why would such a terrifying device be placed inside a child's toy?

Through gritted teeth he said, "Lovely."

Marion showed him a collection of cloth dolls which made Ben think of the sorts of things that miserable parents held up on news stories when they were raising awareness about a case of child abduction. He wondered if he dared risk a glance at his watch to find out how much longer he was expected to endure Marion's company as she toured him around the misery of the doll museum.

"These are our specialist areas," she explained as she led him down a flight of stairs to the ground floor.

He was mildly surprised to see they were coming down the double flight she had initially walked them up. But this time, they were heading down the side without a red rope partition blocking off the stairs. He wondered if he was losing his sense of direction, if he'd ever had one, and that was why he was unable to find his way out of a village or notice that he'd climbed up one side of a building and was being walked down the other.

"This is what the doll museum currently specialises in," Marion said as she threw open a door. "These are our reborns."

He stared in surprise.

The dolls looked surprisingly realistic. Unnervingly realistic. Each was the same size, shape, and colour of a newborn, or very young baby. Marion later told him they were also weighted so that they felt like a real infant being cradled in the arms. She explained that the sales of the reborn dolls were currently the most lucrative area of her business.

Ben studied the doll in the bassinet closest to him and marvelled at the detail that had gone into creating the thing. It had minuscule fingernails and eyelashes and the tiniest delicate threaded veins on its eyelids.

"The artistry is superb," he muttered.

"I work hard on them."

"These are all your own work?"

"The majority. I have some staff working for me now, darling. I've trained them to work in the same way that I work on my dolls." She gave him a smile that was meant to look gracious but came across as smug.

In fairness, Ben thought she had good reason to be smug. The dolls were an amazing accomplishment. They were as creepy as fuck. But he couldn't fault the technical detail.

"Where do you make them?"

"I have a workshop downstairs in the cellar," she told him. "But that's not as pleasant as the rest of the museum." The sound of a distant gong interrupted their conversation and she added, "It also sounds like there's no time to explore any further. Dinner sounds like it's being served. Come and meet my staff."

#23

Marion's staff were the creepiest bitches Ben had ever encountered. A pair of tall women, dressed in some attire that vaguely resembled French maid outfits, greeted him politely as he entered the room. They wore plastic smiles and appraised him with nods of silent and sulky servility.

"This is Vicky and Laura," Marion explained, pointing from one to the other. She didn't make a great point of differentiating which was which. One was an anorexic brunette with a pixie cut. The other was a curvy blonde with a ponytail. "They'll be serving us tonight," Marion said.

Ben nodded and took the seat that was offered to him.

The dining room was intimate, lit by candles on the centre of the table, and warmed by candlelit sconces on the dining room walls. The air was fragrant with the scent of exotic spices and over-cooked vegetables. Everything seemed civilised and sophisticated except for the robotic movement of the maids.

They walked with the sort of stilted action he would have expected to see in badly drawn animation. Their hand-movements were sudden and erratic and seemed almost violent compared to the emotionless features of their unsmiling faces.

Ben became aware that Marion was watching him.

"Why do you have pictures of clowns in the hallway?" he asked.

"Excuse me?"

"I noticed them when I came in. You have pictures of clowns. What's the attraction? And is there any association between the clowns and the dolls you make here?"

She laughed and he thought he heard a defensive note in the sound. "Of course you'd know about clowns," she said. "You're a writer. I suspect you're familiar with the *Commedia dell'arte*."

"I recognise the Harlequin and the Pierrot," he admitted. There were other names he vaguely recalled, Columbina, Pulcinella, and Pantalone, although he didn't bother telling her as much. He had never been so pretentious as to think that a writer had to know every story in the history of stories before being allowed to put pen to paper. "Harlequin and Pierrot are the names of those two clowns, aren't they?"

She nodded. "I grew up with a theatrical family," Marion confided. "It seems so long ago now. But the pictures of the clowns give me a lovely sense of nostalgia. They remind me of family, friends, and a life that I knew a long, long time ago."

"A theatrical family?"

Her smile was tight. "Circus-folk, to be exact," she admitted. "Travelling circus-folk. At least, they were travelling circus-folk until they came here. Then they seemed to settle in this village and that's why Sandalwood is so tightly bound with my heritage."

She didn't bother to elaborate and Ben sensed it wasn't an area that she wanted to discuss in further detail. Deciding to change the subject, he asked, "How long have you known John?"

"Johnny and I go back a long way," Marion laughed. She studied him across the table as she stirred her spoon through a bowl of soup. "I got Johnny started as an agent," she explained. "And, in return, he's managed to help me benefit."

Ben sipped his wine and hoped she wouldn't make a joke about 'friends with benefits'. The woman was as predictable as a *Carry On* script, but without the subtlety and finesse. He considered his soup which smelled vaguely fishy, like an untreated genital infection. The idea of tasting it was unappealing.

"I helped Johnny finance his first agency," Marion explained. "And since then we've been bending over backwards to please each other." She gave Ben a knowing wink and said, "I do some of my best pleasing when I'm bending over backwards."

He smiled as though the comment was amusing. Wilfully, he struggled to keep up his end of the conversation rather than blush and tell her that her jokes were offensive. It was difficult to accept that he was in the company of someone who made his own puerile sense of humour seem sophisticated. Ben knew he was the sort of person who could find farts amusing. When he was dating, he could turn every comment in an evening into some vague blowjob reference. There had been nights he'd spent with Etta where every other remark had been an innuendo about anal sex. But, even though he had an adolescent devotion to the lewd and licentious, he still believed his humour was more mature and sophisticated than Marion's coarse and vulgar banter.

Vicky and Laura, he didn't know which was which, took away the soup bowls and returned with plates and a platter that bore a lump of over-cooked flesh. He couldn't work out if it was beef, lamb, pork, dog or tourist. Ben only knew that it looked both repulsive and obscenely tempting. The day had been a long one, and he couldn't recall eating since he awoke. Anastasia had been licking the toast that Mrs Scum had made, so he hadn't bothered with that. He knew he'd worked up an appetite burning off nervous energy running in circles around Sandalwood. But still, even though it was understandable, the appetite struck him as voracious and unstoppable.

Vicky and Laura brought in tureens of vegetables, but it was the meat that held Ben's attention. Glistening beneath a glazing of gravy and misting the air around it with a fragrant and appetising scent, the meat made his mouth water. He didn't know what sort of creature it had come from. He wasn't even sure if he should be eating it. But he thought the joint looked irresistible.

One of the maids began to carve slices from the bone.

He watched her hand motions.

They were jerky and rigid. She was frowning at the meat with a concentrated effort. The piece she pulled away was perfectly sliced but that didn't stop him from being unnerved by the lack of a human expression on her face as she worked on carving a second slice.

The other maid appeared by his side, spooning dark sprouts onto his plate from a willow pattern tureen. He tried not to flinch. There was something in the way the woman stood, something about her stiff posture and stilted movements that made him want to shrink away from her.

Worse than that, there was a smell.

It wasn't a particularly powerful smell. But it was strong enough to have registered on his senses. When Etta had died, he had visited the funeral home where her body had been on display. Ben recalled that there had been a similar perfume lingering around her. The scent was a noisome combination of faraway decay covered by cloying, floral sweetness. When he had asked about the scent, the funeral director had told him he was catching the combined fragrances of decomposition and formaldehyde.

Ben tried not to think as to why either Vicky or Laura would smell of formaldehyde.

It was enough for him to know, if either of the maids reached out to touch him, he was likely to scream and run shrieking from the Doll House.

"I've been looking forward to getting my lips around some meat all day," Marion told him.

He sighed as he forced the smile across his face. It was another of her cock gags. In some ways it was almost a relief to hear her making a lewd joke. It stopped him from speculating on why Vicky and Laura both looked like extras from a low-budget zombie movie.

"This all looks delicious," he said politely.

"Tuck in," Marion insisted. "There's more where that came from if you want something extra." She laughed indulgently and said, "Of course, if you want something extra, you could always take Laura or Vicky home with you."

He said nothing. Goosebumps prickled up and down his arms and he hoped his face didn't show the stomach-churning unease that came from contemplating such an idea. It was disquieting to share the same room with the maids as they went through the charade of serving food as though it was natural to them. The idea of being intimate with either creature was enough to make him feel nauseous.

He ate the food without tasting it, smiling at Marion's weak jokes as the evening progressed. It was something of a relief when she turned to him after the coffee and said, "I expect you'll need to head off home and make an early night of it if you want to keep to your current writing schedule."

He nodded. He stopped himself from saying anything for fear of sounding too enthusiastic.

"Mind you, you didn't object to having a late night yesterday with Debbie from the Green Man, did you?"

He studied her open-mouthed. As soon as Marion mentioned Deborah's name, Ben remembered everything about the woman he'd picked up in the pub. He remembered chatting with her, he remembered eating the Barnsley chop with her, and he remembered the sex.

Worst of all, he remembered discovering the woman's body in the linen closet.

The confusion of the day rushed through him and he shivered. He had found a mutilated corpse. He had tried to escape from an inescapable village. Someone had taken the mutilated corpse from the house where he was living. And he had convinced himself that the corpse had never been there. It had been a demanding day on so many levels that all he could think to ask was, "How did you know that I...?"

She laughed and pointed upwards. "You saw my viewing platform up there. There's no part of the village I don't see."

"You saw me and Deb-"

"I saw everything," Marion purred. Her lips were curled at the corners with the wickedest glint of a smile. "How long did you go down on her?"

"Excuse me?"

"You were eating her out for hours. You must be one of those men who can breathe through his ears. I've prayed for someone with your stamina to visit the village and it looks like you're the answer to my prayers."

"Did you see what time Deborah left?"

"I didn't see. Why? Are you needing some bedroom companionship? If you don't want to take advantage of Vicky or Laura I can help out with that if you–"

"Goodnight, Marion," he said firmly. "Thank you for a lovely evening."

"I'll see you Saturday, shall I, darling?"

He was going to say he didn't think that was likely but the certainty in her voice made him hesitate. "Saturday?"

"John's already confirmed that you two will be joining me for a meal. It will be so lovely to have two men for the evening. Do you think we should have a spit-roast? Or should I just ask Vicky and Laura to help me organise sandwiches?"

He turned away and walked down the driveway back to the cottage.

#24

"Say Jesus again," Alice insisted.

Tom glanced into the rear-view mirror of the car and didn't bother hiding his scowl of contempt. He could see Alice's face, with a smirk pressed on the fat, full lips, and he knew he hated her. He didn't hate her as much as he despised Ben Haversham. And his loathing for her paled beneath the black fury he wanted to unleash on Marion. But he still hated her. He hated her with a murderous passion.

"Say his name again," Alice taunted.

He was driving Marion's personal Mercedes. It was a polished, black vehicle that sped through the night with slick and speedy ease. The glow of the dashboard was vaguely comforting. The occasional cue from the satnav prompted him to navigate the roads safely. But he still found his thoughts returning to the hatred he harboured for Marion, Ben and now Alice.

"Say his name again," Alice said. "I want to watch you punch yourself."

"How does she do it?" he asked.

"How does she do what?"

The question made him pause for a moment. "How does she do all of it? How did she stitch you up? How is she controlling me? How is she capable of any of that?"

"She's a sorceress," Alice explained. "She's a sorceress and she can do whatever the hell she wants."

Sorceress, he thought numbly. *Thou shalt not suffer a sorceress to live.* His fists tightened on the steering wheel. He knew the command from the Bible but, instead of doing the right thing, instead of burning Marion or tearing her head from her shoulders or making her suffer the righteous wrath she deserved, he was following the woman's instructions and driving her zombie friend back to London. The Bible said, 'Thou shalt not suffer a sorceress to live.' Instead of obeying the word of the Bible, he was acting as the lackey to a sorceress.

"Where does she come from?"

"Say Jesus again and I'll tell you."

His fists tightened their grip on the steering wheel. His head throbbed with a furious ache. Slowly, trying to hide the anger in his tone, he asked again, "Where does she come from?"

Alice sighed as though she was disappointed that Tom wouldn't play along with her game. "No one knows for sure where she came from. They say she's old, as old as the village of Sandalwood. Maybe older. But no one really knows for sure."

Tom's frown deepened. "What do you mean?"

"Some people reckon she was around when that travelling circus pulled up on the site where the Doll House now sits."

"I got the impression that happened centuries ago," Tom said carefully.

"From what I understand, it did."

They drove on in silence for a while as he tried to digest this. "Are you saying she's centuries old?"

"At least."

"But that's impossible, isn't it?" He could hear the hateful notes of doubt and uncertainty in his voice. No one could live for centuries, could they? "You're just saying this to mock me," he decided. "You think I'm stupid enough to believe lies and falsehoods."

"You believe in God and Jesus," Alice sniffed. "So I think it's fair to say you're relatively gullible."

"I have faith in God and–"

He stopped himself abruptly before he could make the mistake of saying that second name. He didn't want to run the risk of losing control of the vehicle whilst he was driving. More importantly, he didn't want to suffer the hurt and humiliation of striking himself again. "I have faith," he admitted. "But I don't believe the lies of a sorceress and her acolyte."

"Believe what you want to believe." Alice sounded indifferent. "I know that Marion Papusa hasn't changed in appearance since I first met her, and that was more than eighty years ago."

He studied her through the rear-view mirror. He wasn't a good judge of ages. He had no idea how to look at person and guess how old they were. It was an ability he had never mastered. Usually, Tom thought people were around eighteen, or somewhere near thirty, or maybe north of fifty-two. But he didn't think Alice looked like she was even in her fifties.

"How old are you?" he asked.

"That's a very impertinent question."

He stayed silent and waited for her answer.

"I first met Marion when I was in my early forties," Alice explained. "I'd been working for John for a decade back then and he took me for a weekend break to his house in Sandalwood." She blushed as she admitted this piece of information.

Tom didn't notice. He was doing maths in his head. If she'd been in her early forties when she met Marion, and that meeting had been eighty-years ago, it meant Alice was-

"You're more than a hundred and twenty years old?"

"Somewhere round there," she agreed.

"But that's not possible. People don't live to that age."

"Marion's at least twice that age. Maybe three times older than me."

"She's a sorceress," Tom growled. "If what you say is true she'll carry on living until someone smites her. But you're not a sorceress. You're…" His voice trailed off. He remembered seeing her sagging breasts and the holes in her chest that were stitched with darning twine. "You're not a sorceress," he concluded.

"No," Alice agreed primly. "I'm one of Alice's immortals."

He wanted to argue but he could see no point. He had shot Alice four times in the chest at point blank range. It wasn't that she had managed to survive the injury. The truth was she had seemed only irritated by the interruption to her routine and annoyed that her blouse had been damaged.

The night sped past them, a blur of black interrupted only by the motorway's overhead lights, flashing past with monotonous consistency.

"How did she make you immortal?" Tom asked.

"The same way she made you immortal."

Tom stiffened. "She's done nothing to me."

"Are you sure about that? Don't you remember the taste that was in your mouth when you woke up in the basement? It wasn't particularly pleasant, was it?"

He wanted to tell her that there had been no unpleasant taste. But he couldn't say that with any degree of confidence. The more he thought about it, the more he realised there had been an unpleasant taste.

"There's some potion she has," Alice explained blithely. "When she's trying to get people under her influence surreptitiously, she'll slip the potion to them in a meal or in a drink. I think that's how she's managed to wield control over so many of the no-hopers that have been sent to her in Sandalwood from John's agency. She has her cook slip the potion into some food cooked by one of her servants."

As he listened, Tom rubbed his tongue uneasily against the roof of his mouth.

"Once she's forced the potion down your throat there's a ritual," Alice went on. "And then, if everything goes as she wants, you become immortal." She smiled tightly, seemingly satisfied with her explanation. "Didn't you notice that there was no blood when you stabbed yourself with the screwdriver?"

His stomach folded uneasily.

"You no longer bleed," Alice told him. "You're impervious to injury. You're immortal."

He remembered the way his tears had been bloody, and he wondered if he should mention as much to her. He stopped himself, not sure it would be wise to let her know about that detail. "I can't really be immortal," he whispered. The idea seemed unlikely, impossible, and unholy. "Are you saying I can never die?"

"If they did it right, someone could kill you," Alice mused. She sounded as though the idea of his death was amusing. "Someone could cut your head off. Someone could burn you until there were only ashes left. Someone could dissolve you in a big bath of acid like they used to do on that TV show about American drug dealers and…"

Tom shuddered and stopped listening.

They had left the motorway and were driving into the heart of the city. The satnav was showing a chequered flag for his intended destination and he realised he had made surprisingly good time. His instructions had been to drive Alice to her home and then return to Sandalwood.

The idea of disobeying those instructions should have been unthinkable. But Tom knew, if he wanted to maintain any sense of his previous self, he needed to make a final attempt to defy Marion's commands.

"I wouldn't worry about immortality too much, if I were you," Alice said. She spoke with unpleasant cheerfulness. "Marion's employing you as a woodsman and her woodsmen never last long. The last few have been destroyed within the same month they were created."

He swallowed thickly. "Destroyed?"

"She works them too hard. Look at you for instance. She had you carrying that body single-handed from the Doll House to the woods.

I'll bet she got you digging the grave alone and filling it in by yourself."

Tom brought the car to a halt outside Alice's home. The satnav told him he had reached his destination. He pondered Alice's words with a sinking of his spirits. He'd worked very hard digging the grave for the body in the powder-blue suit. The blisters that sat on his palms were a testament to the effort he had put into doing her bidding. He'd also worked hard filling in the grave over the figure in the Harlequin costume. He wondered if that had been one of Marion's previous woodsmen. Had he been right to fear that the same fate now waited for him? He couldn't be sure of the definitive answers to those questions, but he felt confident that he would have to find some way of defying Marion if he wanted to avoid an unmarked burial in the midst of the forest surrounding Sandalwood.

"You haven't slept since she roused you, have you?"

"No," he admitted. He wanted to say more but a growing worry in the pit of his stomach made him sure she was revealing an unpleasant truth.

"Now we're here you're going to drive back to Sandalwood and it will be lunchtime when you get back there. Instead of allowing you to sleep or rest Marion will put you to work, either in the packaging department, or working on collection and deliveries of raw materials. Once those jobs are complete, and they're rarely ever complete, she'll get you slaving over the darker jobs she needs doing."

Tom didn't like the idea of doing anyone's 'darker jobs' but it was Alice's use of the word 'slaving' that made him cringe internally. He didn't want to be anyone's slave. He stepped out of the car and went to Alice's door to open it for her.

"This is how she's destroyed so many of her woodsmen in the past." Alice climbed out of the car and looked him up and down with a sneer of disapproval. "You must feel weary now?"

He nodded.

"That's going to be amplified a hundredfold by the end of the week. You'll be staggering through your chores, praying for death. And bits of you will start to drop off."

He studied her quizzically, trying to work out if she was joking or not. He had addressed the injury to his little finger with a roll of sticking plaster, although he suspected that the repair was an inadequate measure. The finger now pointed awkwardly out of his hand and, he suspected, unless he watched it carefully, there was a strong likelihood the digit could fall away and he would be none the wiser.

It was the middle of the night. They were standing on a quiet street in a relatively prosperous suburb of the city. They were close enough to a street light so he could see her features. Tom tried not to shiver as he listened to Alice describe his impending future.

"You'll get a finger caught in some packing crates. It will be easier to tear the finger off rather than pause and take care of yourself. You'll lift something so heavy that your spine will snap. You'll work to the point of exhaustion where something in your brain just gives up. It will happen."

"You didn't want me to be a woodsman," he remembered. "Why not?"

She sniffed sourly. "Don't get me wrong. I'm not sorry that you're a woodsman. You're a religious freak and you deserve this sort of fate. The reason I didn't want you to be a woodsman is because I wanted the pleasure of watching you die quickly and painfully whilst I was still in Sandalwood. Now your end is going to come slowly, and maybe even more painfully. But it's unlikely I'll be around to watch it happen."

"So, what's going to happen to me?" he asked. "What happens if I collapse on the floor with body parts missing and my brain refusing to go on? What happens then?"

Alice's smile had been tinged with cruelty. Now it softened into something he understood was pity. She glanced briefly in the direction of a nearby house and he guessed this was her home. The building was held in shadows and the only one on the road with no interior lights suggesting life inside. Turning her solemn gaze on Tom she asked, "You saw her patching me up, didn't you?"

He nodded.

"She has the power to do that for some. But, for disposable labour like yourself, she'll have you dig your own grave and then lie in it until your flesh rots."

Tom shrank from the notion. He remembered the corpse he had buried in the woods. He remembered the movement he had seen that his mind insisted was the fluttering of leaves in the breeze. He remembered the almost imperceptible shifting of lipless jaws trying to shape the word, 'Help.'

The bleak realisation of his future struck him with brutal force.

He felt ill with the idea that his fate was now in the hands of the hateful sorceress, Marion Papusa. He spoke without thinking in a soft prayer that began, "Please help me, gentle Jesus–"

It was only as he said the name of his saviour that Tom realised he had spoken the word without punching himself. He stared at Alice, aware that she had noticed the same thing.

Her frown was heavy with consternation.

"Jesus," Tom said again. He felt a small tear of blood squeezing its way from his eye and spilling down his cheek. Still, his hand made no attempt to punch his face.

"You're crying blood," Alice said thickly.

He nodded and grinned at Alice as the same understanding swept over both of them. He was crying blood and he was freely saying the name of his saviour. He was no longer in the control of Marion Papusa. He could again be the scourge that his Lord had wanted him to be.

"You said 'Jesus', didn't you?" Alice muttered. "How did you do that?"

He shrugged and smashed her hard in the face.

She went down heavily onto the hard, paving stones. One knee struck the kerb with a hollow thud that made Tom wince sympathetically. Alice made a ferocious attempt to scrabble away from him. She clawed at the pavement, breathlessly muttering words that were supposed to make him reconsider his actions.

Tom stamped on the back of her left leg. It was a hard and violent attack. He put as much force into the action as his body could muster. He felt the snap of bone beneath his boot.

Alice wailed.

Indifferent to her cries, not caring what protests she made, Tom knelt in the centre of her back and then placed his arm around the woman's throat. He grabbed a fistful of hair to try and hold her still. Once she was in a headlock that he thought was strong enough, he grunted and heaved and strained at her.

Alice struggled with all of her might.

She scratched at him with her nails and briefly pulled her head from his grip. As he fought to resume his hold over her, Alice placed her mouth around his forearm and bit with desperate ferocity.

Tom grimaced and punched her until she let go. Resuming his hold around her throat he grunted, heaved and strained until he had finally managed to pull her head from her shoulders. It took a huge effort, but it was more than worth it.

Her decapitated body stopped struggling.

#25

For one merciful moment Ella thought she had been reprieved. The dealer had been walking ahead of them whilst Fat Jay pulled her by the wrist. She was guided through the pub, where the glumly, grumbling patrons remained indifferent and oblivious to her situation. Then Ella was led out into the day's bright sunlight. The hum of traffic buzzed past on the main road outside the Boar's Head. The sweet, city scents of petrol fumes and warm tarmac filled her nostrils.

In that moment Ella thought she had seen salvation.

A man stood outside the doors of the Boar's Head wearing a sandwich board. He had his back to her but his shoulders were broad and his head was hidden beneath the brim of a battered straw hat. Ella didn't think there could be many lay preachers lurking on the pavement outside pubs. She felt sure there was only one lay preacher who ever spent time lurking outside this particular pub. She was lucky enough to know that he was a lay preacher who would do anything to help make her life better.

"Tim," she cried.

Fat Jay glared at her. His eyes spat an unspoken instruction for her to remain silent. It was a foreboding frown that told her there would be repercussions if she tried to get assistance. But, even when his hand squeezed tighter around her wrist, so tight she could feel the delicate bones rubbing together, Ella refused to let him crush her opportunity to cry out for help.

"Tim?" she called more loudly.

The lay preacher began to turn. For the first time she read the lettering on his sandwich board.

'RePeNT THeN, aND TuRN To GOD, So THaT YouR SiNS MiGHT Be WiPeD ouT, THaT TiMeS oF ReFReSHiNG MaY CoMe FRoM THe LORD. (ACTS 3:19).'

They were heavy black words, as dramatic as the tattoo she now bore, and they screamed for attention from the white background. She didn't know much about graphology but she suspected that the combination of capitals and lower case suggested poor levels of literacy. Or maybe tendencies to be a serial killer.

"Tim?"

This time, when she called his name, she had already given up on the idea of it being him. Her hope began to diminish. It wasn't Tim. This man was wearing the same religious sandwich board and wearing the same battered straw hat. But after that there were no similarities between him and Tim. This man didn't have Tim's bodybuilder physique. He lacked Tim's substantial height. When he stepped out of the shadows that had held him, and Ella saw his grey beard and bespectacled face, she understood that he would be of no use helping her against the threat posed by someone as physically menacing as Fat Jay and the dealer.

"Are you alright, young lady?" the lay preacher asked.

"Keep out of this," Fat Jay warned.

The man with the sandwich board ignored him. Staring at Ella he said, "I'm not Tim. But I know a man called Tim. We know each other from the mission. Is that who you thought I was? Tim from the mission?"

Her heart began to race with the renewed hope of salvation.

"I thought you were him," she admitted. "Tim's a friend of mine. A very good friend."

As she spoke she tried to wrest her hand away from Fat Jay's grip. It was an impossible struggle. Fat Jay held her securely and, for all her struggles, she only served to make him tighten his hold until she had to cry out with pain. The sob came out as a pitiful call that she despised for its weakness.

"Do you need help?" asked the lay preacher.

"I told you to keep out of this," Fat Jay said. He said the words with weary resignation. He sounded as though he had already decided that the man would face retribution for daring to be available to offer assistance.

Ella was pushed into the arms of the dealer as Fat Jay stepped in front of the man with the sandwich board. She couldn't see what Fat Jay took from his pocket but she saw the dealer mouth a warning. His eyes were wide with concern as he muttered, "Be careful."

Ella didn't know if the warning was directed at Fat Jay, the preacher or herself. She only knew that it made her shiver with dread for what was about to happen.

The lay preacher seemed oblivious to the escalating danger he faced. His shoulders were squared and he tilted his jaw as though he was savouring the opportunity of defying someone truly godless. It was an expression that Ella had seen a hundred times on Tim's face.

There was an obvious and sanctimonious pleasure in his smile. There was a rigidity to his posture that suggested divine authority.

"The fool has said in his heart, 'There is no God,'" the lay preacher announced. He paused theatrically, stared at Fat Jay and added, "What sayeth thou?"

Ella didn't know what Fat Jay said. She wasn't even sure if he said anything. His hand moved forward swiftly and there was the solid thump of something hitting hard against the sandwich board. She saw the lay preacher's eyes open wide with surprise and then he staggered back.

Whatever glint of superiority had been in his eyes began to fade as his expression turned to confusion.

Fat Jay stepped away from him. His mouth was set in a determined line of resolve. He had been faced with a tough and demanding chore and he had done it without flinching. He grabbed Ella again by the wrist.

She had a moment to glance over his shoulder, time enough to see that there was the handle of a knife protruding through the O in the word GOD. She saw the lay preacher staggering backwards, one hand stretching out, like a drowning man reaching for some form of life preserver.

Then Fat Jay had pushed Ella around a corner, away from the Boar's Head and away from her only hope of salvation. The scream of traffic buzzing past continued as though no one cared that a man had just been murdered and she had just been kidnapped. The pleasing scents of the city that she had savoured before were now the dry and arid stenches of indifference.

"I'll scream," she told Fat Jay. "I mean it. I'll scream until my fucking lungs burst."

He slapped a hand across her face and then pushed her through a doorway. She blinked the pain away and saw that he had taken her to an address that was barely two doors away from the pub. She didn't recognise the building. She had thought all the houses near the Boar's Head were boarded over and abandoned. The air was heavy with dirt, grease, and the fading memories of a pungent pizza. Her heartbeat raced as she realised that screaming would no longer be a useful recourse. She wasn't sure any option would be a useful recourse. Her cheek burnt where he had hit her and she glared at him with eyes that were barely holding back the tears.

"What the fuck is this place?" Ella demanded.

The door slammed closed.

"This is where you learn a little respect," Fat Jay told her.

He slapped his hand again hard across her jaw. The previous blow had been powerful but this one was hard enough to make her head rock. She tried to glare at him defiantly, but it was difficult to do that as a fresh rush of tears smarted at the backs of her eyes.

"Hit me as much as you want," she told him. "That won't change anything. I won't be buying any more of your diluted merchandise. And I'll be warning all my friends to steer clear of-"

She didn't get to complete the sentence. He hit her again and this time the blow was hard enough to make her fall silent.

"That's what you shouldn't have said," Fat Jay told her. He pointed at her with a wavering finger. "You're doing and saying nothing that will have a negative impact on my business. Nothing."

She stared into his eyes and heard the door being locked. The dealer was in there with them and Ella knew, between the pair of them, they intended to kill her.

Ben put the pages down and shook his head. He didn't like the direction of the story he had been writing. He wasn't sure how much of the story was based on reality, and how much was the product of his own sleep-fuelled imagination. But he didn't like the idea that he was writing about the horrible way his best friend had died. How was it even possible that he could be producing such a story?

He almost laughed as that question surfaced in the back of his mind. His one issue with the story that was being produced through his sleep-writing was that the content was touching closely on issues he considered to be too personal. He didn't seem unsettled by the fact that the story was being written by some completely unnatural process with no conscious effort on his part. He was only worried that he didn't like what was happening to one of his favourite characters.

Sighing heavily, he put the pages of his novel with the rest of the manuscript and walked out of the study and into the kitchen. The grandfather clock tocked in time with his footsteps. Absently, Ben pulled a bottle of beer from the fridge and then splashed milk into a saucer for Anastasia. He didn't bother putting dry food down for the cat this time because it didn't seem to eat the dry food on a night.

Even though he had gone through a couple of glasses of wine whilst in Marion's company, he did not have a pleasant alcohol buzz mellowing his mood. Given the amount he had consumed, Ben knew he should have been somewhere between tipsy and staggering. And, as he usually found his spirits mellowed with alcohol, he would have expected to be in an accepting and genial mood. But, if anything, after an evening sidestepping Marion's lewd suggestions and doing his best to rebuff her transparent flirting, he simply felt tired, depressed, and miserably sober.

He chugged on the beer and wished it was something stronger.

The cat jumped onto the table and began to lap at the milk.

It mewed in a disinterested way as he tickled the scruff of its neck. Not wanting to trouble the creature with his unwanted display of affection, feeling as though that was a violation of their writer/cat relationship, he withdrew his hand and took the remnants of his beer up to bed.

The clock chimed twice as he walked past it.

He wondered if it was worth going to bed, or if he should simply dump himself in front of the Silver Reed. If his body clock was going to wake him at 03:10, in just a little over an hour, he didn't see the point in getting into bed and struggling to get comfortable for such little benefit. Thinking about it rationally, he figured he'd be lucky to catch a full hour's sleep.

But that didn't matter, Ben told himself.

If he woke at 03:10, *when* he woke at 03:10, he was determined not to get out of bed and go down stairs to write. He would simply turn over and go back to sleep. He did not intend to do any sleep-writing this evening. If he didn't write any more on the story, there was no danger of Ella dying in the novel. And, whilst it was impossible for him to go back in time and save Etta, he thought it was possible for him to avoid writing the novel so that he could maybe save Ella.

He stepped into the bedroom and stared defiantly at the row of dolls. Before he could stop himself, he found he was counting them. His gaze immediately acknowledged the presence of Wall-Eyed Wally and Adolf. Wally was staring at him with a pitiable expression that he didn't think had been there before. It was an expression as though the doll was urging him to understand something that was just beyond the thing's ability to communicate. He admonished himself for such fanciful thoughts, sure that he was only buying into the silliness of his own paranoid fears. It took him a moment longer to find Al Jolson, and then Luke, and he figured Mrs Scum had rearranged the collection when she had been tidying. He hoped Mrs Scum had rearranged the collection because the alternative explanation was too disquieting for him to contemplate.

"Thirty-five," he said, when he reached the last of the dolls.

He released a sigh of relief when he made the total. Stripping off his clothes, dumping them on the floor, he walked over to the painting of the clown's eye and stared at it.

"You're a hideous fucking thing," he grumbled.

He wondered if he should look into the *CW* artist woman and find out more about her. Was it likely that she had mental health issues? If she thought it was acceptable to produce paintings of scary-fucking clowns, then she clearly wasn't playing with a full deck. He decided it would be interesting to research the woman, and it might give him some insight into what had happened in Sandalwood before he arrived. It would certainly be preferable to working on a story that was now depressing him with its bleak content about the demise of a character he had come to think of as a close friend.

Something shifted behind him.

He turned, his heart lurching, and saw the door was being pushed open by Anastasia. The cat padded stealthily into the room and then leapt onto the bed. It fixed him with a bored expression that rested somewhere between indifference and vague curiosity. Then it settled down in its usual spot.

Chuckling at his own nervousness, Ben walked over to the window and stared out at the Doll House. He wondered if Marion was in her upper room now, peering down on him. Given the way she had talked to him through the evening, she could clearly see into his bedroom and she had obviously been watching him the previous evening when he had been entertaining Deborah. He recalled that he had spent a long time going down on Deborah and, in some small way, he was pleased to discover that his hard work had been acknowledged – even if it was by a sinister voyeur. The idea that Marion could see him now, stark-bollock naked and defiantly glaring at her, did not trouble him. If anything, he hoped, if she was looking at him, she would see it as a gesture of rebellion.

What are you rebelling against? he asked himself. He couldn't think of an answer and felt himself deflate from a stance of proud defiance to puzzled nudity.

"Go to bed, Haversham," he muttered. "You're obviously drunk."

He supposed it was true.

He had been counting dollies. He had been talking to clown paintings. Now he was standing naked at a window in the hope the sight of his nude body would convince an old woman he had no sexual interest in her. If there was ever going to be a textbook definition of insanity, he felt sure that combination of his current actions would be part of the formula.

There was movement outside the Doll House. Again, he could see cars and vans parked in front of the building, black shadows on a midnight silhouette. There were lumbering figures clambering back and forth and a smear of weak yellow light illuminated the pathway for some of them. He could see that large packages were being hefted into the shadows, but he had no idea if the deliveries were being taken in or out of the Doll House.

He didn't suppose it mattered. He had no intention of visiting again. If Marion thought he would be going there on the weekend, then she was mistaken. Even if John insisted, Ben had already decided he would feign a dodgy belly or an unexpected migraine. Anything to avoid enduring the dusty old woman's sex-obsessed companionship for an evening.

He climbed into bed, turned off the light and closed his eyes.

The house was silent save for the faraway tock of the grandfather clock and the rasp of Anastasia's snores. There were no other sounds. Not even the shuffle of the dolls shifting places on their shelves. He smiled without humour and realised that that was a thought he didn't want to have echoing around inside his empty head.

"No more writing tonight," he vowed.

He was adamant that he would keep to this resolution because the story was taking too many unpleasant turns. He didn't like the way Bill seemed to be living in the isolation of some inescapable village. Bill had already fucked a local in the village, and a part of him wanted to make the content of that scene saucier. But he supposed it would be inappropriate to make the scene sexual given that the woman turned up later as a dissected corpse.

He wasn't impressed with the events that were happening to Timmy: the man had gone from being a God-bothering nuisance to some paranormal zombie-scourge. But, Ben thought, it was Ella's strand of the story that was most disturbing. Ella wasn't dying of an unnecessary drug-overdose the way Etta had done. Ella's fate seemed like it was going to be far worse. And, the only way he could help her to avoid that fate, was by not writing the remainder of the story. As consciousness slipped away from him, he vowed that he would not wake at 03:10 and go down to write more on the novel. Even if he did wake 03:10, and even if the urge to write was irresistible, he would simply stay in bed and avoid writing.

#27

He woke up in front of the typewriter. His back was stiff. His fingers were sore. There were fresh pages piled beside the machine. The grandfather clock was chiming twelve and the house was filled with the scent of something meaty and sweet.

"What the actual…?"

He didn't bother finishing the question because the answer was obvious. It didn't matter what he had vowed as he drifted to sleep, or how he planned to take control of his life. Whatever controlled Sandalwood, its inhabitants, and the house, it now controlled him. He was a slave to the powers that ruled the village: another lackey in the employ of powers greater than his imagination.

He scowled at the pages of manuscript and stood up.

There was a flashing light on the mobile phone and he guessed that meant there was a message from John. If he'd been able to summon the energy he would have flipped off the phone. But his fingers ached and he didn't have the enthusiasm to waste time on small, petty gestures. Slowly, he walked through to the kitchen and did himself a mug of instant breakfast coffee. There was a note from Mrs Scum on the fridge, held beneath a magnet.

'Didn't want to disturb you whilst you were in the study. I've put Cumberland Sausage in the slow-cooker. It should be ready for eight tonight. There's enough for two if you have a guest again. X'

A guest? He puzzled to make sense of the comment before understanding swept over him. Did everyone in the village know that he'd fucked Deborah? If they did, he wouldn't mind someone telling him what had happened to the woman after she left. It would be good to know if she was still alive. Not only would it give him some sense of closure, it might even give him an idea as to why he had thought her dissected corpse was stuffed inside the linen closet.

He sipped the coffee grumpily and glared at the meticulous surroundings.

On any day earlier this week, he knew he would have been eager to read through the novel he was writing. He had always enjoyed the seemingly magical process of writing, discovering character traits and foibles as a story progressed, and being pleasantly surprised by unexpected plot twists. He knew he should have been enjoying this process even more because it came with none of the headaches, doubts, and anxieties that were always present when he was writing.

However, because he no longer wanted to know what was happening in the story he was writing, because he didn't want to find out how Ella met her fate, he couldn't bring himself to read the latest pages.

He hadn't even wanted to write them.

In a deliberate attempt to avoid the study, stopping himself from being taunted by the temptation to flick through what had been written, he stepped into the conservatory.

If not for the overgrown foliage at the back of the house, it would have been a light and airy room. The glass walls gave a suggestion of openness that should have made the room pleasant.

Except it wasn't.

There were overgrown trees and bushes at the back of the house that pressed against the conservatory's windows like some hostile triffid invasion. Spatters of bird shit and the detritus of snails and autumnal droppings dirtied the conservatory's glass roof.

Worse, much worse in Ben's opinion, the room was stacked with paintings. On his first night at the house he remembered thinking that there had been an equal division of doll and clown paintings. Now he could see that the balance favoured clowns as a subject. His nostrils wrinkled with involuntary revulsion as he stared at the pictures. There was one on an easel. There was a stack of paintings propped against the conservatory's door. There were two covering one window and a second stack resting in a wicker armchair.

Too many of them showed clowns.

"Lovely," he muttered. "More clown pictures."

There were pictures of clowns juggling. There were pictures of clowns dancing. There were pictures of clowns involved in violent and hostile acts.

"Jesus-fucking-Christ."

He shook his head, not sure he could believe what he was seeing.

In each image it seemed to be the same pair of clowns: Harlequin and Pierrot. *CW* had caught them with a sense of realism that made Ben think he was studying real people dressed in traditional costumes. He also got the idea that these clowns would stink of dirt, sweat, and corruption. There was something about the grass-stained knees of the Pierrot costume, the dirty, frayed cuffs of the

Harlequin's outfit, and the soiled crotches of both clowns, that made him sure they would carry a stench of body odour and rank sweat. These weren't the sorts of clowns a person would employ for a children's party. These were the sorts of clowns he had seen in bizarre pornos.

He knelt down in front of a stack of paintings and began to flick through them.

He had thought the first of the paintings showed the two clowns dancing but that wasn't accurate. On a closer inspection he could see the pair were involved in a fist fight and looked to be circling one another as they each tried to gain an advantageous position for the continuation of their struggle. The Pierrot looked to be suffering the worst of the conflict. Blood poured from his nose. His left eye was swollen to a huge, bloated bruise. There was a hole in his shoulder, as though he had suffered some terrible and violent injury.

Uncomfortable with that image, not sure he liked the brutality of the scene, Ben flicked past the painting to find himself staring at a partially rotted Harlequin lying at the bottom of a shallow grave. The earth was rich in autumnal colours. The few scattered leaves, oak leaves, he thought because of their distinctive handshapes, were caught in vibrant shades of orange and red. And the corpse looked green with putrefaction. The skin had dissolved to reveal bone. What remained was the colour of mould on month old sandwiches. The only part that looked alive was the single remaining eyeball, staring fervently out at the viewer of the portrait.

"Is this for real?"

The sound of his own voice, echoing from the windowed walls of the conservatory, reminded him that he was alone in the house. He tried to think who would want an original painting of a decomposing clown in a shallow grave. He couldn't think of anyone in their right mind who would want such an atrocity. He quickly flicked past the painting. This time he found himself looking at two clowns fucking.

"Clown sex?" he muttered. "What the actual…?"

It was as he was trying to get past the image of the two clowns copulating, unwilling to note the detail that showed the Pierrot being held beneath the larger bulk of the Harlequin, or the artistry that had gone into capturing the brutal violation, that a slip of paper fell onto the floor.

He assumed it had been trapped between two of the paintings, maybe stuck on the back of one. He hadn't noticed it fall, but he saw it as a white card on the woody-brown floor of the conservatory. In paint the colour of the Harlequin's gaudy costume, *CW* had painted the words:

> 'GET OUT OF SANDALWOOD
> WHILST YOU STILL CAN'

Ben studied the note for a long time.

A warning to leave the village? He picked the note up and then tore it into small pieces. Acting quickly, glancing nervously at the conservatory windows, momentarily fearful that he was being watched, he clutched the torn scraps of note in one hand and then took them into the kitchen. After burying them in the bottom of the kitchen's waste-bin, he washed his hands and then went upstairs.

Whoever *CW* had been, Ben felt sure the artist was now trying to force some sort of communication with him. He showered, grabbed jeans and a hoodie, and pushed his feet into a pair of trainers. He hurried out of the house and trotted past Alfred/Albert who was still working on the driveway.

"Afternoon, Mester Writer."

Ben grunted a vague acknowledgement as he jogged past the man.

As it had been the day before, the weather was gloomy and overcast. He pulled up the hood of his jacket to protect his scalp from the elements. Hurrying to the bottom of the driveway, and then turning right, Ben made his way up the hill to the centre of the village.

Halfway up the hill he had a pang of doubt and worried that he wouldn't be able to reach his destination. Yesterday the village had stopped him from finding an escape route. Today it seemed possible that it would stop him from achieving this day's goal.

But, after he'd walked past two shops and the church, he grinned as he realised he was standing outside the village library.

He was cold. He was scared, and he didn't have words to describe his confusion. But he felt thankful that he had managed to find the village library. "OK," he said determinedly. "Let's see if we can find out a little bit more about *CW*."

#28

As an act of defiance, Tom had not driven straight back to Sandalwood. The words of Marion's instructions had echoed clearly through his thoughts: "*I want you to drive Alice back to London this evening. Then you'll come back here.*" But, instead of kowtowing to her demands, instead of obeying the irresistible pull of her commands, he had decided he could make good use of being in the city.

Especially now.

He sat behind the wheel of the Mercedes, examining his bitten arm, and smiling happily to himself. There had been no real pain when Alice bit him and, even though the skin was broken, there was no blood. There had been no blood from his blistered hands. There had been no blood when he jammed the screwdriver into his thigh. There had been no blood when he rammed the screwdriver into his balls. The only blood he had shed since waking in Sandalwood had been those curiously bloody tears that seemed to come when he was concentrating.

Immortal?

He mused on the word and wondered if it could be true.

If it was, if he did have the genuine capacity to defy death, then Tom thought he ought to put that ability to good use. Despite the circuitous way the power had been given to him, despite the fact that it looked like it had come from a diabolical source, this was nothing short of a gift from his great and glorious Lord, the gentle Jesus.

"Thank you, Jesus."

He said his saviour's name and basked in the ability to enunciate both syllables. During the brief period when he hadn't been able to say that single word without punching himself in the face, Tom had felt miserable and lost. Not only did it hurt not to say Jesus's name, but he was worried that Jesus would miss the sound of his praise. Now he could say the word, now that he could properly praise his Lord, Tom realised his life still had purpose. Purpose and immortality. Not only did his life have purpose and immortality but he was resolved to put that purpose and immortality to good use.

He had parked the Mercedes outside the Boar's Head.

And he had slept.

He wasn't sure how long he had slept but, when he awoke, bursting to visit the loo and stiff from being stuck in an uncomfortable posture for so many hours, he knew it was time to act. His finger had fallen off in the night and, whilst a part of him wanted to shove it back into the hole that remained in the curl of the plaster on his hand, he could see it would serve little point, except for being vaguely decorative. It no longer functioned. The colour was disquieting, and it had the odour of an unhygienic butcher's shop.

He disposed of the detached finger in the Mercedes' ashtray and walked into the pub. The Boar's Head was mildly busy and it was only as he strolled inside that Tom remembered he was still wearing the Harlequin costume. A ripple of laughter went through the room and a handful of derisive comments were catcalled in his direction.

"Fuck me! It's Ronald McDonald!"

"Who the fuck is this, Bozo?"

One of the drunks began to whistle the opening bars of *Entry of the Gladiators*.

Tom ignored all the cries as he visited the toilet and pissed for what felt like five minutes straight. When he came out of the toilets the laughter seemed to have subsided. Aside from being graced with an occasional disparaging glance, no one seemed to care about what he was wearing.

Tom sat himself in the corner booth and stared at a pair of familiar faces.

"You've got some nerve showing yourself in here, b-bruv," the dealer grunted. He had a scruffy bandage wrapped around his hand. His John Lennon shades were buckled and revealed eyes that were bloodshot and ringed with dark circles.

Carlos glared at Tom with undisguised fury. "I ought to get a couple of Yardies down here to teach you a lesson."

He reached into his jacket pocket and Tom guessed the man was going for his phone. He reached across the booth's table and grabbed Carlos by the throat of his T-shirt. Without any show of exertion, he yanked Carlos' face downwards so that it smacked loud, hard, and hollow into the table's surface. A pint of beer was knocked over. Golden liquid spilled across the surface. There was the tinkle of a shattering sound as the glass hit the bar's wooden floor.

Carlos grunted in pain.

Tom slammed the man's head down for a second time, but Carlos made no sound this time. When Tom released his hold on the throat of Carlos' T-shirt, the man slipped from his seat and lay sprawled on the floor.

The only sound to have come from Tom during this action had been the musical jingle of the bells on his Harlequin cap.

The dealer considered Tom warily. "What are you wanting, b-bruv?"

Tom nodded at Carlos. "You don't normally work with him, do you?"

The dealer lowered his gaze. He shook his head and said, "Who are you, bruv? Are you the filth? Is this why you're trying to make life d-difficult for me?"

"Who did you work for before you started lackeying for this one?"

The dealer shook his head. "No way. I'm not g-grassing up Fat Jay."

Tom raised an eyebrow. His grim smile shifted into something that looked like an amused challenge. "Fat Jay? I think I heard Etta talk about him," he mused. "He's the one who wears tracksuits and sunglasses and jewellery, isn't he?"

"I'm not crossing Fat Jay," the dealer insisted. He held up the hand Tom had damaged during their first encounter. The bandage wrapped around the palm looked as though it had been used to wipe out ashtrays. "You can stab me with screwdrivers," he insisted. Nodding at Carlos he said, "You can knock me unconscious and leave me on the floor next to him. But you're not capable of inflicting the levels of h-hurt that Fat Jay can inflict."

Tom thought the words sounded like a challenge. He stood up and bent over Carlos' fallen body. Wrinkling his nose with distaste at the chore, he went through the man's pockets. There was a tightly wadded roll of twenties and fifties that Tom figured would cover his current needs. Straightening himself slowly, keen to show anyone watching that he was in no real hurry, Tom walked idly across to the bar.

The bells on his cap jingled softly with every other step.

Given the silence in the room, and the fact that every face was turned in his direction, he figured that most of them had witnessed his interaction with Carlos and the dealer. No one was now laughing at his Harlequin costume. If anything, he could see he was being considered with the obsequious respect that was usually reserved for the most dubious of violent criminals.

Whilst he despised criminals, and the ungodly types who inhabited places like the Boar's Head, Tom had to admit that, on some level, the respect was satisfying. He struggled not to smile and willed himself to remember that he was there to do the work of gentle Jesus.

"Can I get you anything, Sir?" the barman enquired.

Tom met the man's gaze as he handed him the roll of notes he'd taken from Carlos' pocket. "This is to compensate you."

"Compensate?"

"There might be some cleaning to do when I've finished with the two gentlemen in that booth. Also, there might be aspects of my discussion that could make some of your customers take their business elsewhere for the evening. I don't want you losing out because of what I need to get from them."

"That's very considerate of you, Sir."

Tom smiled. He liked the barman. He told himself that gentle Jesus would have approved of the man's eagerness to help. Although, deep down, he suspected gentle Jesus would really just want him to smite everyone in the room.

"Will there be anything else, Sir?"

Tom considered this and then nodded. The bells on his cap jangled musically. He was glancing back at the dealer and Carlos. A tight smile played across his lips as he said, "I could use a mallet and some nails."

The barman said, "I'll see what I can do."

#29

Ben stopped in the foyer of the library and sighed with disgust. "Fucking villages," he muttered. "Fucking creepy little villages."

A woman walking past him scowled but Ben paid her no heed. He was overcome with a sensation of confusion and dislike for Sandalwood and all of its residents, that included the piously scowling harridan shuffling past him as he stood in the foyer of the library.

He had been stopped by the sight of a painting of a cemetery. Ben thought it looked like something from the set of a horror movie. It had been captured in blacks and whites, with silvers of moonlight dancing on the hard edges of anonymous marble tombstones. There were small touches of colour here and there – midnight-blue slashes between clouds in the night sky, a mouldering green of graveyard moss, and the blood-red wound of a fallen poppy petal – but the majority of the image was dark, imposing and disturbing.

It wasn't disturbing because it showed a cemetery, although Ben didn't think that helped. Ben thought the image was disturbing because the artist had included suggestions of ghosts and ghouls in the background. A forest of trees to the rear of the cemetery was dense with screaming faces. Reflections on the glossy surfaces of tombstones showed shady figures that seemed too sinister to comprehend.

"Who in their right mind puts shit like this in a foyer?" he wondered. "Welcome to the library. This scene will now haunt your every nightmare."

He shook his head and hurried past the painting and into the warmth of the library. The place was artificially quiet and musty with the scents of polish, books, and words. A bored librarian was muttering her way through a quiet conversation with the woman who had scowled at Ben in the foyer. She glanced at him and raised a curious eyebrow. "May I help you?"

The scowling woman turned on him as though she was curious to hear his response. In that moment Ben felt a wave of paranoia rush through him. Rather than explain the nature of his visit to the librarian, he pointed at a sign on the wall. Amongst the many posters urging people to read, and advocating the strengths of this title or that series or some other publisher, there was an arrow pointing towards some stairs. The arrow was labelled with the word '*REFERENCE.*'

"It's OK," he said. "I think I know where I need to be."

Paying no heed to their puzzled glances, Ben shuffled past both women. He was conscious of the sounds of his trainers squeaking on the polished floor. The sound abated to a whisper as he climbed the stairs to the reference section and, beneath the sound of his footsteps, he could hear the librarian and the scowling woman still talking in lowered voices.

"His name's Ben Haversham. He's a writer from that London."

"I heard him swearing in the entranceway. Is he on drugs?"

"Probably. He's from that London."

"I don't think I'd want to read one of his books."

"You wouldn't like them. There's a lot of unnecessary swearing."

Ben shook his head. He could picture the two women as the embodiment of every single-star Amazon reviewer he'd ever had the misfortune of encountering. He pushed into the reference section of the library and began to browse the shelves.

It took him less than an hour to find a history of the artist Christina 'Tina' White. It transpired she was an esteemed recipient of the Turner prize and a figure of scorn for those tabloids who liked to rail against the unpleasantness of her subject matter. They had not liked her preoccupation with abandoned buildings and they had ridiculed her interest in graffiti and vandalism. When she began to paint cemeteries with a grim and ghoulish fervour, they had dismissed her as being an attention seeker. One critic, a writer who normally wrote a column about reality TV shows, penned an editorial that said she was, "exploiting the macabre for the sake of exploiting the macabre."

Ben chuckled at this, thinking it ironic that a supporter of reality TV shows should complain about exploitation for the sake of exploitation. "Thank fuck you never saw any of her clown paintings," he murmured. For the first time in days, he smiled to himself.

A male librarian approached him and asked Ben if he wanted access to one of the computers to help with his research. Ben hadn't expected the village library to have access to computers. Sandalwood struck him as the sort of place that was trapped in a fifty-year-old time vacuum. Mrs Scum talked about a satnav as a satellite navigator contraption. Since arriving in Sandalwood he hadn't seen anyone walking down the street chatting on a mobile, or sitting indolently in the pub flicking through Facebook or scrolling through Twitter. He felt a rush of giddy gratitude to the librarian for offering him such a kindness.

With access to the internet he was able to discover that Tina White had been married once. She was divorced after some lesbian scandal that was sensationalised in the newspapers to the point where Ben thought it could have become a TV miniseries. The artist's work had been popular outside the UK where the media weren't as indignant about the dark focus of her paintings.

He found a picture of her from one of the online newspapers. It showed a curly-haired woman who would have been attractive if not for the sneer curling her upper lip. She held a bottle in one hand, with the other she was gesturing at a photographer with her middle-finger upraised. The headline above the photograph said *'PISS ARTIST'.*

Ben decided he would have liked Christina White.

There was something about her face that he thought was vaguely familiar. He reasoned that he must have seen a picture of her at John's – they shared the same agent so that did not seem unlikely. It wasn't that he thought he'd ever met her, but he did think he'd seen her somewhere.

He tried to do further research on the woman but there seemed little information available. She had suffered a period of melancholy and Ben got the impression her condition was chemically exacerbated. She had checked into a private medical facility and Ben recognised the name as a celebrated rehab clinic: it was the same one John had offered to use when Ben confided that his friend, Etta, was in need of professional help.

After her struggle with depression, Tina had subsequently disappeared.

She had not submitted to any of the major competitions for the last year. She had not been involved in any prestigious commissions or even been present at any of the celebrity parties where she was usually found drunk, stoned, or sexually compromised.

"What the fuck happened to you, Tina?" Ben wondered.

He looked away from the computer monitor, stretching his neck and trying to work out how long he had been bending over the machine. He preferred the easy responsiveness of the computer's keyboard to the back-breaking effort that was needed to operate the

Silver Reed. But the advantage of working with the Silver Reed was that he didn't need to be awake for that. His back throbbed and his forehead housed the dull promise of an impending headache.

There was a blonde walking out of the reference section doors.

Ben wasn't sure what it was that made his gaze linger on her. He couldn't say it was because of the familiar way she was walking because she had the stilted Sandalwood gait that he had noticed on Marion's maids, Laura and Vicky, when they were serving at the Doll House's dinner table. He didn't even think it was anything to do with the set of her shoulders because she was holding herself with an awkward rigidity that made him wonder if she too had been sitting for too long at a computer keyboard.

It certainly wasn't her face because, from the little he was able to glimpse, he could see that half of her face was covered by her long blonde hair whilst the other side was obscured by a dark eyepatch.

But he felt sure he recognised her.

"Deborah?" he muttered.

She made no attempt to stop. He supposed, because he had only whispered her name, her ignorance was understandable. He stood up and started to follow.

"Did you find everything you were looking for?" asked the librarian.

Ben nodded and thanked him.

The librarian glanced at Ben's monitor and smiled when he saw something familiar there. "Tina White?" he exclaimed brightly. "Did you know she'd stayed here in Sandalwood briefly?"

"No," Ben said. "I mean yes." He glanced towards the doorway of the reference library. He could still hear the sounds of the blonde's footsteps and wondered if there was still a chance to catch up with her and find out if it was Deborah.

"She attended the unveiling of the painting in the foyer," the librarian told Ben. "I got her autograph."

Ben puzzled over the comment before understanding rushed over him. Who else but Tina White would have painted something so macabre as the cemetery picture? He silently berated himself for not having made the connection when he was reading about the artist's penchant for painting cemeteries.

"She used to drink in the Green Man," the librarian said.

He had the wistful smile of someone who had been waiting for the chance to reminisce. Ben nodded and pushed past the man in search of the blonde that reminded him of Deborah. Her footsteps were no longer audible on the stairway and he rushed down in pursuit. The squeak of his trainers seemed louder than it had before. Every step was like a small squeal of impatience. He suspected the noise he was making would be enough to have everyone in the library glaring reproachfully in his direction.

But he didn't care.

Running through the library's foyer, sparing a final quick glance at the gloomy cemetery scene, he saw the distinctive scribble of the *CW* signature in the bottom right hand corner. There was even a photograph of Christina White next to the huge piece of artwork. It was a black and white picture showing a bespectacled young woman with tight brunette curls. In this picture, far more formal than the one snapped for the tabloid, she wore a smile that looked artificial on her intelligent face. Marvelling at his own ability to overlook the obvious, Ben wondered how he hadn't seen Christina White's photograph and signature when he'd first been looking at the painting.

Shaking his head in silent reproach, he hurried out of the library and scoured the road in search of the blonde. The afternoon was grim with lowering clouds and a drizzle of light rain sweated his brow as soon he stepped outside. There were few people out walking in this weather: a couple bustling beneath a shared umbrella and one solitary man with his shoulders hunched into a too-small raincoat. There was a figure in a white clown costume staring directly at him. He wondered if it was the figure he had seen standing outside the Doll House. The costume, deathly white with huge black buttons and a conical cap, looked the same. Even the unnatural tilt of the clown's head looked similar. Ben wanted to rush across the road to question the figure and ask why they were wandering around a village dressed as a clown.

But, heading down the hill, he could see the stilted movement of the blonde he had been pursuing. His dilemma lasted for less than a few seconds. The clown seemed to be appearing regularly in the village and he guessed there would be a chance for questions when they next encountered each other. Deborah had been missing since Tuesday evening and he wanted to talk with her to help dispel fears of the grisly fate that he thought had befallen her.

"Deborah!"

He hurried after her.

She made no attempt to slow or turn. Instead she continued purposefully towards the bottom of the hill.

"Deborah!"

He increased his speed, waving with one arm and repeating her name.

She made no acknowledgement of him, even though he was sure she had seen him. He watched as she stepped through the gates of the Doll House and began to walk up towards the building. She cast a quick glance over her shoulder and fixed him with a stern and reproachful gaze from her single eye.

He stopped running. The arm that he'd been using to gesticulate fell down to his side. It was Deborah. He recognised her face, even though he'd only known her for an evening. As the ferocity of her glare settled on him, he wondered what had happened to her eye that was forcing her to wear an eyepatch. And he tried to tell himself that he didn't already know the answer to that question.

#30

The phone was ringing when Ben walked back into the house. He ignored it. Given that it was the mobile, he figured the call would most likely be from John. He didn't think anyone else had the number. And, although he was anxious to speak with John, there was something more important he needed to do before talking with his agent.

Swiftly, Ben climbed up the stairs.

He ignored the constant tock of the grandfather clock. He brushed past Anastasia as the cat slipped easily out of the bedroom. Taking a deep breath, steeling himself to cope with the task in front of him, Ben stood in front of the linen closet and placed his fingers on the handle.

The telephone stopped ringing. The only sounds in the house were the grandfather clock and the pounding of his own heartbeat.

He remembered the previous time he had opened the linen closet door. The shock of seeing dissected limbs had been powerful. The idea that something equally grisly might still be lurking behind the door was enough to make him hesitate. But he knew that he had to open the door if he wanted to explore the idea that now plagued his thoughts.

There was no dead body.

He wouldn't let himself sigh with relief. Obviously he was elated that there was nothing sinister lurking behind the door. He thought, if there had been another corpse inside, he would have likely shrieked at the discovery. He would have run, and run, and run, regardless of whether or not the town allowed him to escape. He wasn't sure how such an exercise could have worked in reality. The town's roads seemed to be like a Möbius strip for him in that they were cyclical and never-ending. He stopped himself from pursuing those thoughts, in no mood to explore such a surreal notion. Instead of musing on such fanciful hypotheticals, Ben stared at the thin slats of pine wood inside the cupboard. Some of them were covered with neatly folded towels. Others held spare bedding that was lightly scented with a lingering fragrance of unnaturally floral fabric conditioner.

None of the shelves held dissected body parts.

He glanced down towards the bottom of the cupboard and studied the stain that was there. It was only a subtle stain. It was the memory of an inconsequential wetness that had been spilt a day or two earlier.

Reluctantly, Ben placed his finger against the stain.

It was slightly sticky.

His nostrils curled in disgust. This was where he thought he had closed the door and popped Deborah's eyeball. If that had happened, if that incident had not been a horrific gift from the tortured depths of his imagination, then it went some way to explaining why Deborah was now wearing an eyepatch.

He laughed uncomfortably and realised his logic had several fatal flaws.

If there had been an eyeball in the linen closet, and if he had slammed the door on it and popped it like a grape, that didn't really explain why Deborah was now wearing an eyepatch. It only served to explain that the outside world was just as crazy as the insane interior of his head. It would be impossible to pop the eyeball of a dissected dead woman and think that explained why she was now wearing an eyepatch. Such an explanation made no mention of how she had been reassembled or reanimated.

The mobile phone began to ring again.

He closed the door on the linen closet and then stepped into the bathroom. With meticulous care, he washed his hands and removed all traces of the stickiness that had been lingering on his fingertips. The Imperial Leather produced a pleasant, slippery lather as he rubbed it against his fingers. The fragrance was cloyingly creamy, but that was preferable to the imagined scent of eyeball stickiness that he feared might be on his fingers. He studied his reflection in the bathroom mirror as he washed his hands, surprised to see that the person staring back at him did not look like the sort of raving lunatic who lived in a village of animated corpses.

The person staring back at him looked as normal as any serial killer.

He dried his hands on a scarlet towel and then draped it back over the towel rail. In no hurry to get down stairs, despite the insistent ring of the telephone, he walked calmly along the hall, past the closed door of the linen closet, and down the stairs. The phone was still ringing when he got to the study.

Unhurriedly, he flipped it open and said a curt hello.

"Where the fuck have you been?" John demanded. "I've been trying to reach you all fucking day?"

"Hello, John," Ben said affably. "How are you today?"

"Where the fuck have you been?"

"I was doing some research at the library," Ben said.

"And you didn't think to take your phone with you? Do you know why they're called mobile phones?"

"Did you just phone up to swear at me?" Ben asked. "Or was there something you needed from me?"

"You've not been returning my calls."

"No. I've been busy working on that book you wanted writing."

"Is that all you've been doing?" John sounded more than sceptical. He barked the question as though it was a challenge.

"No," Ben admitted. He glanced around the study and his gaze fell on the painting of the Doll House. "It's not all I've been doing," he told John. "Yesterday I spent the evening having a meal with that skanky old bag from the Doll House."

"Marion said she was going to have you over for a meal," John told him. His anger seemed to have abated slightly. If anything, whilst talking about Marion, Ben thought his agent sounded defensive. "She said she wanted to make you feel welcome."

Ben nodded. "She was going out of her way to make me feel welcome. I suspect she wanted to make me so welcome she would have swallowed. Does she try and fuck everyone who comes into this village?"

"If you'd checked your phone messages, you would have seen I wanted to talk to you about that. I was going to warn you that she can sometimes come across as a little... predatory."

"Predatory? The woman made Peter Sutcliffe look like a Mills and Boon hero from the fifties."

"If you'd checked your messages..."

Ben didn't bother replying. He was staring again at the painting of the Doll House. Tina White had managed to capture a lot of detail in the image. There were suggestions of demons in the clouds. The walls of the Doll House, even though they were held in the silhouette of shadows, looked to be constructed of shady ghoulish figures. Was that how the artist saw the village? Was every surface a reflection of something ghoulish, unnatural, and sinister?

"How's the novel progressing?"

"It's progressing."

"Really?" John sounded sceptical. "Is it really progressing?"

"Yeah," Ben assured him. He flicked through the pages he had typed the previous night and said, "I'm honestly surprising myself."

"How many pages?"

Ben flicked through them and made a rough guess. "I think I've got near on a hundred pages so far."

"Good going," John said. He sounded genuinely impressed. "I take it I'll have a lot of reading to do when I get up there this weekend."

"I might have an idea for another story when this one's finished," Ben told him. "If it sounds feasible we can bounce the idea around and discuss possibilities."

"Go on," John urged. "What are you thinking?"

"I'm thinking of writing a story based on that artist, Christina White."

There was silence from John's end of the phone.

"She did all those paintings that the establishment hated," Ben said cheerfully. "So I thought she'd come across as a pretty cool anti-hero. I figured I could write an interesting story about her career and her disappearance."

"Don't fuck me about, Ben," John growled.

"Fuck you about?" Ben tried to sound innocent. He wasn't sure he managed it. "I'm just suggesting an idea for a story that I think would-"

"Alice hasn't turned up for work this morning," John snapped. "So I'm trying to deal with my office remotely. You haven't been helping by not returning my calls and now, this shit about Tina White-"

"She was a client of yours," Ben said.

"Yes."

"Until she disappeared."

"That's right," John sighed.

"Where is she?"

"She disappeared," John said. "I don't know where she is. That's what disappeared means."

"She spent time up here, in Sandalwood, didn't she?"

"Yes."

"How long ago was that?"

John released a heavy sigh. "Ben," he began. "If you've got an idea for a story about a character like Christina White, then I look forward to discussing it with you over the weekend. I can advise you on what will sell and what I'll publish. But I can't give you any insight into how or where or why she disappeared, because I don't have answers to those questions."

Ben frowned and walked out of the study. He got the idea that John was no longer telling him the truth. In the hall, the smell of the slowly cooking Cumberland sausage was maddeningly enticing. He glanced at the grandfather clock and wondered if the food would yet be edible. It was just shy of six o'clock and he didn't think he could stand the temptation of smelling the food for much longer if he wasn't allowed to eat it.

"Christina White was up here a month ago, wasn't she?"

"What makes you think that?"

"Her paintings are still here."

"Yes," John admitted. "She was there recently. I'm not sure it was as recently as a month ago. But she was the last of my clients to use the cottage."

Ben stepped into the kitchen. Anastasia stood on the table, pacing back and forth with heightened agitation. Ben saw a note beneath the cat's feet, something written in a hand he didn't recognise. He wanted to look at the note but the cat's impatience, his hunger for the Cumberland sausage, and the conversation with John, all got between him and his goals.

"Are we OK to discuss this in more detail over the weekend?" John asked. "I'm struggling without Alice. I've got Jason Connor going into meltdown over some bad review for his latest anthology. And I've just had an email from Kayleigh Walters to say that her husband, Kenny, has gone missing."

Ben nodded and tried to find some sympathy for John's plight. As agents went, he knew that John often went above and beyond what was required for his clients. The fact that Ben was being accommodated in a country cottage to help him overcome his writer's block showed how much personal investment John made. John had clearly made the same arrangement with Tina White and he would likely have to do something to help Jason Connor if the short story writer was having problems. Ben struggled to think who Kenny Walters was, then remembered seeing the man once in John's office. He was a pleasant author, a broad-shouldered giant of a man who had a penchant for wearing a powder-blue three-piece suit.

"You've got a lot on your plate," Ben told John. "I'll let you get on with stuff and I'll see you over the weekend."

"I'm looking forward to reading what you've written," John said.

Ben just managed to stop himself from saying, "Me too." He was bidding John a farewell, pouring out cat treats for Anastasia, and trying to peer inside the slow-cooker when he finally saw the note that the cat had been standing on.

*'Get out of Sandalwood
whilst you still can.'*

#31

Tom slapped his hand across Carlos' face for a third time. This was the blow that finally brought him back to consciousness. It was a wet sound that spattered droplets of blood into the air. Carlos' nose was broken. His eyes were dull with a lack of comprehension. He considered Tom with the reluctant respect that a cowered animal would give to a violent and cruel hand. One burst lip curled into a sneer and he said, "You're a fucking psycho, man." The words came out slurred but they did not lack emphasis. "You're a total fucking psycho."

Tom shook his head and, again, slapped Carlos hard across the jaw.

"Gentle Jesus doesn't approve of your dirty words. Stop using them or there will be repercussions."

Behind Tom, the dealer moaned as though he was agreeing with this sentiment. His cry sounded as though it came from a point of helpless desperation.

The bar had been emptied of patrons. The only sounds came from crackling speakers that poured Britney Spears tracks into the room. That and the broken, anguished sobs of the dealer. The barman remained in his place behind the bar, calmly eyeing the events, but making no attempt to intervene. Given the wad of notes he now held, Tom figured the man would make no attempt to interfere.

"I want you to get Fat Jay down here for me," Tom told Carlos.

Carlos shook his head. "Forget it," he said simply. There was the trace of a resigned chuckle at the back of his throat as he said, "You're asking the wrong man. Fat Jay is a rival on the local turf. Fat Jay wouldn't come down here for me if my life depended on it."

Tom grabbed Carlos by the scruff of his neck and lifted him from the floor. He half dragged, half carried him across the room and stood him in front of the bar. Twisting Carlos' head, he forced him to look up and see what had become of the dealer.

"Are you sure you can't convince him?" Tom asked. "Look at this ungodly specimen and see if you feel motivated."

Carlos hitched a breath. His eyes grew wide with disbelief.

The dealer groaned.

"Are you sure you can't convince Fat Jay to come down here?" Tom pressed. "Because I can get very imaginative with the way I persuade people. And I'm sure you don't want me to get much more imaginative, do you?"

Tom wasn't sure that imaginative was the correct word. He had crucified the dealer on the crossbeams over the bar but he wasn't convinced that crucifixion involved much that was imaginative. It was a form of punishment that had been popular since before the birth of Christ and there had been little imagination employed in its development since those days. On this occasion a twelve-inch nail had been driven between the radius and ulna bones of each of the dealer's wrists. Dark blood wept from his wounds. The fluid had traced lines down his arms and now dripped from his elbows. The dealer's features were twisted into a constant grimace of raw agony. His sobs were a perpetual background to the ambience of the room. Tom thought, standing this close to him, his cries were mercifully drowning out the sounds of Britney Spears. Tom had never been a big fan of Britney.

Carlos stared at his crucified friend and shook his head in disbelief. "Jesus fucking Christ," he muttered.

Tom slapped his face.

"Don't take the Lord's name in vain," Tom warned.

"You're a psycho," Carlos said. He no longer looked like he was concerned by the upset he caused to his persecutor. The words he spoke were directed at Tom but he stared at the dealer, as though he was unable to drag his gaze away from the gruesomely fascinating sight. "You're a real fucking psycho."

"Get Fat Jay to come down here," Tom insisted, "and you won't have to find out just how much of a psycho I really am."

"And what do you want with me?"

The voice came from a newcomer: someone Tom had never seen before.

He was a skinny young man wearing gold bling at his neck and wrists. His blood-red track suit looked like a slovenly piece of attire and Tom suspected it had cost a stupid amount of money for leisure-wear.

"Who are you?" Tom asked.

"This is Fat Jay," Carlos said.

Tom frowned doubtfully. "He's not fat."

"And the birdman of Alcatraz wasn't really a bird," Fat Jay snarled. "Now, tell me: what do you want with me?"

He stepped closer and Tom reckoned he could take the man with a single punch. Whatever formidable power and authority Fat Jay wielded over the local drug community, Tom was confident he would be immune. He had managed to resist the will of a powerful sorceress who controlled an entire village in the north. He figured it would be a lot easier to resist the will of a godless drug-peddler in a scarlet track suit.

"You killed a dear friend of mine," Tom explained. "A young woman called Etta. You sold her drugs and those drugs killed her."

"That doesn't make me a killer," Fat Jay said. "If your friend was stupid enough to use the shit that I sell, I can't be held responsible."

Tom drew a deep breath. The temptation to punch Fat Jay was almost irresistible. He let Carlos drop to the floor and squared himself up in front of Fat Jay. Rather than striking him immediately he wanted to savour the impending moment. He didn't think gentle Jesus would approve of violence. And he knew his Lord and saviour would not want him to take pleasure from hurting any living thing. But he wouldn't deny himself the pleasure of enjoying the opportunity to strike down vengeance upon Fat Jay.

"How did you know to come here this evening?"

Fat Jay glanced at the barman. "A friend of mine said my presence was required."

Tom grinned. He nodded his thanks at the barman and said, "That was good of him. It's saved me from trying to beat the truth out of these two."

Fat Jay glanced at Tom's handiwork. His sneer surfaced as he looked at Carlos' fallen figure. When he glanced over the bar, and admired the way the dealer had been crucified, Tom could see a glint of surprise arching the man's eyebrows above his Ray-Bans.

"Impressive," Fat Jay said. "You know how to inflict pain. If you're looking for work I could always find employment for someone with your skill set."

"I don't need employment," Tom said simply. "I'm doing the work of gentle Jesus. That's more than enough employment for me."

"I can double whatever he's paying."

Slowly, Tom shook his head. He could see that Fat Jay was mocking him and he knew there would be no point in engaging in an argument about their different theological positions. Tom had his beliefs, and Fat Jay was clearly a heretic who deserved a swift and painful death. Tom didn't think there was any common ground they could exploit.

"You wanted me here and now I'm here," Fat Jay said gruffly. "What are you going to do now that I'm here?" He held his arms in a gesture that showed he was open and honest and not carrying any weapons. "What do you want from me, clown?"

Tom turned his head sharply at the final word, perceiving it as an insult. It was only when he heard the jangle of one of the bells that hung from his cap that he remembered he was still dressed as a Harlequin.

"What do you want, clown?" Fat Jay demanded. "Do you want compensation for the dodgy smack I sold to your friend Etta? Do you want to claim her money back?"

"No," Tom assured him. "I don't want financial recompense. I just want to punish you for your involvement in her death."

"And you think you're going to be able to punish me? On your own?"

Fat Jay laughed as though he was genuinely amused by the notion.

Tom nodded. The bells on his cap jangled musically. "I think I can handle you," he admitted. He was going to say that gentle Jesus was his guiding hand and his saviour hadn't let him down so far. The sound of a footfall behind him made him hesitate and turn. He glanced over his shoulder, half expecting to see Carlos making an eleventh-hour attempt to save the day. Instead he saw that half a dozen of Fat Jay's associates, all broad shoulders packed into glossy leather jackets, filed into the bar.

They stood in a row and glared at Tom. One of them held a gun. One cradled knuckle-dusters on his fist. Tom saw one was wielding a baseball bat and then he noticed one lurching towards him with a long-bladed knife.

Before he could stop the man, the blade had thrust deep into Tom's stomach.

As he fell to his knees, they all crowded around him. Tom heard the glee in Fat Jay's voice as the man yelled, "Kill the fucker. Kill the fucker now, boys."

#32

"You're going to die in here," the doll told Ella.

Ella nodded understandingly. She had known this much before the doll started talking to her. She supposed, on some level, she'd been aware that she was going to die by Fat Jay's hand since he had dragged her from the Boar's Head. Yet it seemed, when she heard the words, the sadness began to rush through her.

She didn't want to die.

It struck her that the experience would be empty. She particularly didn't want to die in the basement of the abandoned house next door to the Boar's Head because it was the bleakest place she had ever encountered. There was a piss-smelling mattress in one corner where she had dozed a couple or three times since the door was locked behind her. The corners of the mattress were black with speckles of mould. There was a semi-full bucket in the other corner. Ella had been the one to semi-fill the unpleasant thing. Although she had been in worse places in her life, she didn't think things ever got much bleaker than when a person had to piss and shit in a bucket and then breathe in the fuck-awful fumes that came from such practices.

Aside from those nuisances and inconveniences there was peeling plaster flaking from the windowless walls. There was a single faltering light bulb hanging from the ceiling on a threadbare flex of cable. And there was a sturdy, inescapable, locked and bolted door.

It was, she thought, a place where someone would be expected to die.

Not that there had been any real threats made against her. If anything, her killers were being genial and pleasant. Admittedly Fat Jay and the dealer had been aggressive with the way they took her down to the house's basement. But, once she was locked there, Ella had been given a bottle of vodka.

She couldn't recall how long ago that had been. It might have been a few short hours earlier. It could have been last week. Locked in a grim basement with no daylight, and nothing but vodka, weed and a talking doll for company, her comprehension of time seemed to have diminished.

She'd had nothing to eat since she stole a cigarette and a croissant from Bill's house the morning after she'd acquired her tattoo. There had been painkillers back then, and she could still recall the pleasantly foggy sensation that accompanied those tablets. Bill always kept the strongest painkillers. It was one of the many reasons she loved him.

But that had been a while ago and since then there had been other chemicals, such as vodka and weed, and there had been the confusing passage of time.

And there was the talking doll.

"Are these drugs making you happy?" the doll asked.

It wasn't just odd that it could talk, Ella thought. She was prepared to note that its ability to communicate so fluently was probably the most unusual thing about the doll. It talked easily and discussed her situation as though it was a rational entity with access to her most private thoughts and fears about the situation.

But that wasn't the only odd thing about the doll.

Ella thought it was an odd-looking doll in general. It had angelic golden curls that should have made it look absurdly pretty. But its features were rendered striking because it had one eye a different colour to the other. She wondered why anyone would create such a peculiar doll. It seemed like an odd-condition to foreground.

"Are these drugs making you happy?" the doll asked again.

Ella considered her answer. At some point, she remembered, the dealer had rolled a pair of joints. She'd shared both of those, although she thought the phrase 'shared' was being generous. Neither Fat Jay nor the Boar's Head dealer had bothered with either joint when she offered them their turn. They had simply smiled at her whilst she smoked and smoked. They had smiled and offered her vodka and exchanged knowing glances.

And, as much as she enjoyed the euphoria that came from being off her tits, Ella thought it would be inaccurate to say that the drugs were making her happy. Considering the current way her spirits were plummeting as she reflected on the hopelessness of her plight, and the inevitable doom that was looming towards her, Ella thought the drugs were making her anything but happy.

There had been as much coke as she wanted.

The dealer had given her a glass mirror, a razor blade and a rolled-up tenner. Fat Jay had offered her a hypodermic that was still in its hermetically sealed packaging. He had said that freebasing was way better than merely snorting a line, and he'd said that such treats needed to be savoured with a fresh bottle of the best vodka. And, whilst she knew the vodka he was giving her wasn't technically the best, it was a Poliakov rather than a Crystal Head Aurora, she figured her imprisonment was going to be a lot more tolerable if she took advantage of every chemical distraction that was offered.

"Is this really how you want to go out?" the doll asked.

During her incarceration, Ella had accepted everything she was offered.

She had been surprised to see that she needed a new bottle of vodka, but it was only a passing observation. At the back of her mind she suspected she had drunk enough to seriously compromise any of her remaining decision-making faculties. She knew she would have pondered on the hopelessness of her plight more if not for the distraction of the drugs and alcohol and the unexpected pleasure of the doll's conversation.

"You're going to die in here," the doll repeated.

"I know," Ella agreed. "It's a pretty empty way to go."

As she said the word she read the ink on her forearm. 'EMPTY'.

The doll followed the line of her gaze and nodded approvingly. "Cool tattoo."

"Thanks," Ella said brightly. She paused for a moment, frowning, and asked, "Am I really talking to a doll, or has my mind flipped from a combination of the drugs and the horror of whatever it is I'm currently being subjected to?"

"Does it matter?"

Ella considered this and figured it didn't matter. If she was enduring some form of horrific abuse that was about to result in her death, then she figured it was best not to know about it, especially if it wasn't a death she could avoid. And, if she was talking to a supernatural animated doll, she supposed it would only remain genuinely supernatural as long as she didn't understand whatever uncanny forces had prompted it to come to life and engage her in conversation.

"No," she conceded brightly. "I don't suppose it does matter." Her smile faded as she added, "It's pretty shitty that I've got to die."

"It's pretty empty," the doll agreed. "But lots of people die. Maybe your death can bring about something good."

Ella wasn't sure that was likely. Her life hadn't brought about much good so she didn't think there was much hope of her death having positive benefits. "How could my death bring about something good?"

The doll considered her solemnly. "There's a village to the north of here. A place called Sandalwood."

"And?"

"Your friend Bill is going to be taken there," the doll explained. "He's going to be taken there and he'll face a terrible evil. He's going to have a chance to stop that evil."

Ella reflected on the words for a long moment. "That sounds hella cool."

"Most likely Bill is going to fail," the doll warned.

Ella shook her head. She was struck by the need to defend her friend. Her best friend. "I doubt he'll fail. Bill can be pretty heroic when he puts his mind to it. There's nothing he can't do."

The doll glanced away, as though not wishing to argue the point. "Fail or succeed," the doll said. "You'll be able to guide Bill on how he can overthrow the powerful force that controls the village of Sandalwood."

Ella was nodding earnestly. "OK. What do I need to do?"

The doll's smile turned momentarily sad. Something softened in the odd-coloured eyes. "The first thing you need to do is die. But I think you just did that."

Ella glanced behind herself. She saw that her corpse was sprawled on the cellar's floor. A needle hung from one scrawny arm and her glassy eyes stared blindly towards the ceiling. She refused to let herself cry at the sight of her dead body. She told herself it wasn't really her body.

It was a shell.

It was empty.

She fixed her features into a scowl as she tried to hold back the tears. Even as she watched the dealer and Fat Jay come into the room, and saw them lift her corpse and then drag the body up the stairs, Ella refused to let herself be upset by the sight of her own demise.

Steeling herself to doing something useful, Ella asked the doll, "What do I do now?"

"Now, we have to go and tell Bill how to kill Marion."

#33

Ben wondered if the Black Swan was hosting a fugly convention. If Etta had been with him he would have asked her the question just to see her smile. A fugly convention seemed like the only explanation that would account for all the unattractive and vaguely menacing patrons waiting for the Black Swan's pub quiz to start.

There were a pair of elderly old biddies in one corner, fat enough to require mobility scooters and dressed in gay, garish colours that contrasted with their grim, and grizzled features. Whenever he glanced in their direction, and the bright colours they wore seemed to draw his gaze repeatedly, Ben found they were staring at him with murderous sneers.

He watched a man shamble from the bar, holding a pint in one hand, and walking with the awkward gait of someone trying hard not to shit himself. Half the man's face appeared to be sloping downward, as though he had never fully recovered from a serious stroke. He looked, Ben thought, as two-dimensionally unattractive as a *Batman* villain.

The pub's landlord scowled at Ben. He had overgrown eyebrows and a complexion like the exposed foam rubber from fire-damaged furniture. His scowl made his moustache sit asymmetrically over yellowing teeth. Ben didn't consider himself prone to flights of fancy but he thought he could see genuine hatred in the landlord's eyes. The ferocity of his unspoken dislike was powerful enough to make Ben recoil. There were other stock characters: a woman who was heroin-thin with a top that showed off knobbly elbows and a rash of vitiligo; a man who was zombie-pale with dirty hands and claw-like fingernails and a mouth with lips as red as a wound.

"Are we all ready for tonight's pub quiz?"

The question was boomed through too-loud speakers that sounded to be on the verge of spewing a feedback whine. Ben glanced at the man behind the microphone, the host of the pub quiz, and saw it was another contender for the pub's ugliest specimen competition. This one wore an open waistcoat over an unironed shirt with sweat-stained armpits. He had thinning grey hair on his flaky scalp, with a similar scruff of grey fur dirtying his cheeks and chin. He stared sourly around the room and said, "Get your drinks before we start. I don't want anyone making noise whilst the questions are being asked."

If Etta had been with him, Ben knew she would have whispered, "He's a charming little fucker, isn't he?"

The thought made him smile sadly. He had missed her every day since she died. But there were some days when her absence struck more sharply, and this was proving to be one of them. He decided to finish his pint and go back to the cottage. There seemed to be no point in remaining in the pub and trying to socialise.

He could see Mrs Scum in one corner of the pub. With her plain features and homely style of dress, she fitted in well with the rest of the Black Swan's facially challenged clientele. At first, he hadn't recognised her because she wasn't wearing her tabard. It was only because she was having a drink with Alfred/Albert that Ben was able to place her face. Hoping not to appear rude by disappearing without talking to her, he motioned for the barmaid and asked her to organise drinks for the couple.

"You're that writer, aren't you?"

He nodded.

"You're from that London, aren't you?"

"Yeah." He passed her a ten-pound note to cover the cost of the drinks and told her to take one for herself. One of these days, he vowed, he would ask a northerner why so many of them called the capital 'that London'.

"Can I ask a question about books?" the barmaid said.

"Sure."

For the first time, he properly noticed her and realised that she didn't fit in with the rest of the locals in the Black Swan. She was pretty in an understated fashion. She wore a lengthy blonde ponytail that bobbed up and down when she nodded. Her eyes shone with an awareness that he saw in few of the faces of Sandalwood villagers. In some ways he thought she resembled either Vicky or Laura, whichever of the maids had been the blonde one at Marion's home. But there was something in her eyes that made him think this woman was someone different to the maid. Too many of Sandalwood's locals stared through him as though he was invisible, or they stared past him as though they were lost in their own personal world. The barmaid met his gaze with an earnest frown settling on her lips.

"How would I go about writing a book?"

"What sort of book?"

She stared at him. "Do you want me to be pacific?"

He stiffened. It was one of his pet foibles that no one should ever use the word *pacific* whenever they meant *specific*. But he could see no point in having that discussion with this individual. "Yeah," he said. "Please be *pacific*."

She nodded. "I want to write a book about this place."

"The pub?"

She shook her head and her brows furrowed. Her ponytail swished from side to side. "Sandalwood," she lowered her voice to a conspiratorial whisper that was barely audible beneath the clamour of the pub around them. "It's a funniosity. I reckon there could be a popular book with all the material I've got from living here. How would I go about writing that book?"

He changed his mind about leaving early and ordered another pint for himself. Trying to make the question seem conversational, he asked her why she thought the village merited a book.

"There's comings and goings most every night," she explained. "I know a lot of the traffic is doing deliveries and pickups at the Doll House, but I've always had the impression it's something more sinister than that."

"Sinister?" he prompted.

She shrugged uneasily. "I was walking home past there one night," she explained. "It was late. It was dark. And I'd drunk two glasses of wine through my shift, so I probably wasn't the most reliable witness in the world."

"Go on."

She lowered her voice to a hoarse croak. "I'm sure there were people doing it outside the Doll House."

"Doing it?"

She urged him to understand with her eyes. "Doing it," she repeated.

He remembered the painting in the study and the shadowy figures that were locked together in coital embraces. Was the barmaid telling him that she had seen those shadowy figures in the middle of their carnal passions?

"That sounds…" he began.

He wasn't sure how to complete the sentence. If he said it sounded good, would that make it appear that he was condoning orgiastic excess in front of a local museum? If he said it sounded bad, would that suggest he thought there was no point in her writing a book about the village?

"…what else would you write about in this book?"

"I'd want to write about the clown situation," she said confidently.

"The clown situation?"

She rolled her eyes. "The village is overrun with them. There ought to be a warning on the signs outside the village, in case someone visiting here has that clown-o-phobia…"

Ben considered telling her the condition was called coulrophobia, and then stopped himself, worried such a correction might hamper her desire to confide.

"…because there are always clowns lurking around, especially at night. And especially in the woods." She paused. Speaking so softly he thought she was directing the question at herself, she said, "I wonder if that's why some of the locals refer to the clowns as *woodsmen*?"

"Clowns?" Ben repeated doubtfully. The only clowns he could recall seeing were the ones in the paintings in John's cottage. And the ones in the paintings at the library. And in Marion's Doll House. And, of course, there was the white-faced clown he had seen at the Doll House and the library.

"I've been told that there's something special about clown suits," she told him. Her voice was lowered to something only slightly louder than a conspiratorial whisper. "There's something special about clown suits that allow the wearer to escape from this village if they're trapped."

Ben understood what she was saying. His eyes widened incredulously.

"There are clowns all over the place here in Sandalwood," the barmaid explained. She glanced behind him and her jaw moved wordlessly.

Ben stiffened, suddenly worried she had seen some sort of clown lurking over his shoulder. The idea was enough to make a shiver of ice-cold dread tickle down his spine. Summoning all his courage he turned and found himself facing the scowling pub landlord with the asymmetrical moustache.

The landlord looked past Ben.

"Serve these others," he said, gesturing at a pair of locals waiting further down the bar. "I don't pay you to stand around here channering to Londoners, do I?"

Ben thought the barmaid looked like she was going to snap a rude retort. The moment passed. Her frown of impatience melted into the resigned expression of despondency that he had seen in a thousand faces before. This was the silent contempt he had often seen employees cast at those bumbling superiors who had been elevated to positions of responsibility well above their abilities.

As the barmaid mumbled an excuse and slipped along the bar to serve other customers, the landlord considered Ben with a disparaging sneer.

"You're not from around these parts, are you?"

"No," Ben admitted. He raised the pint he had just bought and sipped it slowly as the landlord continued to study him with a smouldering fury. "That's not a problem, is it?" Ben asked genially. "It's not compulsory that everyone in the bar is related, is it?"

The landlord's lips thinned.

"You're a long way from that London, Mester Writer."

"Yes," Ben agreed. "But, luckily, the warm welcome I'm getting here in Sandalwood is helping to ease my homesickness."

"Are you asking for a leathering?"

Ben could feel the hatred emanating from the man in a sickening rush. He could sense the man's anger and power and knew, if there was a confrontation, the man would be a volatile and uncompromising adversary. Ben had no idea what he had done to merit the man's anger, and common sense told him he should be trying to find a way to placate him. But he sensed things were already beyond that point.

"Are you asking for a leathering?" the landlord repeated. His hands were clenched into fists. His shoulders were thrown back and his chest was puffed out. "Because if you are, I can fuck you up, Mester Writer."

Ben stood up. "Have you considered anger management classes?"

The landlord's face turned the colour of a thunderstorm.

"I could do with a hand here," the barmaid called.

The landlord looked momentarily torn. He glanced from Ben to the barmaid and, slowly, painfully slowly, his posture softened. Seeming to see that there would be no point in furthering the confrontation, the landlord pushed past Ben and went to help serve the fuglies that were wanting drinks before the pub quiz started.

Ben sipped his pint and tried not to let the barman's hostility sour his mood. He thought of joining Mrs Scum and Alfred/Albert but it was only a passing notion. He didn't want to sit with them because of the worry that it might be revealed that he didn't know their names. He preferred the idea of waiting for the barmaid to finish her chores so she could share more details about her idea for a *pacific* book. It wasn't that he thought it sounded like she could write a potential literary masterpiece, but he was curious to hear about any of the other anomalies that had happened in Sandalwood. He thought, perhaps, she might be able to tell him something that helped him better understand the village mysteries he had already encountered. More importantly, it sounded as though she knew about the difficulties that could be encountered for anyone trying to leave Sandalwood.

Was there really a way to escape the village? Could it really be something as simple as a clown suit? Ordinarily he would have baulked at the insanity of such a suggestion. But this was Sandalwood and, given the unusual comings-and-goings he had encountered since arriving in the village, Ben realised it would be unwise to discount an idea just because it wouldn't have sounded sane a week earlier.

The quiz started with a flurry of bossiness from the man with the microphone. He went through a list of rules – absolute silence, no use of mobile phones, judge's decision being final – and then he started to bark his questions.

"Question one: name the artist who painted the cemetery scene that hangs in the foyer of Sandalwood library."

The bar fell preternaturally silent.

Ben watched as each of the fugly customers stooped over a sheet of paper and began to scratch responses.

"Question two: in what year was Marion Papusa's doll museum constructed?"

As the scratching intensified Ben began to wonder if all the questions related to Sandalwood. He could feel his interest in the quiz being piqued. Was there a chance that some question in the quiz might provide one of the answers he needed? Maybe he could learn something of value about Sandalwood, and perhaps some explanation as to why he was unable to escape?

"Question three-"

"I'm going out for a fag break," the barmaid told him. She whispered the words in his ear. They were loud enough to drown out whatever the third question was in the pub quiz. "If you join me in the smoking shelter I can tell you more about my ideas for the Sandalwood book."

"And the clown suits?" he asked.

She looked momentarily puzzled, and then nodded before turning away from him.

Ben picked up his pint and started towards the pub doors. He didn't know where the pub's smoking shelter was, but he could see that the barmaid had disappeared through a 'STAFF ONLY' door behind the bar. He figured she would meet him out there and he doubted it would be difficult to find.

"Question four: What was the title of Nick Fallow's book about Marion Papusa?"

Ben stepped outside into the night's chill air. A mist had rolled from the moors surrounding Sandalwood and he could feel the cool moisture adhering to his face and throat. Lights outside the pub lit the slick cobbles. Ben shivered and began to look for signs of the smoking shelter where the barmaid had suggested they meet. He ended up walking to the rear of the pub, shouldering his way through a yard that was filled with barrels and cases of bottles. The back door of the pub was open and light spilled out into the darkness. The air was sweetened with stale lager and long-fermented yeast. As Ben walked closer he could hear voices inside the pub.

"Where the hell do you think you're going?"

It was a man's voice and he sounded gruff enough to be the pub's landlord.

"I'm going out for my break."

This was a woman's voice. Ben thought it sounded like the barmaid who'd been talking to him. He held himself in the shadows of the pub's rear yard, not wanting to face the volatile landlord away from the sanctuary of the pub's bright lights.

"Have you arranged to meet that writer?"

"What if I have?"

"You shouldn't be talking to outsiders about village business."

"Get off me."

"You know the rules. We don't talk to outsiders."

"I'll talk to whoever the hell I want."

"You'll do as you're damned well told whilst you're working in my pub."

This last exclamation was followed by the sound of a hard, vicious slap. Ben's eyes opened wide and he realised he was listening to some form of violent abuse. He guessed it was the landlord assaulting the barmaid and he tried to work out what he was supposed to do. Chivalry and common decency told him that he needed to intervene but, for an instant, he stood frozen.

The barmaid moaned unhappily. "I'm going out to talk with him."

There was the sound of another slap.

This one tore sobs from the woman.

"Fuck this," Ben decided. He squared his shoulders and started for the back door of the pub. He had let Etta down when she needed him. He was determined not to let this barmaid down at such a critical moment.

A hand fell on his arm, stopping him.

#34

He hadn't noticed Mrs Scum and Alfred/Albert following him. It was the gardener's hand that fell on his arm. He turned and found himself facing the gardener and the cleaner. Alfred/Albert's fingers pressed more firmly against Ben's bicep. Mrs Scum placed a finger to her lips in the universal sign for silence.

Ben glanced towards the back door of the Black Swan. The raised voices had fallen silent, but he thought that was a disconcerting development. Did that mean the landlord had beaten the barmaid into acquiescence? Or was it even more serious than that?

"Let us take you home, Mester Writer," Alfred/Albert insisted.

Ben tried to wrestle himself free from the man's grip. For a doddery old git, Alfred/Albert was surprisingly strong. Either that, Ben thought, or his years of dissolute hedonism had left him too weak to overpower a geriatric gardener.

"Don't cause a scene," Mrs Scum insisted. "It's for the best."

He wanted to say it wouldn't be for the best. He had already let one person down by not doing the right thing. Etta was dead because he hadn't had the courage to do what, he knew, should be done. If he ignored the barmaid's cries for help, or the sounds of the beating she was suffering, or the sinister silence that now whispered through the crack in the door, Ben knew he would not have changed from being the selfish piece of shit he had been whilst he was back in London.

"Get off me," he told Alfred/Albert. "I'm going to go and help that barmaid."

The gardener leant in close to him and placed his lips close to Ben's ear. "Remember what happened to Deborah," he murmured. His voice was so soft that Ben was sure there was no danger that Mrs Scum had overheard. "Remember what happened to her, Mester Writer," Alfred/Albert insisted. "Come back with us now and, maybe there's a chance for you to get out of Sandalwood whilst you still can."

Ben stiffened.

Get out of Sandalwood whilst you still can.

Hadn't those been the words that were written on the note he'd found in the cottage? Ben considered Alfred/Albert warily, wondering if it was possible that the gardener had been the one to write the note. He'd thought the first one had been written by Tina White. The second one, the one that had been waiting for him on the kitchen table, Ben had no idea who it could have come from. He struggled to remember if Alfred/Albert had been lurking outside the house when he found that note.

"What did happen to Deborah?" he asked.

The gardener tugged on his arm. Mrs Scum stepped between Ben and the door at the back of the Black Swan and she urged him to start walking with her.

"Please," she pressed. "None of us want this to turn ugly, do we?"

Reluctantly, hating himself for his weakness and wishing he'd had the courage to take a stand against the landlord, Ben sighed and began to walk away from the pub. He realised he was still holding his pint and, in a fit of impotent rage, he hurled the half-empty glass against the wall of the building. It shattered in a sharp explosion that faded to a merry tinkling sound. The contents left a wet smear on the wall and the misty air was momentarily tainted with the fragrance of real ale.

Ben saw the landlord poke his head out of the pub's back door and he wasn't surprised to see Mrs Scum wave him away. Obediently, the landlord followed Mrs Scum's command and returned to the sanctuary of the Black Swan.

Ben stormed off down the hill.

"Wait up, Mester Writer," called the gardener.

Ben didn't bother waiting. He lurched down the hill at a speed just short of a run. He got to the bottom and then fought his way through the overhanging branches that covered the cottage's driveway. He could hear Alfred/Albert and Mrs Scum all the way behind him. By the time he reached the cottage's front door they had given up shouting for him to slow down or hold on. He guessed that the conspiratorial whispers he could now hear were their discussions on how they should best deal with him.

He wasn't sure if he cared what conclusion they reached.

Ben didn't bother closing the door behind himself. He could see no point. He knew Mrs Scum had her own key to the cottage and he suspected Alfred/Albert would have some way to get in. Going through to the kitchen, still shaking from the unspent adrenaline that pumped through his veins, he tore open the fridge door and then slammed it closed. None of the beers in there were strong enough for what he currently required.

Anastasia stood on the kitchen table and considered him warily.

He didn't like that the creature had picked up on his anger and he forced himself to calm down. Grabbing a pair of saucers from beneath the sink he poured out nibbles and cream. The clatter of footsteps in the hallway told him that Mrs Scum and Alfred/Albert had caught up with him.

"Cooee," Mrs Scum called. "Are you alright in there?"

"Mester Writer? May we come in?"

He stormed past them as he went into the study. The door to the drinks cabinet was locked but it was a flimsy construction and Ben was able to wrench it open with a single forced tug. Inside he found a virgin bottle of Jack Daniels. He snapped the cap from it and savoured the aroma like a connoisseur. Pouring a generous shot into one of the highballs, he chugged a satisfying mouthful that barely touched the sides. The whiskey had a delicious burn that went some way to dulling his anger.

"We didn't want to intervene," Mrs Scum told him.

"We were just trying to help," Alfred/Albert insisted.

"The landlord of the Mucky Duck is a brussen bas'ard," Mrs Scum explained. "He's outside Marion's control and he'd have hurt you badly."

"Outside Marion's control? What the fuck does that mean?"

Mrs Scum clapped a hand over her mouth and shook her head as though refuting the statement. It was Alfred/Albert who responded, sounding like a voice of parochial wisdom in the insanity of the cottage.

"You know what that meant, Mester Writer. You're bright enough to have worked most of this out. Marion runs most of this village and that includes the three of us."

Ben drained his bourbon and glared at the man.

He could see that Mrs Scum was scowling, as though she was uncomfortable with such frank revelations. She clutched at the gardener's arm and shook her head. But Ben could see that Alfred/Albert was in no mood to be silenced.

"Whilst she runs most of this village, she doesn't run everything. The landlord of the Black Swan is one of those she doesn't yet control."

"You shouldn't be telling him this," Mrs Scum hissed.

"He's a bright young man," Alfred/Albert snapped. "I reckon he'll have worked most of this out already." He nodded at the pages of completed manuscript beside the Silver Reed and said, "I reckon most of the answers he's searching for will be written in that there book."

Mrs Scum pursed her lips, but she didn't press the point. She didn't look as though she agreed with the gardener's stance, but it was clear she was no longer going to argue with him.

"The landlord's one of those that Marion shall be using as a woodsman in the future," Alfred/Albert explained.

Ben shook his head. "I have no idea what that means."

"Don't you?"

Mrs Scum glanced at the pages of manuscript as she asked the question and Ben realised he did understand. He wasn't sure why the phrase had meaning but it sounded like something he had written about with reference to Timmy's subplot in his story. He swallowed the contents of his highball and poured himself a fresh drink. He didn't suppose alcohol would help him better understand what was happening but he reasoned it would make the confusion less unbearable.

"The landlord is outside of Marion's control. He would have hurt you badly if you'd given him the excuse."

"Very badly," Mrs Scum concurred.

"What the hell has he got against me?" Ben asked. "I don't think I've seen him before tonight."

"No," Alfred/Albert agreed. "But he's seen you. And he knows you were the last one to be seen with his former girlfriend, Deborah."

Ben sipped at his drink and said nothing. That was something he hadn't expected.

"He would have hurt you very badly," Mrs Scum said quietly. "And we wouldn't have wanted that, would we?"

Ben shrugged. "Why would my welfare be of any concern to you?"

Alfred/Albert looked away.

Mrs Scum said, "We work for Mester John. We know how important you are to his work. He would have been livid if we'd known you were in danger and he'd found out we'd done nowt to help."

Grudgingly, Ben nodded. He knew he should be grateful to the couple for stepping in. He suspected that they had saved him from a substantial amount of physical hurt and a lot of emotional upset. But a part of him still worried that the landlord was going to take out his wrath on the barmaid. And Ben felt sure he should have done something and put the considerations for his own safety to one side for the sake of helping someone else.

He believed such acts of self-sacrifice were something he should have been doing for a long time. Deliberately, he sat down in front of the typewriter.

"Do you need us for anything else?" Mrs Scum asked.

He bit his lower lip and stopped himself from saying he hadn't needed them for anything so far this evening. Keeping the thought to himself he shook his head.

"Are you getting on with some writing?" Alfred/Albert asked.

Ben nodded and sipped again at his drink. He rolled a sheet of A4 paper onto the platen and then rested his fingers on the home keys.

"Should we leave you to it?" Mrs Scum asked.

"If you don't mind."

He waited until the pair of them had shuffled out of the house and closed the door behind them before he stood up and poured himself a fresh measure of Jack Daniel's. The whiskey was beginning to take a hold, burning his throat and warming his belly. His thoughts were becoming pleasantly clouded and his anger at being stopped from helping the barmaid had begun to abate.

More importantly, he was telling himself that he needed to make some sort of plan to escape from Sandalwood.

He returned to his chair before the typewriter but stared thoughtfully at the painting of the Doll House. Anastasia leapt onto the table and positioned herself between him and the Silver Reed. He stroked the cat absently as his mind went through the various options that were available to him.

If there was any hope of escaping from Sandalwood, he felt confident it would be found somewhere inside the Doll House. He had spent an afternoon trying to walk out of Sandalwood and had only ended up tired and still trapped in the village. If he was to believe what Mrs Scum had just told him, that Marion Papusa controlled Sandalwood and its inhabitants, then it made sense to believe that the answers to escape were locked somewhere in her home.

"OK," he told Anastasia. "There's no sense in investigating the Doll House tonight. The place is always too busy during the night. I'm going to find a way in there tomorrow, and I'll find out why, and how, Marion is controlling me."

The cat meowed as though it was agreeing with him.

Ben nodded and said, "More importantly, once I've found out how and why she's controlling me, I'll find a way to break her hold and I'll escape this fucking village."

The carnage was close to being biblical. As his anger began to abate, and as he found himself resuming control over his fury, Tom took a moment to take in his surroundings and appreciate the righteous havoc he had wrought.

Whilst he didn't condone violence, it was, he thought, impressive.

A second figure, this one Tom remembered was called Carlos, was crucified over the bar. His arms were nailed to the main beam. His head lolled forward as though he had died in the process of repenting for his sins. His intestines had begun to spill from the gaping wound in his abdomen.

There was a lot of blood.

The room stank of blood to the extent where its coppery tang tainted Tom's every breath. Its stench was so rich it lined his nostrils and threatened to choke at the back of his throat. Every time he swallowed he could feel traces of the slick liquid oiling his gullet. It was an intoxicating and inescapable flavour and it made him smile.

Blood-reddened the remnants of Carlos' T-shirt. It blackened his jeans and dripped to form a spreading puddle from the toes of his boots. The coils of his intestines, spilling down to his knees, looked like pale and glistening snakes. Or monstrously overgrown worms caught in tableaux as they writhed their way up his body and into his stomach.

"You've done good work," Tom told himself.

Two severed heads were on the floor in a slippery pool of blood.

They did not resemble the neatly severed heads Tom had seen in various films and TV shows. The faces were battered with blackened eyes, missing teeth, and innumerable cuts and scratches. There was no suggestion of a clean cut going through either of the necks. The stumps beneath the faces were ragged and looked as though they had been chewed. The hair was sticky with blood and the faces were dirtied with gouges of missing skin.

But, whilst they weren't pretty or aesthetically pleasing on any level, Tom thought they looked like a good example of the fate that could befall any miscreant who earned the vengeance of his God. This was what happened to all who defied the will of his saviour, gentle Jesus.

He wouldn't let himself be distracted by his achievements. Noises in the pub made him aware that there were still some dangers facing him.

Some of the attackers who had set on him were still alive. A couple of them had enough energy left to groan and whimper. The sounds of their distress were sharpened with obvious agony. Tom could hear someone sobbing in disbelief. He could hear the hitched moans of a person on the verge of hysteria. One of the voices he could hear was blatantly cursing and taking the Lord's name in vain, but Tom reasoned it was forgivable on this occasion. The carnage in the Boar's Head was more than worthy of a little blasphemy.

He continued to glance around the pub, considering the results of his handiwork. Secretly he believed that gentle Jesus would be pleased with him. This was the righteous retribution his Lord deserved. It was indicative of a wrath that, perhaps would have been more appropriate for the *Old Testament*. But Tom still thought Jesus would have been pleased that so many violent deaths had been performed in his name.

"You'll pay for this," Fat Jay assured Tom.

Tom nodded in agreement. Most likely Fat Jay was right. There were red and blue lights splashing their colours on the window outside the Boar's Head and Tom suspected the police were about to make their presence known. If they came in and decided he was responsible for all that had happened in the pub, he knew there would be calls for him to be punished. And if the authorities demanded he be punished, Tom thought it would only be right for him to take that punishment.

But he didn't think it would happen just yet.

Gentle Jesus had other plans for him.

He still had debts to settle. The most important one of those debts was the bill that needed settling in the faraway village of Sandalwood. He had to deal with Marion Papusa and he needed to make sure that Ben Haversham got what was coming to him. He felt confident that gentle Jesus would not allow him to be interrupted from such important work until Tom had settled both of those accounts with interest.

Slowly, he bore down on Fat Jay.

At first, when Tom had been stabbed and then set upon, he had worried that Fat Jay and his cohorts would easily be able to overpower him and kill him. There were lots of them. They all looked menacing and violent. And they each seemed intent on causing him the maximum physical damage they could inflict.

It was only when he saw the blade come out of his stomach, and realised the shiny length of steel was untainted by blood, that Tom remembered he was immortal. The stabbing had caused no pain. It had merely been a little uncomfortable and torn a hole in his shirt.

He wasn't happy about being immortal. He was sure gentle Jesus wouldn't approve of such a diabolical condition. But he was determined to use the gift to his best advantage. For a long moment he allowed his attackers to continue beating him, lulling them into a false sense of security. He took blows to his head, shoulders and back. Then, feinting a slump to the floor, he tripped the first of them.

It was simple enough. He grabbed a man's ankle and pulled with as much strength as he could manage. Once the first man was on the floor, Tom found he was holding the man's knife. With that weapon at his disposal it was easy enough to take down two more.

Slowly standing, and immune to punches, kicks, and knife attacks, he went through them all with brutal determination. He shot punches to faces and throats. He drove his knee into groins. He slammed the blade he was carrying into necks, chests, and stomachs. He grinned with each assault he delivered.

"I mean it, you fucking freak," Fat Jay wailed. "You'll pay for this."

Tom suspected that Fat Jay was right to call him a freak. He could feel spatters of blood and gore on his face and, coupled with the Harlequin costume he was wearing, Tom figured that *freak* was probably the kindest description he could merit.

"Are *you* going to make me pay?" Tom asked. He made a point of looking around the pub, as though there remained a chance that someone might come to Fat Jay's assistance. He stepped over three corpses, glanced up at the two crucified figures above the bar, and then stooped down to look at the barman's decapitated head.

The barman had been one of the first that Tom had decapitated.

Although he had originally thought the barman was on his side, he realised now that the man was the one who had summoned Fat Jay and his helpers to the Boar's Head. It seemed obvious that he had called on them so that they could help to kill Tom. Consequently, Tom thought it was only fitting that he made a point of cutting off the barman's head as a public display of the retribution he was wreaking.

Fat Jay had pissed himself when he saw the execution. The crotch of his scarlet track suit was now black with the stain of his fear.

Tom stepped closer to Fat Jay.

There were bodies strewn across the floor in his path. Some of them were moaning through various stages of distress. Most of them lay dead still. Tom kicked one severed head aside and stepped over a portly torso. He stood over Fat Jay and punched him effortlessly to the floor.

As soon as Fat Jay was down, Tom stamped on one of the man's legs.

There was the satisfying sound of bone breaking: a crunch that was softened by the wet rip of meat tearing. This noise was followed by Fat Jay's howl of agonised disbelief. It was a shriek that rang around the bar and rattled from the glassware.

Tom grinned.

He picked up the mallet and one of the handful of twelve-inch nails he had been given when he was intending to crucify the dealer. Acting swiftly, he slammed the nail through Fat Jay's ankle, pinning him to the pub floor.

Fat Jay had howled before. This time he screamed.

Tom took his time driving the nail deeper so that it was holding Fat Jay securely. Then he went about the leisurely process of going behind the bar and finding a bottle of brandy. Unhurriedly, he sprinkled the contents along the bar and over the floor. He sprayed brandy onto each of the tables and chairs, and then onto the fallen colleagues of Fat Jay.

"You'll pay for this," Fat Jay warned him. "You'll fucking pay."

"I don't doubt it," Tom agreed.

The red and blue lights outside the bar's windows were more noticeable than ever. Tom guessed the police were on the verge of bursting through the doorway. He dropped the empty bottle of brandy into Jay's lap and pulled a box of matches from the pocket of his Harlequin costume.

"What was the point of this?" Fat Jay demanded. He spat the words through sobs of dismayed frustration. "If you're trying to stop drug crime, that's not going to happen. There'll be another dealer on this street selling the same shit I've been peddling by tomorrow night."

Tom shrugged indifferently. "I never expected to wipe out drug crime. I just wanted to avenge the death of a friend." He struck a match and smiled softly at the glow of brilliant yellow light. It brightly shone in the darkness of the bar. "For this reason," he murmured softly, "I remind you to fan into flame the gift of God, which is in you through the laying on of my hands."

Fat Jay seemed not to have heard Tom recite a passage from the Bible. He seemed fixated on Tom's previous comment. "You want to avenge a friend's death?" Fat Jay babbled. "It's not just down to me though, is it? What about the family that let her down? What about the false friends who didn't give her the encouragement or support she needed? What about them?"

"There's only one of her false friends remaining," Tom admitted. He dropped the match and the flame immediately caught on the brandy fumes. He stepped away from the blossoming inferno and started towards the doorway at the back of the Boar's Head. Over his shoulder, speaking more to himself than Fat Jay, he said, "There's only one of those false friends remaining, and I'm on my way up to the village where he's hiding so I can make sure he pays the proper penalty."

#36

Ben awoke stiff and out of sorts with the world. There were more pages of the novel lurking next to the typewriter and he scowled at them. It was sickening to realise he took no pleasure from what was written there. He had always been proud of his writing and the accomplishments he could make with words. But this sleep-writing was no accomplishment. The sleep-writing was simply more proof that he was under the control of Sandalwood's puppeteer. Whilst the idea of reading the rest of the story was tempting, he resisted the urge. He felt sure those pages contained details of Ella's death and he didn't want to subject himself to that. He understood that the description would not be too dissimilar to the fate that had befallen Etta.

It was earlier than he had been waking at Sandalwood.

The sky outside the study window was dirty with smears of the lingering night and smudged by the prospect of a grim day. He had fallen asleep in front of the typewriter and, it seemed, he hadn't bothered with bed the previous evening. Warily, he glanced at the most recent page he had typed and saw, with relief, that he had finished halfway through a chapter. The observation eased his mind a little because, on some level he understood, once he had typed the words *THE END*, his usefulness in Sandalwood would have expired.

He put down food and drink for Anastasia, went for a pee, and had a breakfast coffee. Whilst he was sipping at the drink, and watching another bleak dawn fill the morning sky above the village, he went over the plans he had made the previous evening.

He was going to investigate the Doll House.

The building was so busy on an evening it would have been insane to try and gain access during the night. But, on a morning, when all the deliveries, dispatches, and bacchanal activities had been completed for the night, he thought it might be possible to sneak into the premises undetected.

He frowned and swigged more coffee and wondered what he hoped to find.

The idea of breaking into somewhere as sinister as the Doll House, and then risking the wrath of Marion Papusa, and whatever villagers she had under her thrall, was daunting. But to do that with no real notion of what he was looking for seemed like the epitome of foolishness. Nevertheless, Ben pulled on a fresh dark hoodie and rushed out into the morning chill. If there was a way out of Sandalwood, Ben felt sure it would start at the Doll House.

He knew the location of the garage because of the painting in the study.

It was sited to the rear of the house and he jogged past the main entrance in case anyone was watching. He didn't think anyone would be watching but then, he wasn't sure he was really convinced that Marion Papusa was controlling villagers like some master puppeteer. Logically, that was the only explanation for a lot of the anomalies he had witnessed in Sandalwood but, realistically, the idea still sounded like the fantasy of a deranged mentality.

Dodging through a hedge at the back of the building, he trotted to the large double garage and was pleased to see the doors were open. He had to sneak past a Daimler on his way in and there was something familiar about the vehicle that niggled at his memory. For some reason he had been under the impression that Marion owned a Mercedes. He didn't know if that was because she had the personality of a Mercedes driver, or if she had said something about the vehicle when he had been attending her insufferable dinner party.

Deciding it was something he would think about later, Ben crept into the depths of the garage and found the door he had known would be at the back of the room. He had seen enough boxes going to and fro from the Doll House to feel confident that there would be a way into the building through this route.

Yet still, he felt as though his investigation was vindicated by the presence of the door. "Never underestimate the shrewd observational powers of a writer," he murmured.

The door was unlocked.

He grinned to himself.

Instead of leading into the house the door opened on a descending staircase. He could make out a dim glimmer of light at the bottom and began to walk slowly downwards. The stairs creaked beneath his weight. He wasn't concerned that they wouldn't be able to support him, but he was worried that the noise of each step would give him away.

But, knowing that he needed to get into the house, Ben headed downwards.

He stopped at the bottom and tried to work out what he was seeing.

The walls were lined with boxes. He suspected the basement was the same size as the whole of the house, but it was made smaller by the lining of boxes. They were in various shades of brown and manila. Some were labelled in a cursive hand he couldn't be bothered to decipher. Others were bare. He could see a stairway leading out of the basement, and up towards the house he guessed.

And he could see people.

There looked to be a dozen people in the basement. Each one sat in front of a workstation, armed with an illuminated magnifying lamp and bent over a partially assembled doll. There was no music. There was no conversation. There was no sound other than the splosh of paint being applied to a doll, or the creak of scissors cutting, or the rasp of cable-ties being tightened.

As he walked slowly amongst them, Ben realised that none of the workers were even looking up from their work to glance at him. He remembered Mrs Scum saying that the landlord was outside Marion's control. He wondered if the women at the workstations, because they were all women he now noticed, were all under Marion's control.

How was it possible for someone to control people in such a way?

He wasn't sure he wanted to find an answer to that question. But he suspected the answer might prove his only way of escaping Sandalwood. He held his breath as he walked through the workshop. There was something so disconcerting about the silence of the workers that he felt afraid to share the air they were breathing.

If they were breathing. That was an idea that forced a rash of goosebumps to bristle across his forearms.

He could see they were intent on their work with the dolls. And the dolls they were producing looked lifelike and chillingly realistic. But, despite the fact that the workers were demonstrating some obvious artistic ability, he got the impression they were blind to everything else in the room.

He was about to leave, anxious to get away from them and thankful he had seen another doorway that he hoped would lead into the house, when the glint of something dark on the face of one worker made him pause.

She was wearing an eyepatch.

"Deborah?"

The woman didn't bother looking at him. She continued to dab paint along the lips of the doll she was working on. And yet, even though she was refusing to respond to him, Ben felt certain it was the woman he'd bedded on his second night in Sandalwood. The woman whose dismembered corpse he had found in the linen closet.

"Deborah?"

Instead of stepping closer, he found his natural instinct was to step away from her. A part of his mind was screaming that she was a corpse and he had to get away from her. As he moved, he nudged against a workstation and pushed the hand of a curly-haired brunette.

At first he was shocked to think he had touched one of the workers. It was disquieting to see this one was dressed as a white-faced clown, her head tilted unnaturally to one side, forcing her conical hat to point awkwardly to the ceiling. She glanced up at him with unseeing eyes and then turned her attention back to the doll she was painting. It was only a brief glance, the shortest encounter of gazes, but it was enough for Ben to recognise something in her face.

"Fucking hell," he muttered.

He forced himself not to run up the stairs and into the Doll House. A part of him wanted him to go back the way he had come and flee the house completely. But, sure that the solution to his escape plans lay somewhere in the house, Ben forced himself to walk slowly and steadily up the stairs. Silently, he prayed he would find some answers to the million and one questions that now flooded through his thoughts.

#37

When Marion had given him a tour of the ground floor, Ben came away with the impression that she didn't live in that part of the house. He had an idea that the pristine floor plan, with its polished dining table and glossy surfaces, was a front for guests and visitors. The floor immediately above, and the one above that, seemed dedicated to the rooms and exhibits associated with the doll museum. It was only the highest floor, that single exposed room with its unbroken view of the whole village, the room with the mystical signs chalked on the wooden floors, that looked like it had been stamped with her personality.

He headed warily up the stairs.

It crossed Ben's mind that, when he had entered the building, he'd had no idea what he would say if he was caught. Before he had entered the Doll House he had simply been driven by a determined desire to break into the building and find something inside that would give him a means to escape Sandalwood. If someone had challenged him he might have feigned puzzlement and blamed it all on an episode of sleepwalking. He had reasoned that the explanation was vaguely plausible since, if he was capable of writing most of a novel in his sleep, surely he was capable of sleepwalking into a museum that was only over the road from where he currently resided?

But now he thought he would be justified in challenging any challenger.

What was he doing in the Doll House without permission? What was the owner of the Doll House doing keeping an army of zombie slaves locked, sweatshop-fashion, in the confines of her basement? What was she doing controlling the lives of the villagers and reanimating their dissected corpses? What in the name of hell was going on in Sandalwood? And how much of it was happening because Marion Papusa insisted it should happen?

He hurried up the stairs, fuelled by a sense of righteous justification that filled him with a pious certainty that he would find all the solutions he needed so long as he stood in front of the right person and shouted loudly enough. Yes, he was breaking and entering. But surely that crime paled to insignificance compared to whatever

Marion Papusa was doing as she secured her hold on the village of Sandalwood?

His confidence began to falter as he started up the spiral staircase that led to the uppermost floor of the Doll House. He could hear guttural moans coming from above his head. There was something animal and unpleasant in the sounds. At first, he feared he was hearing some grim and unnatural beast grunting its way through a cruel and tortured sacrifice.

But the reality – the noises of Marion and John fucking – seemed far worse.

It wouldn't have surprised him to find Marion slaughtering an animal in the open attic. It was easy to imagine the spindly woman wielding a lengthy butcher's knife and slashing through unsuspecting flesh. There was something in the emotionless shine of her glossy black eyes that made him certain she could happily cut the throats of lambs, pigs, cows or humans. He felt sure she could end any life without blinking back a tear of remorse. If anything, he thought she would likely have to chew on the inside of her cheeks to keep the smile from twisting her lips.

But there was no beast being slaughtered or sacrificed.

Marion was naked and on all fours, her bony old knees pressed into the centre of one of the chalk circles that decorated the attic floor. John was behind her in a similar state of undress. He was pounding into her with disquieting vigour and it was Marion making the feral sounds that Ben had mistaken for cries of torture and distress.

Ben held himself motionless and hoped that neither one of the couple had seen him. He held his breath and wished he wasn't looking directly at them.

Marion was naked, and it was not a sight he had wanted to behold. Her modest breasts hung downward looking empty, leathery, and unappetising. His gaze was drawn to the tumid swelling of her nipples. Uneasily he noted that they were pointing in different directions to each other. The breasts swayed with each violent thrust that John ploughed into the woman. The motion was almost hypnotic.

Ben wouldn't let himself look at John.

The man was his agent and almost a friend, but that didn't mean that Ben was going to look at his naked body whilst the man was busy granny-fucking the marionette who controlled Sandalwood. He noted the pasty white flesh of John's torso and pot-belly. He saw the unnatural sprouting of dark hairs that snaked down the man's stomach. And he could see John's fingertips digging into the tanned hide of Marion's buttocks as he pushed himself repeatedly into her.

Then he tore his gaze away.

The musty scent of sex touched Ben's nostrils. It was an odour that combined sweat and game, and something vaguely reminiscent of the sea.

He wondered if he was going to vomit.

"Deeper," Marion growled. There was an urgency in her voice that combined anger and desperation. "Make it go deeper," she insisted. "Deeper and faster."

Ben told himself that he couldn't hear the slurp of Marion's vagina clutching wetly onto John's length. He couldn't hear anything. He wanted to believe he couldn't see anything. And he was determined to deny that he could smell anything. He refused to accept that he could taste the fetid flavour of their sex on every breath.

"I'm doing it as best I can," John snapped irritably.

"And you'll do it as I want it if you expect me to supply a replacement dogsbody to fill Alice's shoes."

Ben had been on the verge of creeping stealthily down the stairs. He hesitated, wondering if there might be some advantage to eavesdropping. John needed a replacement for Alice? That was a surprise. The woman had been with the man's agency since for as long as Ben could remember. He had thought she was a permanent fixture. He wondered what had happened to make John get rid of Alice.

"Is this fast enough?" John grunted.

Ben could hear that the pace had quickened. The creak of the floorboards and the slurp of Marion's vagina both sounded to be ringing at a much faster pace than they had previously.

"Is this fast enough, Mistress?"

Marion moaned.

Ben stifled the urge to release a similar cry. He reasoned that the couple were involved in some sort of BDSM relationship. A part of him wondered if it would be worth staying within earshot in case they said anything that might be of use to his escape plans. More likely, he thought, his sanity would be damaged beyond repair if he lingered nearby and continued listening. The couple seemed to be performing their act in the centre of one of the attic's pentagrams. He didn't know if it was relevant or important. He only knew it was highly unlikely they would say anything that was going to help him find a way out of Sandalwood.

A hand fell on his arm.

He wasn't sure how he contained the scream that wanted to leap from his lungs. It was fortunate that John had chosen that moment to thrust deep into Marion, and Marion had released a respondent grimace/cackle of satisfaction. But, even with the sounds of those coitus noises covering his surprise, Ben still felt sure the couple would be able to hear the accelerated pounding of his heartbeat.

He recognised her as the barmaid from the previous evening.

She had a long blonde ponytail, eyes that shone with savvy awareness, and a massive black eye. He could see that his fears about the violent temper of the landlord had not been misplaced. It was automatic to want to mutter an apology or to ask her if she was OK or needed medical treatment.

The barmaid put a finger to her lips and nodded in the direction of John and Marion. Ben understood the warning and tiptoed lightly down the stairs after her. He could hear Marion and John continuing to thrust and grunt together and he felt thankful to be away from the sights and scents of their brutal intimacy.

"You have to be quick," she whispered eventually. "There's not a lot of time."

She was thrusting some white fabric at him, clothes he guessed, and he tried to make sense of the urgency in her tone.

"Not a lot of time?" He kept his voice lowered for fear that Marion or John might overhear. "What are you talking about?"

"I told you last night that I could get you out of the village," she reminded him. "This is your chance."

He stared at her warily. "Are you serious?"

"Put this on," she told him, pushing the clothes into his arms. "Walk away from the sunrise. And you'll be able to get out of Sandalwood."

He studied the clothes sceptically. "This is a clown costume."

"To be pacific," she started.

Determinedly, Ben did not mention her use of the word.

"To be pacific, it's a Pierrot costume." She spoke in a tone that was whispered and lofty with knowledgeable indignation. "And it's the only chance you have of getting out of this village alive."

Ben considered the costume. It was a satiny white fabric with a satiny white dunce's cap, all decorated with large black pom-pom-like buttons. "How the fuck is this supposed to help me escape the village?"

"It's a clown costume and this is Sandalwood," she explained. "There's people who think that clowns can come and go in this village more easily than us normal folk."

As though there are any normal folk in Sandalwood, Ben thought. He didn't say the words. He simply nodded as though she was talking sense.

The barmaid seemed oblivious to his lack of faith in her rationale. She continued talking, her voice lowered and her gaze occasionally strayed upward to the top of the spiral staircase. "It might also be that, if Marion is watching your every move from those all-seeing windows up there, and if she's controlling you when she sees you doing something that she doesn't like, she won't recognise you if you're wearing a Pierrot costume."

Ben studied her for a moment longer. He hated to admit as much, but the barmaid's explanation did make some sense. Since he had arrived in Sandalwood, with the exception of the one evening when he had visited Marion's to dine with her, he had spent his time wearing dark jeans and a black hoodie. He didn't think a Pierrot costume would be an ideal disguise, but it would not be a costume anyone would automatically associate with him.

Above him he could hear the quickening thrusts and grunts of John and Marion as they completed their act. Her howl was a dry and agonised groan. His cry was a bitter grunt of disgust. Ben thought it sounded like the most distressing bout of passion he had ever overheard.

"What's the deal with the dolls?" he asked. "Why does she make them?"

"She does it for the money," the barmaid explained. "She has the skills to make some very lifelike creations. The dolls are the best way she has to capitalise on those skills."

Ben felt a wave of relief rush through him. He didn't like to think what sort of skills Marion had that would be needed for making lifelike creations, but he was pleased to think that the dolls did not cover some sinister exploitation of infants or babies.

The barmaid studied him impatiently. "You'll need to put it on now, if you're going to try to escape," she told him.

Ben came to an immediate decision. He began to put the costume on over his clothes. "How are you going to get out?" he asked.

"I can still leave the village when I want," she said. "I do collections and deliveries for the landlord of the Black Swan."

He paused in process of buttoning up the jacket of his costume. Glancing at the bruise over her right eye he asked, "Why do you keep coming back?"

She shrugged. "One of these days I won't," she said. "One of these days I'll stay out of Sandalwood and I'll write that book I was telling you about last night."

"If you get out of the village, look me up," he said. "I'll put you in touch with an editor who can help with your writing." He finished dressing in the clown costume and was thankful there was no mirror nearby. It felt baggy and loose, and it came with a stupid pointy hat. He suspected he looked ridiculous.

"I won't forget this," he promised.

She smiled thinly and nodded. "Hurry up and get out of here," she told him. She nodded up the stairs and said, "They'll be heading down shortly."

Ben needed no further warning. He hurried down the stairs, past the barmaid, and then sped through the basement to make his way outside. None of the zombies in the basement bothered to look at him. They were all working industriously on creating their dolls. It was, he thought, like walking through an airlock. Every one of the workers in the basement seemed to be holding their breath and working like a lifeless robot.

"Frightening," he muttered.

His arms were trembling with goosebumps. The rush of revulsion he felt was so unsettling he wanted to vomit. But he was very conscious that such activity could likely draw unwarranted interest. Hurrying, he got outside, into the morning drizzle, and began to rush across the road.

He felt ridiculous and conspicuous in the Pierrot costume, but he could understand the barmaid's rationale for why he should wear such a disguise. Given that he had worn little other than his writer's uniform of a black hoodie and dark jeans since arriving in the village, he figured no one was going to recognise him dressed in this fashion.

He was surprised to see a Mercedes parked in the driveway. He wondered who the vehicle belonged to and what it was doing outside the cottage. The front door was ajar, and he tried to remember if Mrs Scum drove a car whenever she paid a visit to the house. If she did, and if she drove a Mercedes, it suggested John or Marion was paying the woman too much. If she didn't, Ben thought he ought to ask her if she knew who owned the vehicle.

As he entered he called out a questioning, "Hello?"

Tom punched him hard across the jaw. The blow was so powerful that Ben had lost consciousness before he hit the floor.

#38

It was not as satisfying as he'd hoped it would be. Punching the man that he blamed for Etta's death, punching him so hard he felt bone crack beneath his knuckles, it struck Tom as an empty experience.

Ben fell to the floor in a lifeless lump.

Tom didn't know if the man was alive or dead. He only knew that kicking his prone body gave no satisfaction regardless of whether his boot connected with Ben's face, stomach, or groin. He tried each point of contact three times before admitting to himself that he was wasting his time. It was going to remain a hollow experience.

He had hoped he would be able to spend a righteous day torturing and tormenting Ben Haversham. Gentle Jesus knew that the man deserved to suffer. It was no more than he deserved for the irresponsible way his actions had impacted on Etta. But now, now he was standing over the man's lifeless body and able to punish him with no suggestion of resistance, Tom understood that Ben was not the one who merited his wrath.

Gentle Jesus had placed him in Sandalwood for a reason and it had nothing to do with beating the snot from a dissolute writer. He delivered a final kick to Ben's stomach, a kick that should have been satisfyingly hard because he felt ribs snap beneath the toe of his boot.

But still, Tom took no pleasure from the assault. If anything, he thought that gentle Jesus might think his actions had touched on being excessive. Then he was storming through the front door of the cottage determined to do the real scourge work that gentle Jesus wanted from him.

He walked boldly through the overhanging willows that lined the driveway and pushed out into the light rain that fogged the morning. He could feel his clown costume becoming drenched by the weather but it made no difference to Tom as he walked. His muscles felt aflame with adrenaline-pumped anger and he was determined to vent his fury on the one person in the village who most deserved it: Marion Papusa.

He stormed straight up to the front door of the Doll House and was pleasantly surprised to see that the door was ajar. Another person, Ben Haversham, he guessed, would likely have seen that as curious or suspicious or even fortuitous. Tom saw the act as proof that the divine hand of gentle Jesus was at play, making his job all the easier.

He pushed into the glossy splendour of the Doll House's entrance hall and tried to decide where best to begin. A young woman, blonde and wearing her hair in a ponytail, stepped out of the shadows. She considered him with an expressionless face, but her attention made him aware of the Harlequin costume. He blushed and considered stammering an apology before remembering that he was the visitation of a holy scourge that was going to purge Sandalwood of evil.

"Where is she?"

"Who?"

"The sorceress. The witch. Marion. Where is she?"

"She's in her attic room," the blonde said. She considered him doubtfully for a long moment before adding, "Are you sure you want to go and see her? She's pretty powerful."

Tom pushed past the woman. "The sorceress no longer has any power over me," he declared. He marched confidently up the stairs and then headed up the second flight. He was surprised to hear himself breathing heavily as he ascended to the building's second floor. He had thought he was in sufficient physical shape to conquer the world. Now it seemed two flights of stairs could potentially cause his downfall.

Not allowing himself to be slowed by the challenge, he rushed up the spiral staircase and blundered into the dawn-lit splendour of the attic. His eyes were momentarily blinded by the brightness. It was only as he blinked them used to the surroundings that Tom became aware of what he was looking at.

The view of Sandalwood was magnificent. He could see every building, street, and tree for miles in each direction. It was a cloudy day, the rooftops and roads were slick with glossy wetness. The leaves and lawns were a polished emerald colour.

He wondered how he had been able to overlook the village's beauty.

It was the sort of sight that would make anyone, anyone blessed enough to experience its splendour, believe in the beneficence of gentle Jesus. With a rush of understanding he decided that his oversight and ignorance were likely some diabolical trick played by the witch.

He blinked again and, this time, he could make out the couple in the attic.

They were both naked and, he thought, well past the age where nudity was acceptable. The man, pasty flesh, a flaccid penis, and a flurry of unseemly dark hairs in odd places, stared witlessly at Tom.

"Who the fuck is this?" he demanded.

The woman, Marion, Tom saw, grinned at him with a serpent's welcome. Her teeth were revealed, denture perfect, as her lipless smile widened. She seemed unmindful of her state of undress. To be honest, he thought she seemed almost proud of her non-existent breasts, emaciated waist and the tuft of greying fluff that didn't quite cover her sexual parts.

"This is the village's current woodsman," Marion told the naked man. She sauntered in Tom's direction and smiled at him with a predatory leer. Her eyes were flinty with an absence of expression. "Unless I'm very much mistaken, this woodsman is the one responsible for Alice's death."

"You are very much mistaken," Tom assured her. "Alice didn't have a pulse when I met her. I suspect she died a long, long time before I first met her."

Marion studied him with a reptilian hostility.

"I stand corrected, Johnny," she declared. "This isn't the man responsible for Alice's death. This is the man responsible for her decapitated body being discovered in the industrial bins behind your offices."

"Holy shit," John exploded.

"Language," Tom warned.

The man seemed unmindful of the warning. He was glaring hotly at Marion. "What the fuck is he doing here? Has he come to decapitate us? Is that what he's doing here?"

"He's probably come to try and eradicate me," Marion said pleasantly. "He sees himself as some sort of religious bane and he believes I need to be purged from this community."

Tom nodded. It was good that she understood. It would make things easier.

"He reminds me very much of the witch-finders that used to call on this village when I first came here," she mused. "They were all full of religion and sanctimony and empty threats."

Tom heard her mention of witch-finders and thought the comment made sense. He had believed she was immeasurably old. He had suspected she was more than merely an old woman with a dusty doll museum. Her words confirmed his suspicions that she had existed for centuries. This information, he realised, would make it easier for him to do what needed to be done to purge her evil from society. There would be no guilt associated with killing an immortal sorceress.

"Shouldn't we be doing something to get rid of this nutter?" John demanded. "Shouldn't we be shooting him, or tying him up, or burning him or something?"

"I have him under my control," Marion said simply.

"He doesn't look like he's under anyone's fucking control at the moment."

"Language," Tom repeated. "Don't make me tell you again."

"He's under my control, aren't you, Tom?"

Tom shook his head. It unnerved him that Marion was slowly advancing on him. He didn't think she would be able to overpower him. He felt confident that he could handle a waif-thin sorceress. But he didn't like having her unpleasant nudity in such close proximity.

"I'm not under the control of any witch."

"He says he's not under your control," John told her.

"He's perfectly under my control," Marion insisted. "He can't even say the name 'Jesus' without striking himself across the face."

Tom tried not to smile. He didn't want her to know that he was no longer bound by that restriction. He wanted to savour her dismay when she heard him whisper the name of his saviour without obeying the commands of her sorcery.

"If he's so perfectly under your control why did he decapitate Alice?"

Marion paused and frowned, as though the consideration hadn't previously crossed her mind. "Perhaps the strength of my control diminishes over distance?"

"Or perhaps you have no control over me?" Tom said. "Perhaps you have no control over me because I'm here, not as your servant, but as a scourge sent here to do the divine work of our Lord and Saviour, gentle Jesus."

The punch caught him off guard.

Tom hadn't even realised his hand was curled into a fist. He had no idea that his arm was building up to the punch and, when he smacked himself in the face, the blow was almost enough to lift him off his feet.

"No," he howled.

He made to lurch at Marion but she stopped him with an absent gesture of her hand. Her smile, serpent-like before, was now perfunctory and matter-of-fact. "Very well," she sighed. "You've proved to have too strong a will to be one of my typical woodsmen. Perhaps I should retire you now before you cause any further damage."

"Retire him?" the man asked.

Marion walked up to Tom and glared into his face.

"Go down into my basement and retrieve a shovel," she said coldly. "Once you have a shovel I want you to go deep into the woods and dig yourself a grave."

Tom stared at her and wondered how it was possible to feel so impotent when he harboured so much justified fury for the woman. His body refused to move. He wanted to lurch at her, or throw a punch at her, or do something to end her life and end her control and wipe the smug smile from the bitch's hateful, haggard face.

"Go into the woods," Marion repeated. "Dig your own grave and then lie there until your replacement comes along and covers you. Do you understand?"

He steeled himself to make a final show of independence. He readied himself to lunge at Marion and punch her and maybe take her head from her shoulders the way he had decapitated Alice. He wasn't sure whether or not the man, Johnny, would try to intervene. If he did, Tom felt confident he could overpower him. But he knew that the most important thing that remained for him to do was to defy Marion and act against the diabolical instructions of her sorcery.

"Do you understand me?" Marion repeated. "You'll go and retrieve your shovel. You'll walk into the woods. You'll dig yourself a grave. And then you'll lie down in it until your replacement buries you."

Tom groaned with the effort of trying to hurl himself at her. He made a final, valiant effort to defy her command and heard himself say, "Yes, Mistress."

Trembling with self-loathing he stumbled out of the attic to go and retrieve a shovel so he could follow her instructions.

#39

"How's it going, Bill?"

"Ella?" He tried not to let her see his puzzlement. "Aren't you dead?"

"Well, slightly," she admitted. "But I'm not letting that stop me."

She was dressed in her usual rape-victim chic. Her stockings were laddered. There was a designer tear in the seam of her dress. Her hair looked so tangled and untidy it made him think she would have headlice. Nevertheless, because it was Ella, and because it had been so long since he had last seen her, Bill rushed to hug her.

"I'm sorry I killed you."

He suspected this was some sort of dream, although it struck him as a remarkably vivid dream. It was a dream so vivid he could taste the blood on his own broken lip. He could see the clutter on the floor that suggested someone had been in the cottage – the clutter included a hammer, a screwdriver and a gun. He could also smell the lingering scent of her deodorant and the fragrance of the last cigarette she'd smoked. Admittedly she was cold, and there was the cumbersome weight of the doll she was holding that sat between them. But, even though it was awkward and likely a dream, it still felt good to have her in his arms again.

"I'm so sorry I killed you."

"You killed me?" She sounded surprised.

"I gave you the money for the drugs that killed you," Bill explained. "I killed you."

Ella laughed. It had been so long since he'd heard the sound he was surprised by its musicality. "Is that what you really think?" she asked pleasantly. "For fuck's sake, Bill. I hope you never write about drugs in any of your stories if that's how ill-informed you are about them. Twenty notes would barely get me enough cocaine to make a fizzy drink. It certainly wouldn't fund an overdose for someone with the immunity I've built up."

"But I…"

She shook her head. "You didn't kill me. I was killed by a combination of my own stupidity and an unscrupulous piece of shit of a dealer."

"Which dealer? Who was it? I'll make sure that they pay."

Her eyes softened as she studied him. "Timmy's taken care of him. He's been a pretty impressive scourge so far, although I think he went a little overboard on you." She touched concerned fingers against his cheek and Bill flinched with a rush of unexpected pain.

"I had hoped Tim would be enough of a scourge to deal with the problems here in Sandalwood," Ella confided. "Although I think it's proved more than he could manage."

"What does that mean?" Bill asked.

"It means Tim's dead. He's been dead for the past few days. But now, Marion's put him out of commission. Permanently."

"What can I do to stop her?"

She broke their embrace and took his hand. In the other hand he was surprised to see that she still held the doll she had been embracing before. He recognised it as the angelic one from his bedroom: the doll with the rich golden curls, the innocent pout of its lips, and the odd eyes of brown and blue. It was the doll he had called Wall-Eyed Wally. He glanced into Ella's face and for the first time noticed her eyes were similarly odd: one brown and one blue. He wondered why he had never noticed that detail before. Common sense told him that he must have noticed the detail at some point but he had never made the connection between the doll's unusual appearance and Ella's distinctive eye colouring.

"Is that one of Marion's dolls?" he asked warily.

Ella shook her head. "She's mine. She's been staying here in the cottage to make sure you've been safe and well."

Bill tried not to speculate how a doll could ever hope to watch out for his well-being. He brushed the matter from his thoughts, vowing to think about it later, when he had more time for such considerations. "You have to tell me," he insisted. "What can I do to stop Marion?"

Ella bit her lower lip. "It's no good burning down the Doll House," she said. "That won't stop her."

"Can I shoot her?" he asked, remembering the gun that he had seen on the floor. He suspected it might have been Timmy's gun. "Will it work if I shoot her?"

Ella shook her head. "Unlikely. Marion's been around for the past three centuries. I doubt a bullet will stop her."

"Not even if I shoot her in the face?"

She considered him with a bemused grin. "Are you thinking of zombie movies?"

Bill blushed and shook his head. "What if we pour water on her?"

"She'll get wet."

"She won't melt?"

"For fuck's sake," Ella groaned. Her tone was rich with good-natured exasperation. "She's not the Wicked Witch of the West and you're not Dorothy. Did you seriously think that was a possible solution?"

He went to rub a frantic hand through his hair and found himself clutching a clown's cap. The absurdity of his costume made him feel ridiculous and he struggled to say something sensible or useful.

"Can I throw salt at her?"

"She's not a fucking slug."

He paced the room before asking, "What if I cut her head off?"

Ella scowled. "Are you still thinking of zombie movies?"

"No. Yes. Perhaps. But surely she can't survive if I cut her head off."

"And if she does?" Ella asked.

"Then maybe I can burn her head, or mince it into small pieces, or do something like that?"

Ella placed her doll beside the typewriter. Her smile was softened by patience and she kissed him lightly on the cheek. Even though he could feel nothing but the chill emanating from her, Bill experienced a rush of warmth when her lips touched his flesh. "If you kill Marion, her death could wipe out this entire village."

"Are you saying I shouldn't do that?"

She said nothing.

"This is a village full of mindless slaves to her authority," he said earnestly. "They're all under her control. Are you saying we should leave her to rule her hapless minions?"

"No," she said. "I'm not suggesting that. But I do want you to know that it won't be easy, and the effects could be devastating."

They considered each other in silence for a moment and Bill realised there were a lot of things he had never bothered to say to her and now there was no time to say them. He had never bothered to tell her that she was his best friend, that he probably loved her more than he had loved any other human. And, without her in his life, he'd not been inspired to consciously write a single page. He wondered if she already knew those things and, even if she did, he wished there was time for him to reiterate each of those sentiments so that she fully understood how important she had been in his life.

The chiming of the clock in the hall reminded him there wasn't time.

"Something needs to be done, doesn't it?"

She studied him levelly. "It's you or her. And, if she wins, it will be a case of her or John's next disposable protégé. And then the next one. And then the next one-"

He held up a hand to silence her. "OK," he said. "I think I know what I have to do. Is John a demon, like her?"

Ella laughed softly. "John is her lackey," she said. "You remember Renfield in Stoker's Dracula?"

Bill shook his head.

"Renfield was Dracula's bitch. He ate spiders and did Dracula's bidding during daylight hours. Xander played a similar role in the episode where Buffy met Dracula."

"You didn't get out much when you were alive, did you?"

"Fuck you, Bill," she snorted. Her cheeks, deathly pale and slightly dirty, flushed with twin spots of high colour. "Don't you get what I'm saying? John is Marion's lackey, like Whistler in Blade or-"

"Could you reference one of my novels?" he suggested. "That way I'd have half a chance of maybe understanding the analogy you're trying to make."

Ella paused and drew a deep breath. Studying him sourly she said, "If you kill John it will cause her some nuisance. But she'll survive. She'll find a new lackey and she'll carry on. You need to stop her. You need to stop Marion."

"It will have an impact on the village, won't it?"

"Yes," she said. "But, if you don't, there's a danger that Marion might try and extend her authority beyond Sandalwood."

Bill nodded and came to a decision. Giving her a final, farewell kiss he said, "Leave it with me. It's about time I tried to do something heroic in this story."

Ben awoke slowly.

The hurt did not surprise him. In his dream he had been uncomfortable and, when Etta had touched his face, there had been the sensation that she was caressing bruises, re-inflaming those sensations of pain and soreness that he would rather have forgotten.

Beside the typewriter were another batch of freshly typed pages. He could tell they were freshly typed because the upper pages curled as though they were still bent into the shape of the typewriter's platen.

Next to the typewriter sat a doll.

He shifted back in his chair, uncomfortable with the way Wall-Eyed Wally was staring at him. The doll had been in his dream. Etta had been clutching it. He had seen that Etta had the same eyes as the doll. He began to wonder if the doll was, in some way, the embodiment of Etta. Had it been watching over him since he arrived in Sandalwood? Or was that just another mental explanation to vaguely justify some of the inexplicable occurrences that he'd met with in the village.

He placed a finger against the doll's pigmented cheek and was stung by a rush of sudden and inexplicable knowledge. The doll had been the one that wrote the notes urging him to get out of Sandalwood. The doll had been the one that he could hear running around the bedroom when the house should have been empty. The doll had been controlled by Etta's spirit.

He pulled his hand away, uneasy that he had been given a glimpse into a supernatural world that he hadn't expected to exist. His fingers were shivering and he found himself staring around the study with a renewed respect for everything paranormal. Swallowing down his nervousness, Ben said, "It's about time I tried to do something heroic."

Those had been the last words he had said before waking. He pushed himself from the chair and started towards the study door. As an afterthought, he paused and glanced at the final page on the manuscript he'd been typing. He could see the words *THE END* in capitals completing the story.

Hairs on the nape of his neck bristled.

On some level he understood that, now he had completed his story, John no longer needed him in Sandalwood. He had served his purpose in writing the novel John wanted from him. Now he had become expendable.

"Ben?"

He stiffened at the sound of John's voice.

His agent appeared in the doorway of the study, smiling genially. He wore the driving cap Ben remembered seeing him wear when they had both arrived in Sandalwood. He was dressed like a gentleman farmer in Harris tweed with an affable smile beneath his dark, neatly-trimmed moustache. "I thought I'd call down early and surprise you," John grinned.

Ben wanted to say that he had been sufficiently surprised when he saw John pounding between the legs of Marion Papusa. He kept the thought to himself.

"How's the writing going?" John asked cheerfully.

Ben picked up the gun from beside the typewriter and shot John in the face.

The boom of the gun firing was an enormous sound in the confines of the study. A look of surprise crossed John's features and then he was falling to the floor with a hole in his forehead.

Ben stepped over him as he hurried out of the house.

If he had ever been worried that he was acting rashly, those fears were now behind him. John had come into the house after not seeing him for a week. He had stepped into the study and asked how the writing was progressing. He hadn't asked why Ben was dressed in a clown suit.

Ben had seen John with Marion and he knew the couple were working together. He suspected the information he had gleaned in his dream was correct. John was some sort of lackey who did Marion's work outside the controlled environment of the village.

Admittedly, that information had come to him in a dream, and he supposed it was somewhat irrational to believe such details as facts. But he had written a novel in his dreams, so he didn't think the details could automatically be dismissed as being unimportant.

Before leaving the house he put down food and drink for Anastasia. He didn't know if he would ever return and the thought of the cat going hungry was the one thing that made him hesitate. But he guessed that, in the grand scheme of things, dealing with Marion Papusa was probably more important than feeding a stray cat with flatulence issues.

With the cat's needs served, he stormed across the road and marched into the Doll House.

The door was open, as though the woman was waiting for him.

The maid with the blonde ponytail glanced up at him and smiled uncertainly. "Why have you come back?"

A wave of understanding washed over him.

She had given him the Pierrot costume on Marion's orders. Marion controlled clowns in Sandalwood and, so long as he was wearing the Pierrot costume, instead of it rendering him invisible to her all-seeing eye, the costume allowed Marion to know what he was doing and control his actions.

Ben raised the gun and shot the maid in the face.

She collapsed where she was standing.

He marched past her fallen body and rushed up the stairs. He didn't bother looking at anything in the museum. He knew Marion would be waiting for him in her attic room. He started towards the spiral staircase and stopped when he saw a Pierrot standing there.

It was the Pierrot he had seen lurking in shadows and corners throughout Sandalwood. It was the Pierrot he had seen bent over a doll in the workstation. It was the Pierrot that had been following him since he'd arrived.

"Don't go up there."

The Pierrot spoke with a female voice. Standing this close to the clown, able to see it properly for the first time, he could see tufts of curly brown hair peeping from beneath the brim of her hat. The white face paint was a thin disguise but, beneath that, he recognised the features of the woman staring at him. It was the artist, Christina White.

"Please don't go up there," the clown insisted.

Was this what happened to John's clients once they had finished their allotted time in the cottage? Did Marion dress them up as clowns, controlling them so they were either lurking in shadows around the village, or working like zombies in the sweatshop below the doll museum?

"Please don't go up there," the clown insisted.

Ben raised the gun and shot the clown in the face. She fell where she had been standing. It was an undramatic and brutal conclusion that chilled him with its cold efficiency. He climbed the stairs, blinked his eyes to get used to the brightness, and fixed his gaze on Marion.

"Mr Haversham," she exclaimed cheerfully. "This is a pleasant surprise. You've caught me during my sky-clad celebrations. I hope my nudity doesn't offend you. Perhaps you'd care to join me in my celebrations?"

He raised the gun and pointed it at her face.

He pulled the trigger and the hammer fell hollowly onto an empty barrel.

"Shit."

He pressed the trigger twice more. Each time the gun made a disappointing click instead of firing a bullet.

"Oh dear," Marion purred with faux sympathy. She stepped closer and pulled the weapon from his fingers. Absently she tossed it into a corner of the room. "You must feel so disappointed, Mr Haversham. You burst in here, hoping to impress me with your potency, and then you find your weapon isn't able to do the job that's needed from it."

"If I can't shoot you, I'll find some other way of killing you," Ben promised.

She shook her head. "No you won't, Mr Haversham."

She spoke with such absolute confidence he longed to prove her wrong. He yearned to rush at her and grab her throat and squeeze until she was no longer able to fight against him. But, instead of rushing to overpower her, Ben stood quietly and nodded his obedience.

She turned her back on him and went to one of the windows. "Look at all the nuisance you've caused me, Mr Haversham."

Obediently, Ben stepped to her side and looked out of the window.

He was close enough to smell the stale and dusty perfume of her perspiration. The scent made him think of mummified remains.

"I see you shot John," she said, pointing at the doorway of the cottage.

Ben followed the direction she was pointing in and saw John walking out of the cottage. He had a hole in his forehead but there was no blood. Ben was beyond being surprised. Sandalwood was clearly a village where anything could happen. Shooting someone in the face was no guarantee of killing them.

"I'm going to have a tiresome afternoon patching him up," Marion grumbled. "Facial holes are the most difficult ones to patch effectively."

Ben said nothing.

"I've had to get rid of a woodsman today," Marion complained.

She pointed to the woods and Ben could see, through a clearing, that a clown was digging a grave. Although there was a lot of distance, and he was viewing the figure through the coverage of trees and branches, Ben recognised the clown as Tom. As he watched, Tom planted his shovel at the head of the grave and then lay down in the hole he had created.

"What's he doing?" Ben asked.

"He's following orders," Marion explained. "He's going to lay there now until his replacement comes along and covers up his mouldering corpse."

"But, isn't he conscious?"

"Oh yes," Marion agreed. "And he'll remain conscious until his brain rots. Maybe longer."

Ben shivered. It seemed like a fate he wouldn't have wished on anyone. The idea of being buried alive, and being unable to do anything except suffer the indignity of live burial and gradual decay, seemed like the epitome of cruelty.

"Did you finish writing your story?"

He didn't consider lying. He suspected she would be able to read his thoughts. "Yes," he said. "It's finished."

She nodded laconic approval. "I heard gunshots before you came up here," she said turning on him. "How many of my staff will I have to replace?"

He shrugged. "I shot them in the face, the same as I shot John. If you can repair him surely you can repair whoever I shot?"

Marion slapped him hard across the jaw. "Don't be so fucking impertinent," she snarled. "I can repair John. I need him for my work outside Sandalwood. But it's hardly worth the time or the effort for drones that I use in the village. It's easier to replace those than repair them. So, how many of my staff will I have to replace?"

"I shot the blonde maid," he remembered. "The one who works as a barmaid in the Black Swan."

Marion rolled her eyes. She did not look particularly upset by this news. "I was thinking of getting rid of her anyway. Who else?"

"Christina White."

"You recognised her?"

"Yes. She was wearing a clown costume but I recognised her. She was one of John's clients, wasn't she?"

Marion nodded. "It's a shame you killed her but, perhaps, that's for the best. I take it you know what fate you can expect here, don't you?"

He glared at her and said nothing.

"I need a new white-faced clown," Marion told him. "And it looks like you're already dressed for the part."

He gripped his hands into fists and tried to lunge for her.

His body refused to move.

"What will I be expected to do as your clown?"

She cackled and drew a finger down his chest. Her smile was lascivious and triumphant. "Why, Mr Haversham," she began. "As long as you're my clown, you'll do whatever I demand of you."

#41

Jason Connor toyed with his scotch and wondered whether or not to order a refill. It was not particularly late, and the oblivion of a good measure of scotch did seem appealing.

The landlord considered him with a scowl of mistrust and Jason reflected that his was the only unfriendly face he had encountered in Sandalwood. He had heard that this was the village where Ben Haversham wrote his last novel, *The Doll House*. From what he'd read in the newspapers, Haversham had gone missing after submitting the manuscript to his editor, and now there were stories about him living as a recluse and hiding from a public who didn't understand his work.

He considered asking the landlord if Haversham had ever visited the Black Swan. The sneer that constantly curled the man's upper lip was enough to make Jason think twice about trying to obtain such information.

He glanced up at his reflection in the bar's mirror and was surprised to see a white figure at the back of the room. He turned quickly, sure he had just seen someone dressed like a white-faced clown. The figure had been in the mirror, he was sure they had been in the mirror, but he couldn't see anything resembling a white-faced clown in the bar.

A barmaid tapped him on the shoulder and asked if he was OK.

"Yeah," he said. "Just getting used to this village," he admitted. "And trying to convince myself I'm not seeing clowns around every corner."

"Clowns?" the barmaid laughed. "You're not the first person to think you've seen one of those in Sandalwood." Her laughter momentarily sobered as she said, "You ought to have a word with Marion, the woman who runs the doll museum. She can tell you all about the history of clowns that are associated with this village."

Jason thanked her and said that sounded like something he might pursue.

His smile remained after the barmaid had disappeared to go and serve another customer. She was attractive, despite the heavy tattoo on her inner forearm and the fact that her eyes were different colours. If he was being honest, the disparity of eye colours reminded him of one of the dolls that watched him as he slept in the cottage.

"Are you going to be here long?" the barmaid asked, returning to him.

He shrugged easily. "I'm here to complete a writing project," he explained. "It's a series of short stories that my agent wants with some urgency."

The barmaid nodded. "That sounds like hard work."

"Ordinarily, I'd agree with you," he admitted. "But, I think it must be something about this village life, it seems since I got here, this collection is practically writing itself."

THE END

About the Author

Ashley Lister is a prolific writer of fiction, having written more than fifty full length novels and over a hundred short stories. Aside from regularly blogging about poetry and writing in general, Ashley also teaches creative writing. He lives in Lancashire, England.

www.ashleylister.co.uk

Other titles from Ashley Lister:

PayBack Week
Death by Fiction
Raven & Skull
Old People Sex (and other highly offensive poems)

How to Write Short Stories and Get Them Published
How to Write Erotic Fiction and Sex Scenes

Coming soon from the same author: *Blackstone Towers*

#1

The lift doors opened with a sad electric sigh. The light from within, light that was the dirty yellow of a smoker's handkerchief, fell sickly on the reception floor. It splashed on the uniform white shoes of Elsa and Anya, the night-shift cleaners for the apartment building. The yellow light looked like stains of piss on their otherwise pristine shoes.

Elsa started toward the open door, pushing her cart of cleaning supplies before her. One of the wheels squeaked, a lazy whistling sound that didn't fare well against the flat acoustics of the reception. The bottles of bleach and the spray-guns of offensively floral-fragranced cleaning fluid wobbled nervously in their basket on the top of the cart.

Anya placed a hand on Elsa's arm and stopped her. It was not the first time the woman had hesitated at the lift door. This had been her habit every night that Elsa had worked with her. Anya had nails like talons and, even through the rayon sleeve of her uniform, they scratched sharply at the sensitive flesh of Elsa's bicep.

"Wait," Anya whispered.

Her voice was low and urgent, as though she feared they would be overheard.

"What for?" Elsa asked.

Anya was peering into the confines of the empty lift. Her haggard features, already wrinkled with age, shrivelled with suspicion as she stared at the polished mirrors, the gleaming chrome work, and the blonde wood that glistened beneath the jaundiced lights.

"What are we waiting for?" Elsa pressed.

"It's nothing." Anya let go of the woman's arm and, grudgingly, urged her younger colleague to move into the lift before her. Elsa took a couple of steps and then paused before entering.

"What was that about?"

Anya shook her head and tried to push past her. Her cheeks were flushing with a rouge of embarrassment. Her gaze went in every direction but it refused to meet Elsa's.

"Tell me," Elsa insisted. She had been working at Blackstone Towers for less than a fortnight and Anya had been delegated as her supervisor. The woman's habits wavered between irritating and annoying but this regular hesitation at the lift doors was now becoming a real source of frustration. "Tell me what's wrong with the lift."

"There's nothing wrong with the lift."

"Then what are you looking for?"

Anya frowned. "I'm making sure Mrs White isn't there."

"Who the hell is Mrs White?"

"You'll think I'm crazy."

Elsa already thought the woman was crazy. She didn't bother voicing that opinion. She suspected Anya could read as much from her cold expression. "Who is Mrs White?"

Churlishly, Anya said, "Mrs White is the ghost that travels in the lift."

Elsa crossed herself. Her parents had raised her to believe that it was never done to talk of ghosts. Especially not this late at night. Her fingers went to her throat and she took a moment's solace from the reassuring presence of her crucifix. It was cool and satisfyingly solid to her touch.

"There's no ghost in the lift," Elsa said nervously.

Anya glanced guardedly through the doors. "No. Not tonight. Not right now. No."

The doors started to close. They nudged against the obstacle of Elsa's cart, making the bottles of bleach and the spray-guns of chemical cleaner tremble. Apologetically, the doors bounced back to their housings.

"Not tonight," Anya repeated. With obvious reluctance, she stepped past Elsa whilst pushing her own cart into the lift. "But there are enough nights when Mrs White is in the lift. And I've made a personal vow never to ride with her."

After a moment's hesitation, Elsa pushed her cart into the lift and joined Anya.

"You're serious, aren't you?"

"Blackstone Towers is an old building," Anya said as she pushed the button for the fifteenth floor. "Old buildings collect ghosts." As if sensing her subordinate's scepticism, she asked, "Have you been in apartment four on the thirteenth floor yet?"

Elsa blushed. She had been in that apartment. It was one of the empty flats they were meant to keep clean in readiness for a prospective tenant. She remembered it was as cold as a Warsaw winter in there. Worse, even though there had been no one in the apartment, she had felt as though she was being watched by someone who didn't approve of her being there. It was a disquieting sensation that had left her shaking with unease until she could escape.

Goosebumps prickled up her arms as she tried to nudge away the memory. She had recently been suffering from unpleasant dreams and she had a vague suspicion that those dreams were set in room four on the thirteenth floor. Now, listening to Anya's lowered voice, hearing her whisper confidences as they stood in the creaking elevator and it trembled through its ascent, Elsa tried to suppress a shiver at the thought of what she could have encountered in there.

"I didn't like that place," Elsa admitted.

"That's because it's haunted," Anya assured her. "Apartment four on the thirteenth. Apartment twenty-one on the fifth. Apartment five on the eighth. The penthouse suite on the fifteenth. And the elevator. The elevator is haunted by Mrs White."

Elsa could feel a glut of questions running through her thoughts. She wanted to know who the ghost was, where she'd come from and why she haunted the elevator. The question she eventually asked was, "Have you seen her?"

Anya met Elsa's gaze and nodded slowly. "I think so."

Elsa silently waited for the woman to continue.

"It's an elevator," Anya said. Her tone was shrill and edged with a sharp sliver of defensiveness. "The doors open and sometimes there's someone standing there. You get in with them and you don't talk. You rarely make eye contact. I may have shared the lift with Mrs White. Or maybe I just shared the lift with a miserable old woman who had soulless eyes, smelled like death, and didn't want to talk."

A ghost that smelled of death?

The goosebumps prickled Elsa's forearms with enough severity to make her tremble. She studied Anya with renewed respect and asked, "What does Mrs White do?"

Anya paused for a moment. When she breathed out her sigh was heavy. She was staring into one of the lift's mirrored walls, her gaze fixed directly on Elsa, as though it was only safe to communicate through the secrecy of their reflections.

Standing side by side, both wearing the hotel's uniform of white shoes and white tabard over pale jeans and a pale shirt, they looked like before and after photographs demonstrating the negative effects of tobacco, alcohol, drugs or age. They shared a similar height. They both looked to have used the same shade of dirty blonde to colour their mid-length bobs. They even shared the same ice blue eyes, as though there was some suggestion of shared heritage from their Eastern European ancestry.

Elsa hated looking at Anya's wrinkled features because she feared, unless she found some way to escape her job at Blackstone Towers, she would one day end up living the same life that had clearly broken this woman.

"What does this Mrs White ghost do?" Elsa asked again.

"Most times she just stands there," Anya admitted. "She stands in silence and she does nothing. Then there are times when she's disappeared between floors. I've known staff leave the job because of that. They've been riding down in the elevator and they've found themselves next to an elderly woman. And they're thinking they should smile nicely because otherwise the senior management will find out that they weren't arse-kissing to the tenants and they'll get their bonus docked. And they glance away for a moment, maybe to polish the chrome panel by the door, or wipe down one of the hand rails. And, when they look back, the old woman has disappeared."

Elsa swallowed. Her hand moved swiftly and unconsciously through the motion of genuflecting. "I'd leave if that happened to me," she vowed.

"It's not the worst thing I've heard of Mrs White doing," Anya said guardedly.

The lift was travelling upwards, taking its time to reach the top. The mechanisms above groaned with age and weariness. The metallic coils of an unseen cable slithered against the thin panels of the walls. Elsa wanted to know what else Mrs White had done but she wasn't sure she should hear about it whilst she was using the lift. Drawing a deep breath, steeling herself in readiness for the revelation, she said, "Go on."

Anya licked her lips before responding. Her eyes glanced to the corners of the lift. "Sometimes she talks to people."

Elsa shook her head. Her heartbeat seemed to be racing and she felt sure she had never heard anything more disturbing in her life. Nevertheless, trying to defy her fears, trying to prove that she wasn't another witless migrant bringing her country's backward superstitions with her into her new homeland, she asked, "What's so wrong with that? Talking is only talking, isn't it?"

"Everyone she talks to has come to an unpleasant end."

The lift lurched to a stop at the fifteenth floor and the doors slid open.

There was a figure standing at the door and Elsa almost screamed in terror. She had one hand over her heart, with the fingers of the other clutching at her crucifix as she scrabbled to move backwards. It was only when the man backed away, smiling apologetically, that she realized he was one of the hotel guests.

"*Przepraszam pana,*" Anya muttered, pushing her cart past him. "'Scuse us, sir."

Elsa drew a deep breath and forced herself to calm down sufficiently to walk past the man. She smiled a servile apology and pushed her trolley out of the lift in pursuit of Anya. She figured the man was an associate of Mr Knight's, the current resident of the penthouse suite. She wondered if it might even have been the mysterious Mr Knight himself and she turned back to glance at him, wondering what a person looked like when they could afford to live in the penthouse suite of the prestigious Blackstone Towers.

He hadn't seemed particularly striking, she thought.

If anything, he'd looked like a plain-faced young man dressed in the typical inner-city night-time attire of a black hoodie with black jeans and black trainers. He hadn't been particularly unappealing to look at but she had not seen anything remarkable about his features that made him striking. He was standing in the lift with a finger pressed on the button that would take him to the ground floor.

Behind him, Elsa could see an elderly woman.

Worse, the elderly woman was reaching out to tap the young man on the shoulder. Considering the expression on her face, it looked like she had something to say.

Printed in Great Britain
by Amazon